The Monk Series

Mr. Monk in Outer Space

Mr. Monk and the Two Assistants

Mr. Monk and the Blue Flu

Mr. Monk Goes to Hawaii

Mr. Monk Goes to the Firehouse

MR. MONK
GOES TO GERMANY

A Novel by
Lee Goldberg

Based on the USA Network
television series created by
Andy Breckman

AN OBSIDIAN MYSTERY

OBSIDIAN
Published by New American Library, a division of
Penguin Group (USA) Inc., 375 Hudson Street,
New York, New York 10014, USA
Penguin Group (Canada), 90 Eglinton Avenue East, Suite 700, Toronto,
Ontario M4P 2Y3, Canada (a division of Pearson Penguin Canada Inc.)
Penguin Books Ltd., 80 Strand, London WC2R 0RL, England
Penguin Ireland, 25 St. Stephen's Green, Dublin 2,
Ireland (a division of Penguin Books Ltd.)
Penguin Group (Australia), 250 Camberwell Road, Camberwell, Victoria 3124,
Australia (a division of Pearson Australia Group Pty. Ltd.)
Penguin Books India Pvt. Ltd., 11 Community Centre, Panchsheel Park,
New Delhi - 110 017, India
Penguin Group (NZ), 67 Apollo Drive, Rosedale, North Shore 0632,
New Zealand (a division of Pearson New Zealand Ltd.)
Penguin Books (South Africa) (Pty.) Ltd., 24 Sturdee Avenue,
Rosebank, Johannesburg 2196, South Africa

Penguin Books Ltd., Registered Offices:
80 Strand, London WC2R 0RL, England

Published by Obsidian, an imprint of New American Library, a division of
Penguin Group (USA) Inc. Previously published in an Obsidian hardcover
edition.

First Obsidian Mass Market Printing, December 2008
10   9   8   7   6   5   4   3   2   1

To Valerie and Madison

AUTHOR'S NOTE

This book was written in Los Angeles, California, and in Lohr, Germany . . . and in hotel rooms in Munich, Cologne, London, and Montreal and in the many airplanes and trains that shuttled me between those destinations.

I am indebted to Hermann Joha, Elke Schubert, Jasmin Steigler, the staff of the Franziskushohe, and the kind people of Lohr for their advice, guidance, and good humor on all things German. I also owe thanks to Justin Brenneman, Dr. D. P. Lyle, Kristen Weber, Kerry Donovan, and Gina Maccoby. And, finally, this book would not be possible without the creativity and enthusiasm of my friend Andy Breckman and the entire *Monk* writing staff.

While much of what I have written about Lohr and the surrounding area is true, a lot of it isn't. I am entirely to blame for any errors of fact, geography, logic, or good taste, intentional or otherwise.

The story in this book takes place prior to the events in the episode "Mr. Monk Is on the Run." While I try very

hard to stay true to the continuity of the *Monk* TV series, it is not always possible, given the long lead time between when my books are written and when they are published. During that period new episodes may air that contradict details or situations referred to in my books. If you come across any such continuity mismatches, your understanding is appreciated.

I look forward to hearing from you at www.leegold berg.com.

1

Mr. Monk and the Assistant

It's a tough job being somebody's personal assistant. You have to answer their phone, manage their correspondence, run their errands, pay their bills, arrange their schedule, and basically do whatever tasks, menial to major, they are too busy or self-absorbed or distracted or pampered or disinterested to do themselves.

I know that there are plenty of other occupations that require a lot more education, talent, courage, patience, skill, and endurance. And there are many jobs considerably more demanding, degrading, disgusting, or dangerous than being a mere personal assistant.

Sure, it might not be as deadly and unpleasant as crab fishing in the Arctic, or as risky as defusing land mines in Afghanistan, or as disgusting as trudging through the human waste in the New York sewer system. But, believe me, being a personal assistant is a lot harder than you think it is.

It involves more than fetching coffee, making restaurant reservations, and picking up dry cleaning. You have to be equal parts shrink, social worker, and mercenary to not only second-guess and satisfy the

ever-changing professional, personal, physical, and emotional needs of your employer, but to also predict and manage the impact that he will have on people around him and that they will have on him.

Your intellect, your integrity, your ethics, and your physical endurance are put to the test every single day in ways you never could have imagined.

And you can forget about working only nine to five. Being a personal assistant is a full-time job that never ends. It's 24/7. You're on call more than any doctor, firefighter, or cop but for a lot less pay, negligible respect, and no benefits.

Your life and whatever needs you may have are trumped by the whims of your employer. You exist on this earth to serve him.

Now take all of that and multiply it by a thousand. That's what it's like when you're the personal assistant to a brilliant detective, like I am to Adrian Monk.

Brilliant detectives are able to see things we can't, amid the insignificant details and white noise that normal people like us simply tune out.

They can find connections between objects, events, and behaviors that anybody else would consider random, coincidental, or just fate because, well, most things are.

They can spot inconsistencies that would go unnoticed by anyone else because we have other priorities and simply aren't paying close enough attention.

They interact with the world in an entirely different way than you and I do. They observe the way we live instead of living the way we do.

That's what makes the detectives brilliant. And that's what makes them completely incapable of dealing with everyday life and the basics of simple human interaction. It's the reason why so many brilliant detectives are considered "difficult" and "eccentric" by most people who meet them.

Adrian Monk's brilliance comes from an obsessive-compulsive disorder and myriad phobias, all of which finally overwhelmed him when his wife, Trudy, was killed in a car bombing that has remained unsolved, and has haunted him to this day. He was fired from the San Francisco police force after her death and now makes his living consulting on homicide cases with Captain Leland Stottlemeyer.

Monk goes through life making sure that everything is in its place, following detailed rules of order that exist only in his mind and nowhere else. So he's sensitive to anything that's out of place and he has an uncontrollable need to put things back where they belong. Or, at least, where he thinks they belong.

To him, an unsolved murder is a story missing an ending, a puzzle missing a piece, an extreme and fatal example of disorder in an orderly world.

He *has* to set it right.

To do that, he needs someone to manage his life, get him where he needs to go, and keep away all the things that can distract him or provoke his phobias so that he can get through the day without a nervous breakdown. And, if things go really well, maybe he can solve a murder, too.

But it's not easy dealing with a man who regularly disinfects his box of disinfectant wipes with a disinfectant wipe, who measures his ice cubes to ensure they are perfect cubes, and who once demanded at a crime scene that the police rearrange the cars in an adjacent parking lot alphabetically by their license plates, and then in groups by their make, model, and year of manufacture, so that he could concentrate.

I know I've complained to you about my job before and, until recently, that was all I could do to relieve my stress. But that changed a short time back when the San Francisco police walked off the job in a contract dispute

and Monk was temporarily reinstated to the police force as captain of Homicide.

He was put in command of a trio of other detectives who'd also been discharged from the force for mental health reasons. One detective had a violent anger-management problem, one was a paranoid schizophrenic, and one was slipping into senility.

As different as their problems were, all three of them had one thing in common: They each had an assistant to help them.

It was a revelation and a relief for me.

Until then, if I wanted advice I had to search for wisdom and guidance in the exploits of fictional assistants like Sherlock Holmes' Dr. Watson, Nero Wolfe's Archie Goodwin, and Hercule Poirot's Captain Hastings. Those days were over. I'd finally found real people who could understand and sympathize with my daily struggles.

I wasn't alone anymore.

Now the three assistants and I get together about once a month at a coffee shop in the Marina District to vent about our troubles and give each other advice. I look at it as free psychological counseling, since two of the assistants are mental health professionals.

Occasionally we even have guests. A couple of months ago, we met a guy who works in Santa Barbara with a detective who pretends to be a psychic. Imagine that. His plight made us all feel a bit better about our own situations.

Jasper, a psychiatric nurse who assists the paranoid-schizophrenic detective, brought a guy to our last meeting who works with an Atlanta investigator who is a pathological liar. The assistant's name was Gavin and the fibbing detective he works for was Steve Stone.

"At least I *think* that's his name," Gavin told us. "It could be a lie. He lies about everything. Most of my

time and energy is spent trying to parse the truth from whatever he says and then tell it to the cops he consults with."

"How do you do it?" I asked.

"I keep a running list of what he says and then at the end of the day, I strap him into a lie detector and question him about each comment," Gavin said.

"He lets you do that?" Jasper asked.

"He knows I'll quit if he doesn't," Gavin said. "But he's become pretty good at fooling the machine. So sometimes I'll slip him some Sodium Pentothal."

"You drug your boss?" I asked, shocked.

"Who doesn't?" said Sparrow, a young woman with so many piercings on her body she looked like a magnet dropped into a box of needles. She reluctantly assisted her grandfather Frank Porter, a retired SFPD detective who, despite his senility, was still a better investigator than most cops with perfect memory.

"I don't," I said.

"I've met Monk," Sparrow said. "You should."

There actually was an experimental drug Monk could take if he wanted to that would relieve most of his obsessive-compulsive tendencies. But it robbed him of his detecting skills. It also made him an insufferable jerk. Monk was already insufferable, but at least he wasn't a jerk.

"The problem is that Stone has developed immunity to truth serum," Gavin said. "So most of the time I've got no choice but to rely on my intuition and watch for his tells."

"Tells?" Jasper asked, rapidly thumb-typing notes into his PDA. Everything we talked about was going into his thesis, the exact topic of which changed on a weekly basis.

"Body language, little tics, unconscious habits," Gavin said, scratching his closely trimmed beard.

"Like the way I'm scratching my beard, which I'm sure reveals something about my emotional state, though I'm not self-aware enough to know what it is."

"You want me," Sparrow said.

"No, I don't," Gavin said.

"Yes, you do," Sparrow said. "That's why you're scratching your beard."

"Maybe his beard just itches," I said.

"When men want me," Sparrow said, "they scratch."

Gavin cleared his throat and continued. "What I'm saying is that there are some unconscious mannerisms Stone does whenever he's telling a whopper. But even those mannerisms can be false. It's a constant battle with him."

"So why do you keep doing it?" asked Arnie, the balding anger-management counselor who worked with a notoriously violent ex-cop named Wyatt.

I thought that was a funny question coming from Arnie, considering that Wyatt had shot him three or four times and had thrown him out a window at least twice, and that was just since I'd met him.

Gavin thought about the question for a long moment, as if it was something he'd never considered before. But I was sure he'd thought about it many times. I figured he was probably just deciding how honest he wanted to be with himself and with us.

"Stone is funny, smart, caring, and a true genius. But his constant lies ruined his career as a cop and alienated everyone around him. Nobody can trust him. So now he doesn't have anybody left in his life except me. It's sad. And without me, I worry about what he might do."

"You feel sorry for him," I said.

"I admire him," Gavin said.

"And you like to feel needed," Jasper said, nodding

sagely. He's not sage, but he's got the nod down. I think they teach it in shrink school.

Gavin shrugged. "I'm certainly not in it for the money."

We all nodded in agreement like a row of bobble-heads.

Hearing Gavin's story, I almost felt guilty about how well things were going lately with Monk. He still had all his obsessive-compulsive problems, but somehow they seemed more manageable these days, for him and for me. Or maybe I was just getting used to it.

But there was no question that things were humming along for him professionally lately, too. He solved cases so quickly, it seemed to me that he could probably start doing his work over the phone without visiting the crime scenes at all.

"Sometimes I think that maybe if I stick around long enough, and try real hard, I can save him," Gavin said. "The way he saved me."

I understood how he felt, more than I cared to admit to everyone in the room.

"What did he save you from?" I asked.

"Mediocrity," Gavin said. "Before I met him, I was in telemarketing. I called people in the middle of their dinner and tried to sell them crap they didn't want. Now I'm helping solve big murder cases. I'm doing something important with my life. What were you doing before?"

"Writing my thesis," Jasper said.

"Running group therapy sessions," Arnie said.

"Bartending," I said.

"Enjoying life," Sparrow said. "I'm really looking forward to going back to that."

Gavin looked at the rest of us. "Do you want to go back?"

"I never left," Jasper said. "I'm still writing my thesis, only now it's about the woman I'm working for. It's going to break new ground in the understanding of paranoid schizophrenics."

"I used to spend my days in an office with a lot of miserable, angry people before Wyatt came along," Arnie said. "Now I'm leaping out of speeding cars."

"Wyatt *pushed* you out," I said. "You were in the hospital for two weeks."

"I've become a man of action," Arnie said. "I'm going to get a few scrapes and bruises."

"Don't men of action usually have more hair?" Sparrow said.

"Tell that to Bruce Willis," Arnie said.

"You aren't Bruce Willis," Sparrow said.

"But I *feel* like I am," Arnie said. "And that's worth all the trouble Wyatt causes me."

Gavin looked at me. "What about you? Could you go back to bartending?"

I shook my head. "Serving drinks was never my goal in life. I'm not sure I ever had a goal, which is probably why I've bounced around so many jobs. This is the longest I've worked in one place. But the truth is, I don't think I could quit working for Mr. Monk."

"Are you afraid of what will happen to him?" Jasper asked.

"I'm afraid of what will happen to me," I replied.

2

Mr. Monk and the
Balance of Nature

It was a beautiful Monday morning, the kind that makes you want to jump onto a cable car and sing "I Left My Heart in San Francisco" at the top of your lungs.

But I wasn't in a cable car. I was in a Buick Lucerne that my father bought me when my old Jeep finally crapped out. It was only later that I discovered the real reason for Dad's largesse. He'd actually bought the Buick for his seventy-seven-year-old mother, who'd turned it down because she didn't want the same car that everybody else in her retirement community was driving. Nana was afraid she'd never be able to pick her car out from the others in the parking lot.

So Nana got a black BMW 3 Series and I got a car that my fifteen-year-old daughter, Julie, won't let me drive within a one-mile radius of her school for fear we might be seen. Supposedly Tiger Woods drives a car like mine, but if he does, I bet it's only to haul his clubs around on the golf course.

The day was so glorious, though, that I felt like I was driving a Ferrari convertible instead of a Buick. My glee lasted until I turned the corner in front of

Monk's apartment and saw the black-and-white police car parked at the curb and the yellow crime scene tape around the perimeter of the building.

I felt a pang of fear that injected a hot shot of adrenaline into my bloodstream and made my heart race faster than a hamster on his wheel.

Since I'd met Monk, I'd visited lots of places cordoned off with crime scene tape, and the one thing they all had in common was a corpse.

This wasn't good. Monk had made a lot of enemies over the years and I was afraid that one of them had finally come after him.

I double-parked behind the cop car, jumped over the yellow tape like a track star, and ran into the building. I was terrified of what I would find when I got inside.

The door to his apartment was open and two uniformed officers stood in the entry hall, their backs to me, blocking my way.

"Let me through," I said, pushing past them to see Monk facing us. He was perfectly relaxed, his starched white shirt buttoned at the collar and his sleeves buttoned at the wrist. Believe me, for him that's hanging loose.

I gave him a big hug and felt his entire body stiffen. He was repulsed by my touch, but at least his reaction proved he was alive and well.

"Are you okay?" I stepped back and took a good look at him and his surroundings. Everything was neat, tidy, balanced, and symmetrical.

"I'm a little shaken," Monk said. "But I'm coping."

"What happened?" I asked, glancing back at the two cops.

They were both grimacing. Either they'd eaten something that disagreed with them or they'd been talking to Monk. Their name tags identified them as Sergeant Denton and Officer Brooks.

"I was burglarized," Monk said.

"What did they take?" I asked.

"A sock," Monk said.

"A sock?" I said.

"A left sock," Monk said.

"There's no such thing," Officer Brooks said. "Socks are interchangeable."

Monk addressed Sergeant Denton. "Are you sure your partner graduated from the police academy?"

"Maybe you just misplaced the sock," Sergeant Denton said.

"I don't misplace things," Monk said.

That was true. His life was devoted to making sure that everything was in its proper place.

"When did you notice it was gone?" I asked.

"I washed my clothes in the basement laundry room this morning and brought them back up to my apartment to fold," Monk said. "Then I heard the sanitation truck arriving, so I put on my gloves and boots and went outside to supervise my trash collection."

Officer Brooks stared at him in disbelief. "You supervise your trash collection?"

"Don't ask," I said to the officer, then turned back to Monk. "So then what did you do?"

"I came back inside to resume folding my laundry," Monk said. "And that's when I discovered that I'd been brutally violated."

"You lost a sock," Sergeant Denton said.

"And my innocence," Monk said.

"Did you look for it?" I asked him.

"Of course I did," Monk said. "I searched the laundry room and then I ransacked my apartment."

"It doesn't look ransacked to me," Officer Brooks said.

"It was a ransacking followed by a ran-put-every-thing-backing."

"Socks disappear all the time, Mr. Monk," Sergeant Denton said.

"They do?" Monk said.

"Nobody knows where they go," the sergeant said. "It's one of the great mysteries of life."

"How long has this been going on?" Monk asked.

"As long as I can remember," Sergeant Denton said.

"And what's being done about it?"

"Nothing," the sergeant said.

"But it's your job," Monk said.

"To find lost socks?" Officer Brooks asked.

"To solve crimes," Monk replied. "There's some devious sock thief running rampant in this city and you aren't doing anything about it. Are you police officers or aren't you?"

"No one is stealing socks," Sergeant Denton said.

"But you just said there's a rash of sock disappearances," Monk said.

"It happens," I said. "I've lost tons of them."

"You've been victimized, too?" Monk said. "Why didn't you say anything?"

"Because they weren't stolen," I said.

"Then what happened?"

"I don't know," I said.

"Then how can you say they weren't stolen?" Monk said. "Socks don't just disappear."

I was surprised and a little disappointed that Monk was becoming so unhinged over this. He'd been doing so well the last few weeks.

"Why would anyone want to steal your socks?" Officer Brooks asked.

"They are very nice socks," Monk said. "One hundred percent cotton."

Sergeant Denton sighed. "We're leaving now."

"You haven't even taken my report yet," Monk said.

"We do that and then we have to detain you until someone from psych services arrives and does an evaluation, which could take hours," Sergeant Denton said. "I don't think any of us want that, do we, Mr. Monk?"

"Somebody broke into my home and stole my sock," Monk said. "I've secured the crime scene. What I want is a thorough investigation."

"Can you handle him?" Officer Brooks asked me. I nodded.

"I'm a consultant to the police," Monk said to them. "I work directly with Captain Leland Stottlemeyer in Homicide."

"So why didn't you call him?" Officer Brooks said.

"That would be overreacting," Monk said. "It's only a sock, for God's sake. It's not like someone was killed."

"It's nice to know you have some sense of perspective after all," Sergeant Denton said. "There's hope."

"There's never hope," Monk said.

The officers turned their backs to us and walked out.

Monk looked at me. "They are shirking their duty."

I didn't feel like arguing with him. "It's not a very valuable item, Mr. Monk. I suggest you just forget it and buy another pair of socks."

"And what do I do with the remaining sock?"

I shrugged. "Use it as a rag to clean around the house. That's what I do."

"You clean your house with your socks?" Monk said, his eyes wide with shock. "That's barbaric! I don't even want to think about what you do with your underwear. Not that I ever think about your underwear. Or anybody's underwear. Oh God, now I am seeing underwear. I have underwear in my head. What do I do?"

"You could throw the sock out."

"I can't," Monk said. "It will haunt me."

"It will?"

"I'll always know that a pair has been broken and that somewhere out there is a sock waiting to be re-united with its other half."

"The sock isn't waiting," I said. "It's a sock. It has no feelings."

"I will pursue my sock to the ends of the earth," Monk said. "I won't rest until the balance of nature has been restored."

"One sock is all that it takes to knock nature off balance?"

"Can't you feel it?"

The phone in the living room rang. I answered it for Monk. It was Captain Stottlemeyer.

"Perfect timing," I said. "There's been a crime."

"That's why I am calling," he said.

"You already heard about the sock?" I asked.

"I heard about a murder," the captain said. "What sock?"

"The one Mr. Monk lost and that's going to haunt him until he finds it."

In other words, Stottlemeyer could forget about Monk concentrating on any murder case as long as his sock was missing.

"I see," Stottlemeyer said. "You don't get paid enough."

"Neither do you," I said.

"But I don't have to see Monk every day if I don't want to," he said. "And I get to carry a gun and drive a car with a siren."

"You're blessed," I said.

"I wouldn't say that," he said. "My wife left me and my last steady girlfriend turned out to be a cold-blooded murderer."

"I guess life has a way of evening things out," I said.

"With my help," Monk added.

Stottlemeyer heard that. I could tell from his sigh. "Could you ask Monk to pick up the extension?"

I did. Monk got on the line in the kitchen. We could see each other through the open doorway.

"I want to report two officers who are shirkers," Monk said. "Flagrant shirkers."

"I've got a murder here, Monk," Stottlemeyer said. "It's a tricky case. I could use your help on this one."

"I've secured this crime scene," Monk said. "I can't just walk away. Vital evidence could be lost."

Stottlemeyer sighed again. I could visualize him rubbing his temple, fighting a growing Monkache in his skull.

"I'll make a deal with you, Monk. If you come over here, I'll reassign Randy to the Sock Recovery Task Force and send him to your place to lead the investigation."

"You have a Sock Recovery Task Force?" Monk said.

"We do now," Stottlemeyer told him.

Monk smiled. Balance was being restored.

Any other cop would have been pissed off about being taken off a homicide case and sent to Monk's apartment to look for a lost sock. But not Lieutenant Randy Disher, the captain's enthusiastic and loyal right-hand man. Disher was just thrilled to be heading a task force, *any* task force, even if it existed in name only to satisfy the crazy obsessions of a single psychologically disturbed ex-cop.

It was still a task force. And Disher was the top dog.

Disher didn't say this to me, but it was evident from the way he bounded into Monk's apartment, with his notepad out and a big smile on his face.

"What have we got?" Disher asked.

Monk told him. Disher took detailed notes.

"Can you describe the sock?"

"White, tube-style, size ten to twelve," Monk said. "For the left foot."

"That's a pretty common sock," Disher said. "Would you be able to identify it if you saw it again?"

"Absolutely," Monk said.

I wondered how he'd do that, but I kept my mouth shut.

"I'm on it," Disher said. "I'll develop a detailed timeline, retrace your steps from the laundry room, and question the suspects."

"What suspects?" I asked.

"The ones that will emerge in my investigation," Disher said.

"It's a lost sock, Randy," I said.

Monk leaned close to Disher and spoke in a whisper. "I would start with the new tenant in apartment 2C."

"Why?" Disher whispered back.

Monk tipped his head towards the window. The three of us looked outside. A young man in his twenties was making his way down the sidewalk on crutches. He was missing his right leg.

"That's him," Monk said. "He's obviously an unbalanced individual. I knew it instinctively the instant I saw him."

"He's missing a leg," I said. "That's not a crime or a reflection of his character."

"He doesn't have a *right* leg," Monk said. "So he'd only be interested in socks for his left foot. And you'll notice he's wearing a white sock."

I didn't notice. "That doesn't make him a thief."

"The day after he moves in, one of my best left socks is stolen," Monk said. "Coincidence? I don't think so."

So that was what this was all about. The new tenant had upset the delicate balance of Monk's world. He

couldn't stand the idea that someone with just one leg was living above him. It had probably been all Monk could think about since the man moved in and that irrational anxiety had manifested itself in a lost sock.

I felt like a detective who'd just solved a case.

"I'll question him," Disher said, tipping his head towards the man outside.

"You're not serious," I said. "You'll offend him."

"I'll use finesse," Disher said.

"There is no way to ask a one-legged man if he stole his neighbor's sock and not be offensive."

"I don't see how it's any more offensive than asking the same question of someone who has both legs," Disher said.

"You're right," I said. "So if I were you, I wouldn't ask anybody that question."

"But you aren't wearing a badge," Disher said. "I am. Being a cop means asking the tough questions."

"He doesn't shirk his responsibility," Monk said.

I didn't want to be there when Disher started his questioning. I visited Monk's apartment almost every day and I wanted to be able to face his neighbors without embarrassment or shame.

"You wouldn't want to shirk yours either, Mr. Monk. You have a murder investigation to consult on."

Monk nodded. We got the address of the crime scene and the names of the victims from Disher.

"This shouldn't take long," Monk said.

"You don't know anything about the case yet," I said.

"It's a murder," Monk said. "How hard could it be?"

"It's not like it's a lost sock," I said.

"Exactly," he said.

Monk had no ear for sarcasm. Thank God for that. If he did, I probably would have been fired years ago.

3

Mr. Monk Takes the Cake

Eric and Amy Clayson were a beautiful couple leading a beautiful life. They were in their thirties, with fashion-model, airbrush-perfect bodies and complexions, living in a wonderful, very contemporary Telegraph Hill apartment that was full of light and had a spectacular view of the bay. The Claysons were the ideal twosome pictured in advertisements for every product or service that promised health, vitality, sex appeal, and endless happiness. The only thing wrong with this picture was that the Claysons were dead.

But even in death, they looked great. There was no sign of violence or bloodshed, just their bodies frozen in rigor mortis like two toppled mannequins in a window display.

Eric was shirtless and wearing pajama shorts. His wife was in a nightgown and a thin robe. They were both on the floor beside the dinner table, their chairs still upright. On the table sat an open wine bottle, two glasses, and a half-eaten piece of birthday cake, with two forks on the edge of the plate.

When we came in, a team of forensic guys was wait-

ing impatiently to bag the items on the table and two
attendants from the morgue were waiting just as impatiently to bag the two corpses on the floor. I'd seen
them lingering and fidgeting like that before. They'd
undoubtedly been told by Stottlemeyer to wait so
Monk could survey the scene.

Before we could get there, we were intercepted by
Captain Stottlemeyer, who pulled us aside for a quiet
briefing and rubbed his bushy mustache with his finger. That was his tell. He was stressed.

"The victims are Eric and Amy Clayson. They sell
real estate together. They were discovered this morning at eight a.m. by their maid," Stottlemeyer said.
"The ME pegs their time of death at about midnight."

Monk cocked his head and regarded the bodies from
an angle. "They were poisoned."

"That's what the ME thinks, too," Stottlemeyer said.
"We'll analyze the wine, the cake, and their stomach
contents. We shouldn't have any trouble identifying
the poison and what was tainted with it."

Monk walked over to the table, holding his hands in
front of him like a director framing a scene.

"What's the tricky part?" I asked the captain.

Stottlemeyer brushed his mustache again and gestured towards a tight-lipped man who was standing
by the picture window, grimacing at the view. He had
a military-style haircut and seemed uncomfortable in
his dull gray suit.

"That's Andrew Walker, U.S. Marshals Service," the
captain whispered. "The Claysons were in the witness
protection program."

At the mention of his name, Walker whipped his
head around. He had the supersensitive hearing of a
Doberman pinscher and probably the same groomer.
He marched straight over. I was afraid he was going to
either shoot us or bite us.

"What are these civilians doing here?" Walker said. He spoke through gritted teeth, as if his jaws were wired shut. Or maybe he was trying to speak and growl at the same time. "It's bad enough our security was breached without widening the hole with two outsiders."

"That's Adrian Monk over there and this is his associate, Natalie Teeger," Stottlemeyer said. "If you want this case wrapped up quick, Monk is the guy who can do it."

Walker glanced at Monk, who was scowling at the cake, his nose nearly touching the dried white frosting.

"I'm not impressed," Walker said.

"He hasn't done anything yet," I said.

"I'm trained to assess the capabilities of an opponent in a nanosecond."

"He's not an opponent," Stottlemeyer said.

"The same criteria apply," Walker said. "He's a lightweight."

"Why were the Claysons in witness protection?" I asked.

"It's need to know, honey," Walker said.

"They're dead, Walker," Stottlemeyer said. "What difference does it make now?"

"It reveals our methods," Walker said.

"Which you ought to be changing anyway, since they clearly don't work," Stottlemeyer said, then turned to me. "The Claysons were lovers working as accountants for a mob family in New Jersey. The government threatened the couple with twenty years in prison unless they told us where the mob was stashing their money."

I watched Monk. He was roaming around the apartment, straightening things on shelves and wiping away dust.

"They agreed to talk in return for protection, immunity from prosecution, and a big wedding in Manhat-

tan," Stottlemeyer continued. "They went off on their honeymoon and never came back. The government gave them new faces, new names, and new lives here in San Francisco. Everything was dandy, until now."

No wonder the Claysons looked like the ideal couple leading the ideal life. They were fake, inside and out. But I appreciated the symbolism of them literally starting their lives anew on their wedding day. They were criminals with a sense of romance.

Monk stopped in front of the TV. The screen was black but the DVD player was turned on. He rolled his shoulders and cocked his head from one side to the other. He wasn't straightening himself out; he was solving the crime. He hadn't said a word yet, but I knew we were done here.

I glanced at Stottlemeyer. He knew it, too.

"We made sure they could never be found. But someone inside the Justice Department must have talked," Walker said. "There aren't that many people who knew who they were and where they were. I am going to find the leak and plug it with a bullet."

"There is no leak," Monk said.

"Then how did the mob find them?" Walker said. "Even if Big Carlo DeSantini himself bumped into them face-to-face on the street he wouldn't have recognized them."

"If this was a mob hit, why were they poisoned?" Stottlemeyer asked. "Why not shoot them or stab them or throw them off their balcony?"

"Dead is dead," Walker said.

Stottlemeyer shook his head in disagreement. "But you'd think that DeSantini would want to make it as messy and brutal as possible to send a message to anybody else who is thinking about cooperating with the government: We'll find you and you'll die a horrible death."

"The mob didn't find them," Monk said.

"The Justice Department was a week away from seeking multiple indictments against the DeSantini family," Walker said. "The Clayson murders last night torpedo the entire case. You don't see the connection?"

"The Claysons weren't murdered last night," Monk said.

I jumped in before Walker could shoot Monk where he stood.

"I think what Mr. Monk means is that, technically, it was this morning," I said. "The ME says they died after midnight."

"It was dark out," Walker said. "In my book that makes it night."

"They weren't murdered this morning either," Monk said.

Walker turned to Stottlemeyer. "This imbecile is the best detective you've got? That doesn't say much for law enforcement in Frisco." He turned to Monk. "I see two dead people on the floor. What do you see?"

"I see two people who were murdered a year ago," Monk said.

"Don't you think they'd be a little more ripe? Besides, I was at their wedding a year ago, posing as one of the bartenders, and they were very much alive."

Stottlemeyer rubbed his temples. "Monk, do you think you could be a little less cryptic and get to the point?"

Of course not. Monk had to have his fun. I knew it and Stottlemeyer knew it, but Walker didn't, and his face was turning an ominous shade of red. Ominous for Monk, not for Walker.

"The whole story is right here," Monk said, and hit PLAY on the DVD machine.

It was a wedding video. An attractive couple were taking their vows in front of a dour-faced judge in what

appeared to be a grand banquet hall in an old hotel. I assumed, since we were talking about a wedding, that the couple were the Claysons before they got their new faces. Their old faces weren't so bad either.

"What the hell were they doing with their wedding video?" Walker said. "It's a major security breach. If anybody saw that, it would have blown their cover."

They were romantics at heart, so of course they kept the video, regardless of the risk, which didn't seem too high to me.

"I don't see how," I said. "It could have been the video of a friend or relative's wedding."

"It got them killed, didn't it?" Walker snapped at me. At least his teeth didn't break my skin.

"No, it didn't," Monk said. "But it does show the murder being committed."

"How could it?" Walker said. "That video was shot a year ago."

"Now you're getting it," Monk said.

"I'm not getting a damn thing," Walker said.

"Just spit it out, Monk," Stottlemeyer said. "Who killed them?"

"I don't know who did it." Monk looked at Walker. "But you do."

Walker marched up to Monk and got nearly nose to nose with him. "I ought to kick your ass right here, right now. Are you accusing me of being the leak? Or are you saying that I murdered them myself?"

Monk took a step back to put some space between them and bumped into the TV. "Neither. Here's what happened. Somehow the DeSantini family discovered that the Claysons, or whatever their names were before, were going to cooperate with the authorities and that they would be entering the witness protection program that night. The couple would soon have new names and faces and would be next to impossible to

find. So the wedding was the DeSantinis' last chance to kill them, but the couple was too well protected."

"You're damn right they were," Walker said. "All the guests were thoroughly checked out, there was security at all the entrances and exits, and all the servers were U.S. Marshals. Not even a mosquito could get in that room and bite them."

"But the DeSantinis got to them anyway," Monk said and skipped the DVD forward, freezing the video on the happy couple cutting the wedding cake. "It's traditional for newlyweds to save a piece of cake and put it in the freezer to eat on their first anniversary. So someone poisoned the piece of cake, knowing that wherever they were, and whoever they'd become, the couple would eat it in twelve months, which happened to be how long it took the Justice Department to prepare their case. The cake was a time bomb. The Claysons were dead before they left the wedding. They just didn't know it."

I looked back at the couple, and at the cake on the table. They were celebrating their anniversary last night. That was why the wedding video DVD was in the player and the TV was still on. They were probably watching it when they died.

Until death do us part. It was a tragic romance that was doomed from the start.

"It was the best man," Walker said. "He was the one who saved the piece of cake and wrapped it for them. The DeSantinis must have gotten to him. But I was the stupid sonofabitch who kept the cake frozen and made sure it was in their freezer here when they arrived. So you were right, Monk. I was the one who killed them."

"You were being thoughtful," Stottlemeyer said. "You didn't know the cake was poisoned."

"I knew they shouldn't take anything with them

from their old lives, not even a piece of cake," Walker said. "I'm turning in my badge and taking early retirement."

"Over this?" Stottlemeyer said.

Walker gestured to Monk. "And him. I completely underestimated his abilities. That kind of mistake could get someone killed."

I have to admit I took pleasure in Walker's misery and pride in Monk's success. Walker was a jerk and deserved to be knocked down a peg. And I was pleased, and relieved, that Monk's incredible roll was continuing. I was losing count of how many murders he'd solved lately right at the scene.

"Can I go now, Captain?" Monk asked.

"Sure," Stottlemeyer said.

Monk started to go, but Walker stepped in front of him, blocking his way, and held out his hand.

"I owe you one," Walker said.

Monk shook his hand, then motioned to me for a disinfectant wipe. I gave him one. "As it happens, I could use the federal government's help on a case."

"What is it?" Walker said, watching Monk wipe his hands. It obviously offended him.

"I'm missing a sock," Monk said.

Walker narrowed his eyes at Monk. "Are you messing with me?"

"I never make a mess," Monk said.

"But he does a hell of a job cleaning them up," Stottlemeyer said.

4

Mr. Monk Sees His Shrink

Even though Walker was indebted to Monk for solving the murder in less than thirty minutes (fast even by Monk's standards), the marshal was unwilling to dedicate the full resources of the Justice Department to finding a lost sock.

"Our resources are stretched a little thin and we have to prioritize," Walker said. "We're fighting a war on terror at the moment."

"You don't think thousands of missing socks is terrifying?" Monk asked. "Our enemies could be using psychological warfare to undermine the stability of American society."

"By making socks disappear," Walker said.

"It's insidious and ingenious," Monk said.

Walker didn't buy it. I couldn't blame him. I had a hard time imagining Osama sitting in his cave thinking of ways to steal my socks.

But Walker's refusal to help didn't dim Monk's spirits. He still enjoyed his post-crime-solving high. At least he'd set part of the world right. His sock drawer would come next.

When we got back to Monk's place, the crime scene tape was gone and we found Disher sitting to the right of the one-legged man on the front steps of the building. They were both drinking from cans of Coke and smiling.

Monk whispered to me as we approached the building from my parked car. "Randy has shrewdly lulled the suspect into a false sense of security to lower his defenses. He's going in for the kill."

I'll admit I was surprised to see them hanging out together. I'd assumed the one-legged guy would be offended by Disher's questions and the thinly veiled—not to mention ridiculous—accusations they probably contained.

Monk covered up his right eye with his hand as we neared the steps and turned his head at a slight angle to regard the two men.

"Hey, Monk, back so soon?" Disher said.

"I solved the case," Monk said.

"I solved mine, too," Disher said and whipped out a plastic evidence bag from behind his back. Inside the bag was a white sock. "Look familiar?"

"It's my sock." Monk took the bag. "Thank you, Randy."

"My pleasure. This is Nick," Disher said, motioning to the new tenant. "And this is your neighbor Adrian Monk and his assistant, Natalie Teeger."

Nick offered me his hand. I shook it.

"Welcome to the neighborhood," I said.

"Thanks," Nick said. "It's really peaceful and everybody here is so friendly."

"Why isn't he in handcuffs?" Monk said, ignoring Nick's outstretched hand.

"Because he didn't do anything," Disher said. "The culprit is static electricity. Your sock got stuck inside the dryer. After you left, Mrs. Sandowsky in 2B did a

load. The sock got mixed with her stuff. Is something wrong with your eye?"

"No," Monk said.

"So what's the problem?" Disher asked.

"The problem is that there is no problem," Monk said. "I can see everything that's in front of me and not in front of me. Would you mind sitting to his left?"

Monk gestured to Nick without looking at him. Disher moved to the other side of Nick. The legged side.

"You thought I stole your sock?" Nick said to Monk.

"No," Monk said.

"Are you being honest with me?"

"No," Monk said.

"Nick was just telling me about his adventure climbing alone on Mount Kilimanjaro," Disher said with boyish eagerness. "He got his leg stuck between two boulders and had to cut it off with his pickax to save himself."

"My God," I said. I remembered reading an article about him in the *San Francisco Chronicle* a few months back. It was a horrifying and yet undeniably captivating tale.

"And you left it there?" Monk said.

"Yeah," Nick said.

"You should go back and get it," Monk said.

"It's a little late for that."

"You know what they say—it's never too late to pick up your leg," Monk said.

"Actually, it is," Nick said.

"That's not what they say," Monk said. "And they wouldn't say it if it wasn't true."

"Who are 'they'?" Disher asked.

"They are the people you should listen to when they say something," Monk said. "They know what they are talking about."

"I ate it," Nick said.

"You ate it?" Monk said, looking at Nick despite himself and then turning away, repulsed. "Your own leg?"

"Amazing," Disher said. "I thought I was tough, but you're like five times tougher."

"I had no choice, Randy. I was alone in the snow for days. I had no idea how long it would take them to find me. It was a matter of survival," Nick said. "Life or death."

"You should have chosen death," Monk said.

"What Mr. Monk means is that he admires your bravery and sympathizes with your sacrifice," I said, hustling Monk past them. "You'll have to stop by sometime for coffee."

Monk gasped. "What if he wants something to eat?"

I hoped Nick hadn't heard that. I hurried Monk into his apartment and closed the door behind us.

"How could you be so rude?" I said.

"I have to move out," Monk said. "Help me pack."

"He's a hero," I said.

"He's a cannibal and you invited him here for a snack," Monk said. "What were you thinking?"

"He's not going to do it again," I said. "It was an extreme situation."

"So is this," Monk said. "I'm very tasty to cannibals."

"What makes you say that?"

"It's the one thing I've been absolutely certain of my entire life."

"You've got to be kidding," I said.

"Look at me. I'm clean, healthy, trim, and I stay away from all germs and chemicals. I'm lean, delicious, prime-cut, organic meat. That's why I've never gone to Africa."

"That's why? I thought it was because you're afraid of travel, foreign countries, zebras, airplanes, Tarzan, monkeys, khaki, giraffes, salted peanuts, lions, quicksand, thatched roofs, scorpions, jungles, loincloths, deserts, meerkats, spears, and—"

"—cannibals," Monk interrupted. "Most of all, cannibals. If I stay here, I'll be my neighbor's next meal. I have to find a new apartment in a building that doesn't allow children, pets, or cannibals."

"Mr. Monk, Nick is a great man. Someone to be respected, not feared. Do you realize the unbelievable courage it took for him to cut off his own leg? Can you imagine the pain and suffering he endured? But he survived. He's an example of the endurance of the human spirit in the face of unimaginable adversity," I said. "You'd see things differently if you'd just put yourself in his shoes."

"Shoe," Monk said.

"You're impossible," I said.

"I'm whole," Monk said. "At least until his stomach starts growling. Once you've tasted human flesh, that's all you can eat."

"How would you know?"

"It's what they say," Monk said.

"Them again?" I had to meet these people and give them muzzles. I looked at my watch. "You know what your problem is?"

"Yes. I have a cannibal living in my building."

"You can't accept anyone who isn't just like you. You have no tolerance for diversity. It's the differences between people that make us special."

"Diversity is great," Monk said. "As long as it's clean, even, and symmetrical."

I don't know why I bothered to argue with him. He was never going to change, which reminded me of something. I glanced at my watch.

"You're going to be late for your appointment with Dr. Kroger if we don't get moving."

Monk had never missed his thrice-weekly appointments with his shrink, nor had he ever been late to one. They were the highlights of his week. To be honest, I cherished them, too. It was the only time off that I got on weekdays.

"Let's go out the back," Monk said, making a beeline for his kitchen door, one hand over his right eye.

"But I'm parked in front," I said.

"I don't want to go past the cannibal," Monk said. "What if I trip? I'd be injured prey, easy pickings."

"Then you might want to watch where you're going with both eyes."

"If I do that, I might see something," Monk said. "Or not see something, which would be much worse."

Dr. Kroger's office was on Jackson Street in Pacific Heights and within walking distance of Monk's apartment building on Pine. It was a beautiful day for a walk, but we drove there as usual. By taking the car, we could get to a crime scene in a hurry if Monk got a call from the captain after an appointment. But that wasn't the real reason we almost always took the car. We were both too lazy to make the hike up the steep hill and Monk didn't want to arrive in Dr. Kroger's office with a single bead of sweat on his skin.

We got there a few minutes early, which gave Monk the opportunity to organize the magazines in Dr. Kroger's waiting room by title, subject, and date. It was a ritual that I think helped him to relax and gather his thoughts for the session.

Dr. Kroger emerged from his office a few moments later and escorted out his previous patient, a meek woman I'd seen once a week for years. She never once met our eyes or acknowledged us. All I knew was that

her name was Marcia, so I'd created a dozen imaginary scenarios about her to entertain myself. Since Dr. Kroger was the shrink of choice for the SFPD, my latest story was that she was a detective booted from the force for her raging nymphomania.

"Good afternoon, Natalie," Dr. Kroger said, flashing a smile that showed all his perfectly straight, whitened teeth. If his teeth hadn't been so straight, Monk never would have become his patient. Monk couldn't look at someone with crooked teeth for five minutes, much less years on end. "How is your day today?"

"The usual," I said.

"By that she means a living hell," Monk said.

He was right.

"Are you speaking for her or for yourself?" Dr. Kroger asked.

"I'm speaking for all of humanity," Monk said.

"That's quite a burden you're taking on, Adrian. Perhaps you'd find your day slightly less hellish if you concentrated more on your needs and less on those of humanity."

Dr. Kroger had a very relaxing way of speaking, regardless of what he was saying. His voice gently stroked and comforted you. It was like listening to the tide, if the tide charged a couple hundred dollars an hour.

"That's easy for you to say," Monk said. "You don't know what I've had to face today."

"I'm eager to hear all about it," Dr. Kroger said, motioning Monk into his office and dismissing me with a friendly nod. I was free to go for an hour of Monkless bliss.

On a cold or rainy day, I might have hung around in the waiting room and caught up on *Cosmopolitan* and *Vanity Fair*. Instead, I walked up the street to Alta Plaza, which has some of the best views in the city from its grassy hills and stone steps.

From the north end of the park, I could see clear across the bay to Marin County and from the south side, I could gaze upon the San Francisco skyline. The view wasn't bad inside the park either. There were usually some tanned, muscular guys to see on the tennis courts. Sometimes they were even shirtless. Today was one of those days.

I bought an Eskimo Pie from a pushcart vendor, found a bench with views of the bay and the bods, and took it easy. There were worse ways to kill an hour.

My mind wandered. I thought about Nick cutting off his own leg to free himself from the rocks and then having to eat his limb to stay alive. I am pretty sure that if I'd been in his position, I would have died with my leg pinned in the rocks. I have a hard time just removing a splinter from my finger.

I figured that Nick was probably writing a book about his experiences, and there was probably a movie in it, too, so he was going to do all right financially. But how did it feel to have to carry that memory around with him? To be reminded of it every time he looked at himself in the mirror or simply tried to walk across the room? How did he deal with the insensitive remarks from people like Monk?

I watched the men playing tennis and thought about Nick climbing mountains by himself. He must have been a very strong, physically active man. So how did it feel to be disabled now? How was he coping with the fact that he would never be that man again?

All those unanswered questions made Nick fascinating to me. And very attractive.

I was pretty certain Monk wasn't asking himself what Nick was thinking and feeling. That would require tolerance, empathy, and understanding.

Monk looked at Nick and saw imperfection, disorder, and horror. I looked at Nick and saw mystery, character, and emotional complexity.

We'd be having that coffee together very soon, preferably without Monk around.

I figured Monk would be okay with that.

I finished my ice cream and headed back down the hill to Dr. Kroger's building. I walked into the waiting room just as Dr. Kroger and Monk were coming out of the office.

"You were a big help today, Doctor," Monk said.

"I am pleased to hear that, Adrian," Dr. Kroger said. "I think you're in a real good place right now."

"I'm moving," Monk said.

"I meant emotionally and psychologically. I wasn't talking about your apartment. You've made so much progress, Adrian. I don't think running away is the best way to cope with your fears."

"It certainly is when you're being pursued by a one-legged cannibal," Monk said. "We can talk about it next week, if he hasn't eaten me."

"I'm afraid not," Dr. Kroger said.

"You don't think I can outrun him?" Monk said. "He's on crutches."

"I meant that I'm not going to be here next week," Dr. Kroger said. "I'm leaving tomorrow for Lohr, a small village in Germany, to attend an international psychiatric conference."

Monk looked at him in shock. "You're leaving me?"

"I'll be back in a week."

"How could you do this to me?" Monk said.

I was tempted to ask the same question. Without Dr. Kroger to support him, Monk would have a complete mental meltdown and I would have to deal with it on my own.

"This isn't about you, Adrian," Dr. Kroger said. "I have a life of my own beyond my sessions with you."

"I believe you are mistaken," Monk said. "And if you really think about it, I am sure that you will agree."

"I haven't taken any time off in years," Dr. Kroger said. "This trip will enrich my understanding of human behavior and give me a chance to relax. It will be good for me and for you. In a way, it's perfect timing."

"How can you possibly say that?" Monk cried out. "Didn't you hear anything I told you today? I am in crisis. I need help now more than ever."

"And you'll get it," Dr. Kroger said. "I've arranged for Dr. Jonah Sorenson to see you while I am away."

Monk gasped. "The one-armed guy?"

"He's an exceptional psychiatrist and a wonderful human being."

Monk had seen Dr. Sorenson for one session last year when Dr. Kroger briefly flirted with retirement. The session lasted less than five minutes.

"But he's got a big problem," Monk said.

"Not that I can see," Dr. Kroger said.

"He's only got one arm!" Monk shrieked.

"I don't see that as a problem," Dr. Kroger said.

"Are you blind?"

"In fact, I see his disability as an asset in your treatment. By sharing your feelings with him, and discovering what a sensitive and knowledgeable person he is, you'll feel less threatened by people who are physically different from you."

In theory, that was a great idea. In practice, it was never going to work. I knew it with absolute certainty and I had no psychiatric training whatsoever, except for what I learned listening to Dr. Laura on the radio. So why didn't Dr. Kroger realize it? Then again, maybe he did and just didn't care. All he wanted was a vacation from Monk.

I could sympathize. I almost got away for a Monk-free week in Hawaii but he showed up uninvited on the plane. He was armed with a fresh prescription from Dr. Kroger for Dioxynl, the mood-altering drug that re-

lieved his phobias and enabled him to fly without fear. I've always suspected that Dr. Kroger put Monk up to it to avoid being harassed night and day while I was away.

"Dr. Sorenson is unbalanced," Monk said. "How can you leave your patients in the care of an unbalanced person? That's a clear case of malpractice."

"I'm going to Germany tomorrow, Adrian, and nothing you say or do is going to change that." Dr. Kroger stepped into his office and closed the door in Monk's face.

Monk didn't move. He just stared forlornly at the door.

"We have to go now," I said.

"I'm staying right here," Monk said.

"What good will that do?"

"If he thinks about it for a moment, I'm convinced that he'll come to his senses and cancel his trip."

"He seemed pretty adamant about it to me."

"I felt that I got through to him at the end," Monk said. "As he was closing the door in my face, I could see that he was wrestling with some major doubts."

"There were no doubts," I said.

"We'll see when he comes out," Monk said.

"He's not coming out," I said.

"Great," Monk said. "I'll stand here until my next appointment. If you want to see real endurance, and the true strength of the human spirit, just watch me."

Monk put his hands on his hips and planted his feet in place and stared firmly at the door. I guess that stance was supposed to mean he was in this for the long haul. I'm sure the door was very intimidated.

"I'm not going anywhere," Monk yelled. "And neither are you."

There was no response. Monk shifted his weight.

"You'll thank me later," Monk yelled.

There was no response.

"Or you could thank me now," Monk yelled. "Either way is fine with me."

"Doesn't the back of his office open onto an atrium?" I asked.

Monk nodded.

"And doesn't that atrium have a door that leads to the tenant parking garage?"

Monk shifted his gaze to me. "You don't think he would do that, do you?"

"I think he already has," I said.

Monk opened the door. The office was empty. Dr. Kroger had fled.

"I'm doomed," Monk said.

I was, too.

5

Mr. Monk Falls Apart

As soon as we got in the car, Monk wanted me to drive him to Dr. Kroger's house. I refused.

"That would be invading his privacy," I said.

"I'm family," Monk said.

"You're one of his patients," I said.

"It's the same thing," Monk said.

"No, it's not, Mr. Monk. It's crossing a line. He is a doctor and you are his patient. You are not his family. He is paid to listen to you and offer his guidance and advice."

"We've gone past that," Monk said.

"You have," I said. "He hasn't. He's a professional and I'm not going to help you stalk him."

Monk sulked for a long moment before speaking up again. "He doesn't see me three times a week because he's paid to. He cares about me."

"I'm sure that he does, Mr. Monk. He wouldn't be much of a doctor if he didn't care about his patients."

"It's more than that. I share all my fears and anxieties with him."

"You share them with everybody," I said. "The ones you don't exhibit in your behavior you have

listed, indexed, and leather-bound for people to reference."

"But he knows them all by heart. He actually listens. He's there for me," Monk said. "Or at least he was."

"He still is," I said. "But he has a life. That's his priority. You are his job."

"I see," Monk said. "The only reason he cares about me, listens to my problems, and offers me emotional support is because I pay him. If I didn't, he'd be gone."

"I'm afraid so," I said.

"That's the way it is," Monk said.

"Yes, it is," I said.

I felt like we had made a real breakthrough. Perhaps, I thought, I should consider becoming a shrink. I seemed to have a knack for it.

"Is that how it is with you?" Monk asked.

So much for my knack. I didn't see that question coming. The car suddenly felt very cramped to me. I broke into a sweat.

"What do you mean?" I asked.

I knew what he meant, of course. I was just trying to buy some time to think of how I was going to talk myself out of this one.

"Would you still care about me if I wasn't paying you?"

"You hardly pay me as it is, so it's a moot point," I said with what I hoped was a lighthearted smile, which is hard to pull off when, in fact, you have a heavy heart. A two-ton heart.

Monk stared at me. I cleared my throat.

"You aren't just a job to me, Mr. Monk. I honestly care about you. And I would whether I worked for you or not."

"Then is it so hard to imagine that Dr. Kroger might feel the same way?"

He had a good point. I pulled over and looked at him. I didn't want what I was going to say to appear tossed off.

"You're right, Mr. Monk. I'm sorry. I don't know how Dr. Kroger feels about you and it was wrong of me to assume that I did."

Monk nodded. "Apology accepted."

"Thank you," I said, and glanced over my shoulder to check for traffic before moving back into the street.

"So will you take me to his house now?"

"No," I said.

"Fine," Monk said. "I'll just have him arrested."

"On what charge?"

"Abandonment," Monk said.

"That's not a crime," I said.

"It is when you go off on a vacation and leave your children home alone unattended and unsupervised," Monk said.

"You aren't his child. You're his patient."

"Same thing," Monk said.

"You're an adult," I said.

"That's open to debate," Monk said.

I couldn't argue with him there. Monk started to make a strange mewling noise.

"What are you doing?"

"I'm weeping," Monk said. "Can't you see that?"

"There aren't any tears," I said.

"I'm tearless weeping," Monk said.

"You can't weep without tears," I said.

"Then what am I doing?"

"I have no idea," I said.

"Dr. Kroger would know," Monk said.

I took Monk to his apartment. He told me he was too depressed to work, not that we had any cases anyway, and he sent me home. I watched him creep in the back way to avoid the cannibals, and then I drove away.

*   *   *

I made pork chops and Caesar salad for dinner. But when I set the plates down on the kitchen table, Julie rolled her eyes theatrically and groaned. I don't know where the audience was that she was playing to, but the performance wasn't entertaining me.

"What's wrong?" I asked.

"We always have the same things for dinner," she said.

"Last night we had spaghetti."

"With salad," she said. "And we had chicken the day before."

"Chicken isn't pork," I said.

"It's meat," she said. "With a salad."

"You don't like meat and salad?"

"It's boring," she said.

"What do you want instead?"

"I don't know," she said. That's what she always said. I was expected to read her mind.

"You always have complaints, but never any suggestions. How am I supposed to know what you want to eat? I don't have a crystal ball."

No sooner did I say that than I cringed. My mom used to say the same thing to me. Is it inevitable that we all eventually become our parents? Would Julie be saying that to her daughter in fifteen years?

"We could go out," she said.

That's all she ever wanted to do. Food wasn't good unless you ordered it off a menu.

"We're eating at home. This is what is being served. If you don't like it, there's cereal in the pantry."

I started to eat. It was tasty, if I do say so myself.

She glared at me. "Cereal is breakfast food. You don't eat breakfast food for dinner."

"Now you sound like Mr. Monk," I said.

Julie gave me a withering look, with all the wither a teenager can muster.

"You always have to blow everything out of proportion. I don't like the culinary monotony in this house, so you compare me to a crazy person. That's really mature."

"Culinary monotony?" I said. "Where do you get this stuff?"

"I read, Mom."

"I can't remember the last time I saw you open a book or a newspaper."

"I don't read cave drawings either," she said. "There's this new thing called the Web—maybe you've heard of it."

"When did you become so snotty?"

She was talking her way right into being grounded when my phone rang, sparing her. I answered it.

"Help," Monk croaked.

"What is it, Mr. Monk?" I glanced at Julie, who poked at her food with her fork like she was preparing to dissect a frog.

"He's up there," he said. "I can hear him hopping around on one foot."

"Good," I said. "You should feel secure knowing exactly where he is."

"It's the incessant beat of imminent death," Monk said. "Hop. Hop. Hop."

"I'm sure it's not that bad," I said.

"Hop. Hop. Hop."

"Try earplugs," I said. "Or cotton balls."

"Hop. Hop. Hop."

"Put a pillow over your head," I said.

"Hop. Hop. Hop."

"I get the point, Mr. Monk. I'm sure he'll sit down soon for dinner."

"That's what I am afraid of," Monk said.

"Good-bye, Mr. Monk." I hung up and looked at

Julie, who was eating her food with an overly dramatic show of joylessness.

"It could be worse," I said. "You could be eating your toes."

She looked at me as if I was losing my mind. I wasn't. Yet. That was still a couple of hours away.

The first call came at about one a.m. I clawed my way out of a deep sleep and reached blindly towards my nightstand for the phone. I knocked it off the table and almost fell out of bed searching for it on the floor in the darkness.

I was dangling out of my bed, my head nearly touching the floor, when I found the phone and answered it.

"Yes?" I said.

"He's stopped moving," Monk said.

"Isn't that what you wanted?" I said. "Go to sleep."

"How can I sleep, not knowing where he is?" Monk said.

"Get a grip, Mr. Monk." I am not very sympathetic when I am rudely awakened and I'm nearly upside down, with all the blood rushing into my groggy head.

"He could be outside my door right now, licking his lips and sharpening his pickax."

"Relax," I said. "He's never eaten anyone's flesh but his own."

"Maybe he wants to broaden his palate," Monk said. "And break the culinary monotony."

Culinary monotony? Again? I struggled up into a sitting position in bed.

"Have you and Julie been talking?"

"No," Monk said. "But do you think she would talk to me? I could use someone to talk to. Put her on."

"I am going to bed," I said. "Don't call back."

I left the phone off the hook, lowered the volume, and shoved it under a pillow. And then I went back to sleep.

Here's a piece of advice. Always remember to turn off your cell phone when you're charging it or you could get a call at 4:42 a.m. from an obsessive-compulsive detective having a mental meltdown.

I didn't hear the call, since the charger is in the kitchen. But Julie heard it. She padded into my room and shook me awake.

"What is it?" I asked. "Are you sick?"

She held the cell phone out to me. "It's Mr. Monk. He's sick."

I took the phone from her and shouted into it. "I told you not to call."

"It's a medical emergency," Monk said hoarsely.

"So call 911," I said.

"I did," Monk said. "But they wouldn't come."

"What's the emergency?"

"I can't swallow," he said.

"Why not?"

"I forgot," Monk said, and began tearlessly weeping. "I've forgotten how to swallow. I'm going to die."

"What did the 911 operator tell you to do?"

"She told me to swallow."

"Good advice," I said and removed the battery from my phone.

When I arrived at Monk's house the next morning, I found him in his bed, fully dressed, holding a can of Lysol in each hand, aimed at the door.

"Have you been lying like that all night?" I asked.

"I'm under siege," he said.

"There's nobody around," I said.

"Germs," Monk said. "They are everywhere."

"That's not exactly a revelation," I said. "You've known that all of your life."

"But they weren't coming to get me before," Monk said.

"What makes you think they are coming now?"

"I can feel it," Monk said and started spraying all around him until he was surrounded by a cloud of Lysol mist.

"Is it safe for you to be breathing that stuff?"

"It's disinfectant," Monk said. "It's safer than air."

I didn't share that belief, so I stepped out of the room. I used the moment of privacy to ponder my next move. Monk was falling apart, his shrink was on his way to Europe, and I was completely alone. It could only get worse. What was I going to do?

On the bright side, Monk seemed to have remembered how to swallow.

The phone rang, so I answered it.

"Good morning, Natalie," Captain Stottlemeyer said cheerfully. "How is Monk today?"

"A complete wreck," I said.

"Even though Randy's dogged investigation led to the recovery of his lost sock?"

"Dr. Kroger went on vacation," I said.

"Oh hell," Stottlemeyer said.

"Monk didn't call you?"

"Thankfully, no."

"He called me twice last night before I disconnected my phones," I said. "Why didn't he call you?"

"He knows I would have shot him to put him out of his misery," Stottlemeyer said. "And mine."

"It was a serious question," I said.

"He used to call me all the time, day and night, to complain about dust bunnies and potholes and God knows what else. My wife was furious. She wanted me to get a restraining order against him. So I finally had

to tell Monk that he was ruining my marriage and that if he called me at home again, I'd fire him. I guess it hasn't sunk in yet that I'm divorced. Please don't remind him."

"You'll have to give me something in return," I said.

"How about a murder?" he said.

"You're going to kill Monk for me?"

"I am standing beside a dead guy and I have no idea who killed him," Stottlemeyer said. "I'm thinking that a murder case might be exactly what Monk needs right now."

I never thought that I'd ever welcome the news that a person had been murdered, but I'm ashamed to say that, in this situation, I did.

6

Mr. Monk Loses Count

Ever since I started working for Monk, a lot of my mornings have begun with a corpse. I used to find that strange and unsettling. Now it's typical. I don't want to say I have become blasé about it, but it just goes to prove that over time you can get used to just about anything.

Nine out of the ten cases Monk takes on begin in the morning. The sun rises and somebody stumbles on a corpse left behind the night before. I really have no statistics to back this up, but it seems to me that most murders happen at night.

I can see why. If I was going to commit a crime, I'd do it in the dark so nobody could see me doing my nasty deed. There is also something about doing wrong in the bright light of day that makes it feel even *more* wrong. When you're giving in to your dark side, you instinctively want to do it in the dark.

It just feels right—not that I've given in to my dark side all that often. But when I have, with the possible exception of indulging in something decadently fattening, it has been at night.

This may seem like pointless musing to you, but I do a lot of pointless musing while looking down at a dead body. It helps distract me from things like Clarke Trotter's caved-in skull.

Captain Stottlemeyer, Lieutenant Disher, and Monk don't have that luxury. They have to pay attention to all the details of the crime, no matter how gory or sad. And Monk picks up even more details than anybody else.

Well, usually he does. The investigation into Clarke Trotter's murder was starting out a little differently.

We were in Trotter's one-bedroom apartment in North Beach, which is nowhere near a beach, but don't get me started on that. Even without a stretch of sand, the rent on seven hundred square feet in this neighborhood will set you back twice as much as my mortgage payment.

The apartment was furnished in what I like to call Contemporary Single Guy. All the furniture was big, black, and upholstered in leather (men love their animal hides). The living room was dominated by an altar to the god of electronics—a massive flat-screen television surrounded by stacks of devices. I could pick out a Play/Station, an Xbox, a DVD player, a TiVo, a Wii, a satellite receiver, a cable box, and an amplifier. There was a lot more stuff, too. I just didn't know what it all was.

The coffee table was covered with more electronics—a laptop, an iPod, an iPhone, a BlackBerry, a dozen remotes—and a smattering of men's "lifestyle" magazines, like *FHM*, *Stuff*, and *Maxim*, and empty cans of Red Bull. It was a mess.

The owner of this mess, the aforementioned and very dead Clarke Trotter, was in his bathrobe and lying sideways on the couch. He was a bit pudgy, although I wouldn't call him fat. But it was clear the only exercise he got was on his Wii. There was congealed grease in

his hair and splattered over the couch, carpet, and coffee table.

Stottlemeyer, Disher, and I stood behind the couch. A bunch of forensics guys were dusting and photographing and putting things in Baggies. The CSI crew reminded me of Willy Wonka's Oompa-Loompas, only not as adorable or musical.

Monk stood absolutely still in the doorway to the apartment, his hands gripping the wall on either side of him as if the room was listing under his feet.

Stottlemeyer glanced at Monk, then back to us. "What's traumatized him this morning?"

"I think it's the spot on your tie," Disher said.

"Thanks for pointing that out to him. I've only worn this once and now he's going to make me incinerate it."

"He's obviously noticed," Disher said. "Look at him."

"I don't think it's my tie," Stottlemeyer said. "You've only got seven holes in your belt."

"I do?" Disher said, looking down at himself.

"Everybody knows you need six or eight. You've upset the time-space continuum. You're going to have to go punch another hole in it." Stottlemeyer glanced back at Monk. "Isn't that right?"

"I've lost count of my blinking," Monk said.

"You count your blinks?" Stottlemeyer asked.

"I always do it in the back of my mind. It's how I maintain my sanity."

"Is that how you do it?" Stottlemeyer said. "If I had to count my daily blinking, it would drive me insane."

"I don't know how many times I've blinked so far today," Monk said, his voice tinged with hysteria. "I've lost count."

"So start again," Stottlemeyer said.

"I've kept track of my blinks since the day I learned how to count."

I bet if I asked, he could have given me the exact date of that fateful day.

Monk made that strange tearless weeping sound. "My mom kept track for me before that."

"She did?" I asked.

It was a rhetorical question, of course. I've long since stopped being shocked by the things Monk's mother did to completely screw him up for life. It was no wonder that his father went out for Chinese food one night and never came back. Or that Monk's only brother, Ambrose, never leaves the house.

"Didn't you count Julie's blinks for her?" Monk asked.

"Nope," I said.

"Then how did she know how much you loved her?"

"I told her," I said. "Every day. I still do. I also give her lots of hugs and kisses."

Monk shook his head. "There's no substitute for the comfort and certainty of a mother's accurate blink count."

"What difference does it make how many times you've blinked?" Disher asked.

"It's your foundation. It's who you are," Monk said. "Now I have no center. Who am I? What am I? Where do I go from here?"

Stottlemeyer marched impatiently up to Monk.

"You are Adrian Monk, a detective, and you're walking into this apartment and solving a murder."

He grabbed Monk by the lapels and dragged him into the room.

"But my count—" Monk began.

"Consider yourself reborn," Stottlemeyer said. "You're at blink number one. Most of the people I know would kill for a fresh start."

"Maybe that's what happened here," Disher said.

I looked at the dead guy on the couch. "He was killed so someone else could start their life anew?"

Disher shrugged. "It's one possibility."

Stottlemeyer turned to Monk. "What do you think?"

Monk stood by the couch. He seemed lost. He blinked.

"Two," he said.

Stottlemeyer massaged his temples. "Randy, tell Monk what we know. Maybe that will get things rolling."

Disher referred to his notebook. "Clarke Trotter is a thirty-seven-year-old lawyer, recently single. Works as general counsel for San Francisco Memorial Hospital. He left his wife two months ago for another woman. He moved in here; his wife stayed in their house in San Rafael with their five-year-old daughter. She's seven months pregnant."

I looked at Trotter. What a lovely guy, leaving a pregnant woman and sticking her with caring for their kid. If he was still alive, I'd be tempted to murder him. Following that train of thought led me to an obvious suspect.

His wife, of course.

But it couldn't have been easy for her. It's nearly impossible to find a babysitter to watch the kids while you go to the movies, much less kill your scoundrel of a husband.

I noticed Stottlemeyer looking at me. "I know what you're thinking. I'm thinking it, too." He looked at Monk. "How about you?"

Monk was just standing there in some kind of stupor, blinking and counting.

"Twelve," Monk said.

"Where did you get all of this dirt on Trotter?" I asked.

"From his cleaning lady," Disher said. "They always know everything. She was also the one who found his body."

I'd hate being a maid or custodian—and not just because of the cleaning, low pay, and lack of respect. They always seem to be the first ones to find dead bodies, whether it's in homes, hotel rooms, or offices.

"The medical examiner thinks Trotter was walloped with a blunt object, like a frying pan," Stottlemeyer said. "We're basing that on the shape of the head wound and the splatter pattern of cooking grease around the body. There must have still been some grease left over in the pan from whatever Trotter made himself for dinner."

"The killer cleaned the kitchen from top to bottom to cover his tracks," Disher said. "He even put the frying pan, sponge, and scrub brush in the dishwasher."

The kitchen opened onto the living room and was spotlessly clean. The counters gleamed; everything was neatly arranged. Even the dishrags were neatly folded and hung. It looked more like an operating room than a place where food was prepared.

I nudged Monk, figuring the sight of such cleanliness might lighten him up. "Look, a clean kitchen. It's sparkling."

Monk looked at it and simply nodded.

"Whatever evidence was on the frying pan and cleaning utensils has been washed away," Disher said. "But we have the crime lab checking the drains and pipes just in case."

Stottlemeyer shook his head. "We won't find anything. This is the work of a pro."

"Or an avid viewer of *CSI*," I said.

"I hate that show," Stottlemeyer said. "I'd like to punch the guy who had the brilliant idea of doing a show that teaches crooks how to avoid being caught."

"It's actually three shows," Disher said. "There's

also the one in Miami and the one in New York. I think they should do one in San Francisco."

"Why don't you suggest it to them?" Stottlemeyer said.

"I have," Disher said. "I jotted down a few ideas for the characters. But they are taking their sweet time getting back to me."

"Let me guess. It's loosely based on your life," Stottlemeyer said.

"It's mostly focused on my exciting adventures," Disher said.

"What exciting adventures?"

"You know," Disher said. "Like this."

"You find this exciting?"

"It could be," Disher said. "Imagine if three ninja warriors cartwheeled through the window right now."

Stottlemeyer turned to Monk. "What do you think? Are we looking for ninjas?"

Monk shrugged.

"Surely you've got some observations," Stottlemeyer said.

Monk shook his head. "I don't even know who I am. How can I know who the murderer is?"

"Look around," I said. "Do your thing."

"I did," he said.

"You haven't done this," I said, and proceeded to do my imitation of his Zen-detective thing.

I walked around the room like a chicken directing a movie. I cocked my head from side to side and held my hands in front of me as if I was framing a shot.

"That's not quite right," Disher said. He walked through the apartment, rolling his shoulders and squinting. "This is what he does."

We both turned to face Monk.

"I don't do that," he said.

"So show us what you do," I said.

"This is it," Monk said.

"You aren't doing anything," Stottlemeyer said. "Haven't you noticed anything since you got here?"

"I've blinked thirty-eight times since I walked in the room," Monk said.

"About the murder," Stottlemeyer said.

Monk glanced at the body, then at the apartment. "Like what?"

"Like to get in the building, you have to have a key or get buzzed in. Like there are no signs of a struggle," Stottlemeyer said. "Like the killer must have been someone that Trotter knew or was expecting or didn't consider a threat, like a pizza delivery guy."

"Sounds like you have it covered," Monk said.

"I don't have anything, Monk. I was hoping you might give me something more to go on. You've solved dozens of more complicated and bizarre murders than this in less time than it has taken you to blink forty times."

"Forty-two," Monk said.

Stottlemeyer sighed. "This is going well."

"Can I go home now?" Monk asked him.

"No, you can't," Stottlemeyer said. "You're going with me to question our likeliest suspect."

"If you have a suspect already," he asked, "what do you need me for?"

"I need you to be you," Stottlemeyer said.

"I am." Monk groaned. "God help me."

7

Mr. Monk and the Likely Suspect

We found Emily Trotter, Clarke's estranged wife, having lunch at her mother Betty's house in Sausalito, a self-consciously and premeditatedly picturesque village across the bay from San Francisco.

The house was a contemporary Victorian-style home pinned uncomfortably between two identical condominium complexes with wood-shingle siding and cottage-style decks. The manicured front lawn was such an intense green, and the flowers were in such glorious bloom, that I had to touch the plants to convince myself that they were real.

Emily was profoundly pregnant, her bulging belly looking as if it might burst open at any moment, which might be why the sofas in her mother's immaculate house were clad in thick plastic slipcovers. The widow had dark circles under her bloodshot eyes and her hair looked like dry tumbleweed.

I remembered when I looked like that.

She may have been the likeliest suspect, but I had a hard time imagining her getting up off the sofa, much

less schlepping into the city, clobbering her husband with a frying pan, and doing the dishes afterwards.

Monk and I sat on a matching sofa across from Emily. He ran his hand appreciatively over the plastic as if it was fine suede. Stottlemeyer and Disher stood while Betty went back and forth from the kitchen, serving us cookies and tea.

Everything about Betty seemed to be starched, from the beehive hairdo on her head to the apron around her waist. Monk watched her carry the tray from her sterile kitchen with something akin to awe.

"You think that I killed him?" Emily asked Stottlemeyer with exaggerated incredulity.

"He left you for another woman and you're the beneficiary of his life insurance policy." Stottlemeyer shrugged. "We'd be fools not to consider the possibility."

"And my daughter would have to be a fool to have done it," Betty said. "I didn't raise a fool, except when it comes to love."

"Thanks, Mom," Emily said. "That's exactly what I need right now, another I-told-you-so."

Betty set a plate of perfectly square cookies in front of us and handed us each a neatly folded cloth napkin with edges so sharp they could have drawn blood. Monk picked up the napkin almost reverentially and set it carefully on his lap without unfolding it.

I felt a chill that had nothing to do with the temperature in the room. There was something about Betty and this place that was giving me the willies.

"I didn't say 'I told you so,' " Betty said. "But, for the record, I was against the two of you getting married."

"There is no record," Emily said.

Disher held up his pencil and notebook. "Technically, there is."

"You're right, I had plenty of reasons to murder my

husband," Emily said. "But as much as I hated him for what he did to me, to our family, he was still my daughter's father. I couldn't have done that to her. I don't know how I am going to tell her the news. It will break her heart."

"Better her heart breaks once rather than repeatedly," Betty said. "He would have disappointed her throughout her life."

"Darla was his princess," Emily said. "He never would have hurt her."

"You think walking out on her pregnant mother and shacking up with another man's wife doesn't hurt her?" Betty said.

"Your cookies are very square," Monk commented.

"Perfectly square," Betty said. "Aren't you going to have one?"

"I just like looking at them," Monk said.

I shivered again.

"His lover was married, too?" Stottlemeyer asked.

"Claire and her husband, Eddie, were our best friends," Emily said. "We used to play bridge together every Wednesday."

"I don't know what she saw in Clarke," Betty said.

"I do," Emily said, as a tear rolled down her cheek. "He was a teddy bear. There was no safer place to be than in his arms."

After everything he'd done to her, there was still some love left for him in her heart. Or maybe it was just hormones. When I was pregnant, my mood swings gave my husband whiplash.

"Oh, spare me." Betty quickly handed Emily a tissue from the box on the coffee table and used another to wipe away an errant tear that had dropped onto the plastic slipcover. She folded the tissue and stuffed it in a pocket of her apron. "He was a child who never grew up."

I saw Monk watching Betty. He seemed at peace for the first time since yesterday. I felt another chill and couldn't figure out why.

"You have a beautiful home," Monk said to Betty.

"Thank you," Betty said.

"It's so comforting," Monk said.

Comforting?

"Where were you last night?" Disher asked Emily.

"I'm seven months pregnant and I have a five-year-old daughter, Lieutenant. Where do you think I was?" she said. "I was at home."

"Can anyone confirm that?"

"My daughter, I suppose."

"What time did she go to bed?" Disher asked.

"You think I slipped out after she was asleep?"

"It could happen," Disher said.

"Look at me. I can barely walk," Emily said. "And I wouldn't leave my daughter alone, not even to go murder my husband. What kind of mother do you think I am?"

It was a convincing alibi as far as I was concerned, but I guess it helps to be a mother to really understand that.

"I admire how your napkins are folded," Monk said to Betty. "Did you iron them?"

"Of course," Betty said. "Doesn't everyone?"

"In a perfect world," Monk said. "If only we could live in one."

"I do," she said and gestured to the home around her.

I shivered again and that's when it hit me. If Mrs. Monk were alive today, she'd probably look just like Betty. And her house would look just like this one, covered in plastic and about as homey as a morgue.

"You could have hired someone to kill him for you," Stottlemeyer said.

"That would require money," Emily said. "And Clarke keeps me on a very tight budget."

"Not anymore," Stottlemeyer said.

"Where would my daughter find a killer? In the Yellow Pages?" Betty shook her head. "You should be ashamed of yourselves for even asking her these questions."

"I am," Monk said. "Deeply."

"You haven't asked any yet," I said pointedly.

"The person you should be talking to is Eddie Tricott," Emily said. "Claire's husband. He was furious about the affair and he's wealthy. Who knows what he might have done."

"Has it occurred to you that the murder might have nothing to do with my daughter or Clarke's sleazy affair?" Betty asked.

"No," Stottlemeyer said.

"Clarke was general counsel for San Francisco Memorial," she said. "He made a lot of enemies over the years winning malpractice suits brought against the hospital by patients. Maybe one of them had enough and sought revenge. It happens on *Boston Legal* all the time."

"If you've seen it on TV, then it must be possible," Stottlemeyer said. "We'll have to look into that."

"Do you have any other questions?" Emily said, struggling to her feet. Disher gallantly gave her a hand. "I have to go pick up my daughter at nursery school and tell her that her father is dead."

"I think we're done for now," Stottlemeyer said. "Thank you for your time, Mrs. Trotter. We're sorry for your loss."

"It's my daughter's loss," Emily said. "I already lost him."

I got up and started to follow Stottlemeyer and Disher to the door. But Monk didn't move. I looked back at him, sitting on the sofa with the folded napkin on his lap.

"It's time to go, Mr. Monk."

"You go," he said. "I'm staying."

"We're done asking questions," I said. "We're leaving."

"I'm not," he said.

"You have to," I said.

"I'd rather not," Monk said.

Emily looked at Stottlemeyer. "Is he crazy?"

"He might be solving a murder," Stottlemeyer said. "Is that it, Monk? Are you on to something?"

"Her cookies are square," Monk said. "Her napkins are folded and ironed. There's no dust anywhere. All the furniture is covered in plastic. It's paradise."

My idea of a paradise doesn't include plastic slipcovers, but maybe I don't have much of an imagination.

"Thank you," Betty said. "That's what every home should be."

"I can't go," Monk said.

"You can't stay, Mr. Monk," I said.

"Why not?"

"Because you don't live here," I said.

"I'd like to." Monk looked imploringly at Betty. "Can I?"

"You want to live with me?" Betty said in disbelief.

"I accept." Monk leaned back on the sofa, making himself comfortable. His body squeaked against the stiff plastic.

"That wasn't an invitation," I said.

"Of course it was," Monk said to me before turning back to Betty. "You don't have any cannibals living nearby, do you?"

"Cannibals?" Emily said. "Is he insane?"

Stottlemeyer marched up to Monk, grabbed him by the arms, and yanked him off the couch.

"You'll have to excuse my friend," Stottlemeyer said. "He's having some personal problems."

Stottlemeyer led Monk out the door. Disher followed, and I was right behind them, when Betty spoke up.

"Wait," she said.

Betty took four cookies off the plate, set them on a napkin, and handed them to me. "Take these with you. Maybe they will make your friend feel better."

"Thank you," I said and walked out.

Stottlemeyer, Monk, and Disher were waiting for me in front of the car.

"That was pathetic," Stottlemeyer said to Monk, who began to weep tearlessly, which only seemed to irritate the captain even more. "You can't go on this way."

"I know," Monk whined. "Let me go back."

"You take a step towards that house and I will shoot you," Stottlemeyer said.

"I could be so happy there," Monk said.

"You're fired," Stottlemeyer said.

"What?" Monk said.

"You heard me. You're humiliating yourself and the department. You're a mess."

"Yes, I am."

"You hate messes. So clean this one up," Stottlemeyer told him. "That's what you do best, isn't it?"

I had to admire the logic of Stottlemeyer's approach. I'm pretty convinced that no one understood Monk, or handled him better, than the captain did. He just lacked the patience for it.

"I need help," Monk said.

"Then get it," Stottlemeyer said. "Do whatever you have to do, but do it now, before it's too late."

"What about this case?" Monk said.

"We'll just have to muddle on without you," Stottlemeyer said. "You weren't exactly a big help today anyway, were you?"

The captain and Disher got into their car and drove off. I regarded Monk.

"He's right," Monk said, watching them go.

"So what are you going to do?"

"The only thing I can do," Monk said and rolled his shoulders. "Pack your bags, Natalie."

"Where are we going?"

"I have an appointment tomorrow at four p.m. with Dr. Kroger," he said, "and I am going to keep it."

8

Mr. Monk Takes Flight

A better person than me would have stopped Monk from chasing his shrink all the way to Germany. What Monk was proposing was an extreme and disturbing case of stalking. The sensible thing to do would have been to stop him for his own good.

Maybe.

And maybe not.

There was another way to look at the situation. Monk started to fall apart the instant Dr. Kroger announced his trip, and it was getting worse with each passing hour. I was convinced that the only thing that would stop his inevitable slide into total madness, and mine along with it, was Dr. Kroger's wisdom, compassion, and guidance.

And yet it was Dr. Kroger's unavailability that was causing all of Monk's misery.

So in a twisted way, going to Germany was the only logical solution for Monk.

I know I was right because as soon as Monk decided to go to Germany he became more focused and, for the first time in twenty-four hours, almost relaxed.

I wasn't fooling myself, though, about the obstacles in front of us.

It was a twelve-hour flight to Germany, which would be no easy feat for a man who was afraid of flying and anything foreign to him—that included, among other things, kiwi fruit, French films, polyester, the Beatles, zebras, and anything labeled "Made in China."

Yet Monk was ready to travel immediately to Germany despite his raging fears and phobias, and so was I, which should tell you how desperate we both were to resolve his plight. I also took his determination as a sign that we were doing the right thing.

The way I saw it, Monk was so determined to restore his mental health that he was overcoming one of his biggest fears to get the help he needed.

That had to be significant progress in his therapy, right?

Okay, maybe I was deluding myself, but who could blame me?

Dr. Kroger, maybe. But besides him, nobody.

I also had a couple of very good reasons of my own for not stopping Monk. Payback, for one. I was convinced that Dr. Kroger had encouraged Monk to intrude on my vacation to Hawaii, so I figured turnabout was fair play. I wanted to see the look on Dr. Kroger's face when Monk showed up in Lohr.

Does that sound petty to you?

Me, too, but I've never held myself up as any kind of saint, which brings me to my truly selfish reason for not talking Monk out of chasing Dr. Kroger to Germany.

I deserved this trip.

The perks of this job are few and far between. In fact, they are nonexistent. But now Monk was willing to pay my way to Germany and, while it was hardly going to be a vacation for me, at least it would be an exciting change of scenery.

Was I taking advantage of a bad situation?

Probably, but I was sure that once we got there I'd suffer dearly for it and would regret going on the trip.

Did that stop me? Nope.

I quickly booked the tickets, arranged for Julie to stay with friends, bought some Germany guidebooks, and packed my bags.

The spur-of-the-moment plan was for Monk and me to catch the soonest, and cheapest, economy-class flight out of San Francisco to Frankfurt. Once we arrived, we'd rent a car and drive to Lohr, which according to the guidebooks was about an hour from the airport, on the river Main.

We didn't know where Dr. Kroger was staying, but from what I could tell, Lohr was a small town at the edge of the Spessart Forest. I figured it wouldn't take much detecting skill to find the conference he was attending. We'd worry about where we'd be staying once we got there.

Ordinarily, this lack of careful planning would have presented an intolerable level of uncertainty for Monk. But this was an unusual situation and he was willing to accept the unacceptable. I saw it as yet another encouraging sign of personal growth for Monk that was miraculously and ironically occurring in the midst of one of his worst psychological and emotional crises.

I hoped Dr. Kroger would see it the same way.

Under normal circumstances, just the prospect of packing for the trip would have been an insurmountable obstacle for Monk. He would have wanted to bring six months' worth of food, water, eating utensils, dishes, and bed linens in addition to his clothes and toiletries. It would have taken a week of careful planning, another week of packing, and then he would have needed a freighter to transport everything to Germany.

So the only way that Monk could even contemplate this trip, much less actually embark on it, was if he was drugged up to his eyeballs. He knew it and I knew it.

As soon as I dropped him off at his place, he took Dioxynl, the wonderful experimental drug that relieved his obsessive-compulsive disorder and subdued his phobias. He was able to pack everything he needed into one suitcase and was ready to go when I picked him up an hour later.

But this Monk was a different man than the man I'd dropped off. He was sitting on his suitcase eating potato chips out of a big bag. His shirt was open at the collar and untucked.

I pulled up to the curb in front of him. He threw his suitcase into the back of the car and hopped into the passenger seat beside me.

"Ready to fly, babe?" he said with a big smile. Obviously, the drugs had kicked in.

"I wish you wouldn't call me 'babe,' Mr. Monk."

"You can call me 'babe' if you want to," he said.

"I don't," I said.

"How about 'boychick'?"

"How about 'Mr. Monk'?"

He shook his head. "Why so formal? I'm not your geometry teacher. It's me, the Monkster."

"The Monkster?"

"Aka the Funster," he said.

"Since when do you have an 'aka'?"

"You really have to loosen up. If you were any stiffer, you'd be a sculpture. Want a chip?"

He offered me the bag. I stared at him in amazement.

Monk actually wanted me to stick my dirty hand inside the bag he was eating from and take a chip.

"Sour cream and onion," he said. "They're yummy. It's like they are predipped."

"No thanks," I said.

He shrugged, wiped his greasy hand on his pants, and set the bag between us.

"It's right here if you change your mind," he said and started whistling.

The only thing more horrifying than spending twelve hours imprisoned in an airplane with Monk was spending it with the Monkster.

That was why I'd brought sleeping pills. I intended to spend as much of the flight unconscious as I possibly could, blissfully unaware of whatever Monk was doing.

It was a sad commentary on the two of us that the only way we could travel together was if we were completely drugged, but it could have been worse.

Monk could have been himself.

Without the drugs, he would almost certainly flip out on the plane and, with the heightened airline security these days, he'd either be gunned down by an air marshal or imprisoned for endangering the passengers with his disorderly conduct.

So relying on pharmaceuticals was clearly the best way to go for us, for the other passengers, and for humanity.

We got through the security checkpoint at the airport and boarded the plane without incident. Our airline was Air Brahmaputra, the cheapest flight into Frankfurt that I could find.

Monk is a cheapskate, whether he's drugged or not.

We were traveling on an old Air Canada plane. The only reason I knew that was because Air Brahmaputra hadn't even bothered to re-cover the seats or the worn carpets adorned with the previous airline's name and maple-leaf logo.

The stewardesses were dressed in colorful saris with bare midriffs and spoke with heavy Indian accents. In-

dian music played on the sound system. I could see that the flight would be like spending twelve hours on hold with Dell customer support. Now I was doubly glad that I'd brought sleeping pills.

Our two seats were in an odd-numbered row in the middle of the plane. Monk didn't even notice the numerical incongruity, or if he did, he didn't care.

I took the seat by the window so I could rest against the bulkhead when I passed out.

Monk took the aisle seat so he could get up and wander around the plane, as he'd done on the way to Hawaii.

The seats were narrow and stiff and there was no legroom at all. If the passenger in front of me reclined his seat, we'd be sleeping together. I sat up to get a peek at him. He wasn't bad-looking. If I was lucky, he was also charming, single, and loved kids.

I stayed awake until the beverage service began. Monk had a Coke and talked the stewardess into giving him a dozen bags of peanuts to go with it.

I washed down my pill with a glass of water, and within a few minutes I was asleep.

When I awoke eight hours later, the seat beside me was empty, my bladder was ready to burst, and everybody was singing Wayne Newton's "Danke Schoen."

I squeezed out of my seat and saw Monk. He was wearing lederhosen—Bavarian leather shorts with wide suspenders—and leading a parade of singing passengers down the aisle. He looked ridiculous.

My bladder wouldn't wait for them to pass, so I jumped out in front of him and hurried down the aisle to the restroom. While I was inside, I wondered about how Monk had gotten the lederhosen and where he'd changed into them. He was going to be in for a shock if he was still wearing the outfit when the drugs wore off.

When I emerged from the bathroom, Monk was

heading down the opposite aisle towards the back of the plane. He waved at me. I waved back.

I was pretty certain that what he and the passengers were doing violated all kinds of in-flight regulations, but the stewardesses didn't seem to mind. They sat in the galley reading magazines and munching on snacks.

I asked one of them for a bag of peanuts and a bottle of water and went back to my seat. The Monkster joined me a few minutes later. He was drenched with sweat. It was an amazing sight. Until that moment, I don't think I'd ever seen a bead of perspiration on his skin.

He wiped his brow with his sleeve. "Wow. Don't you just love to travel?"

"Haven't you slept at all?"

"How can you sleep when there is so much to do?" he said.

I'd never thought of a flight that way.

"Nice outfit," I said. "Where did you get it?"

"A couple of German guys up in row thirteen gave it to me," Monk said. "I want to fit into German society as effortlessly as I do into our own."

"And they just happened to have a pair of lederhosen in their carry-on bag?"

"It's what they were wearing in Frisco," he said.

That must have been an interesting sight to see.

"Have they been cleaned since they were worn?"

Monk shrugged. "They passed the smell test."

"You sniffed the shorts?"

"You know what they say—if you can't smell it, it isn't there."

Who *are* these people and why do they keep saying such stupid things?

"What did you do with your slacks?" I asked.

"I shoved them into your bag," Monk said.

"They are going to be a wrinkled mess," I told him.

He gave me a playful punch on the shoulder. "Loosen up, babe. We're on vacation."

That's when a little boy, who looked no older than six or eight, came up to Monk. His nose was running. He wiped it on his sleeve.

"Can I have a balloon doggie, too?" the boy asked.

"Of course." Monk turned to me. "Tissue, please."

This was more like the Monk I knew. Perhaps the drugs were beginning to wear off. I reached into my purse and handed him a tissue.

He wiped the kid's nose with it, then held it against his nose and said, "Blow."

The kid did.

"One more time," Monk said.

The kid did.

"Isn't that better?" Monk pinched the tissue closed and shoved it into his pocket.

He reached into another pocket and came out with a slim balloon, which he blew up and twisted into the shape of a French poodle.

Monk handed the dog to the delighted child. "Be sure to take him out for walks."

The kid ran back to his seat. Monk smiled. "Wasn't he adorable?"

"You wiped his runny nose and put the dirty tissue in your pocket."

"What was I supposed to do with it?"

"Put it in the seat pocket in front of you," I said. "Or drop it on the floor."

"That would be littering," he said. "I'm not a litterbug."

"But you put it in your pocket," I said.

"It's snot," he said, "not nuclear waste."

"Where did you get those balloons?"

"The stewardesses had them," Monk said. "But

they aren't very good at making them into things. So I stepped into the breach. Pretty soon all the kids wanted one."

"All?"

I stood up and looked back and noticed, for the first time, that just about every kid in the plane was holding a balloon shaped into some kind of animal or wearing one as a crown.

So were a few of the adults. And one of the stewardesses.

I sat back down and stared at Monk. "Where did you learn to do that?"

Monk shrugged. "It just came naturally. Would you like me to make you one?"

"No thanks," I said.

I made a mental note to tell Dr. Kroger about this. I was pretty sure that the sudden ability to make balloon art was one side effect of Dioxynl that nobody knew about.

Maybe Dr. Kroger could write a paper on it. Maybe that opportunity would make up for Monk's unexpected intrusion into his vacation.

Maybe Dr. Kroger would eventually see what was about to come as a blessing in disguise.

Yeah, right. Even I didn't believe that.

9

Mr. Monk Arrives in Germany

I spent the rest of the flight reading up on Lohr in the Germany guidebooks while Monk roamed around the plane, mingling with the passengers like it was a cocktail party. He didn't return to his seat until we were descending to Frankfurt.

We arrived at the airport at eleven a.m., right on time. The airline was cheap but punctual.

I stood up and pushed Monk into the aisle the instant our plane came to a stop at the gate.

"Relax," Monk said. "There's no hurry. Germany isn't going anywhere."

My friends and family mistake my mad rush to get off airplanes for joy at being home or eagerness to begin my trip.

It's not. It's what I call "situational claustrophobia."

I don't have any problems with claustrophobia except when I wake up in a sleeping bag or am in a plane at the end of a flight. In both situations, I feel smothered and cramped and have to escape as quickly as possible.

Weird, huh?

I even have nightmares sometimes about being zipped up tight in a sleeping bag on a plane when it arrives at an airport.

Everybody is probably a little bit crazy. Well, that's my bit.

I pushed, elbowed, and squeezed my way through the narrow aisle and out of the plane. I didn't see Monk again until I got into the airport, where I had to endure nasty looks from all the passengers I'd bruised and trampled and shoved aside in my rush to escape.

Monk was accompanied off the plane by a young woman who could have been a professional fashion model. She had an impossibly perfect body and eyes so radiantly blue that she could probably instantly hypnotize anyone she glanced at.

"If you're ever in Berlin, give me a call," she said as she slipped a piece of paper into Monk's shirt pocket. "I'll show you around."

"I'd like that, Elke," Monk said.

"I have to warn you, Adrian—we might not ever make it out of my apartment."

Elke gave him a kiss on the lips that would have made most men spontaneously combust, but Monk took it calmly.

She looked at me as she did it, as if daring me to stop her, and then she hurried off.

Monk watched her go. "She must have a very nice apartment."

"I don't think that's what she meant," I said.

"What did she mean?"

"Never mind," I said. "What's the story with her?"

"She's a photographer. We had a great conversation while you were asleep. She even invited me to join her club."

"What is it?"

"It's called the Mile High Club," Monk said. "I asked

her to send me an application and said I would think about it."

I didn't bother explaining to him what the membership requirements were. I was much more interested in what he'd said that would make a beautiful young woman want to throw herself at him. Maybe she just couldn't resist a man in lederhosen.

We headed to customs. Monk went ahead of me and handed his passport to the agent in the glass booth. The agent wore an ugly green uniform that seemed to change the color of his skin. He looked like he was suffering from jaundice.

"What is the purpose of your trip?" the customs agent asked by rote in a heavy German accent.

"I have an appointment with my psychiatrist," Monk said.

The agent looked up at Monk. "He's in Germany?"

"On vacation," Monk said. "He's attending a conference in Lohr."

"Is he expecting you?"

Monk shook his head. "It's a surprise."

"How long are you staying in Germany?"

"Until he comes back to Frisco or I am sane," Monk said. "Whichever comes first."

"Are you telling me that you're crazy?"

"Hell no," Monk said. "Just deeply disturbed. But it's okay. I'm jacked up on mind-altering drugs."

"You're drugged," the customs agent said.

"Who isn't these days?" Monk said.

The customs agent studied Monk. The man was clearly trying to decide whether or not to let an insane junkie into the country. I felt a pang of anxiety. What if the agent denied Monk entry? After a long moment, the agent sighed and stamped Monk's passport.

"Have a nice trip," the agent said.

Monk walked on into the baggage claim area. I

stepped up to the same booth. The agent glanced at my passport, then up at me.

"Are you with that last guy?" he asked.

"Yes, sir," I said.

"Lucky you," he said and stamped my passport.

We collected our bags and went into the terminal. Near the exit to the street, there were several counters where you could rent cars, buy food, or exchange currency.

I went first to the currency exchange counter to swap Monk's cash for euros. He took some crisp euros from me and went to a hot dog stand while I went to a rental car counter to arrange our transportation.

I got the keys and paperwork, then I found Monk, who'd bought himself six different hot dogs, loaded them up with condiments, and put them in a carryout box.

"They have an amazing selection of sausages here," Monk said. "I didn't know which one to pick, so I took one of each."

I was astonished. Hot dogs were at the top of Monk's list of hazardous foods that should be outlawed. They were right up there with mixed nuts, granola, and scrambled eggs.

"You know that a sausage is seasoned ground meat stuffed into animal intestine," I said. "And you know what intestines are usually stuffed with."

"I don't see your point," Monk said, taking a bite out of one of the hot dogs in his box and squirting sausage juice on his shirt.

"Forget it," I said. Why was I looking for trouble? If Monk was happy, I should be, too.

We went outside to catch our shuttle to the rental car lot. On the way to the shuttle stop, we passed a row of cream-colored taxis. All of them were Mercedes-Benzes. I wondered where the cheap taxis were.

The shuttle came right away. It was a large Mercedes-Benz van. I'd never seen a Mercedes-Benz van before. As we drove through the airport, I saw several silver-and-blue police cars. They were all BMW 5 Series sedans. If the bus drivers and cops in San Francisco saw this, they'd all want to move to Germany.

"This must be a very rich country," I said to Monk.

"They certainly make a hell of a hot dog," Monk said, his mouth full. "Wanna bite?"

"No thanks," I said.

The rental car company shared a portion of an airport parking structure. The shuttle dropped us off in front of a little car called a Seat. I thought it was a strange name for a car.

We put our suitcases in the trunk and got in. I briefly studied the road map. Monk belted himself into his seat in the Seat and immediately fell asleep. I hadn't even started the engine yet. One second he was awake, the next he was in a coma.

I didn't mind. It made it easier for me to concentrate on my driving in an unfamiliar locale.

After a few minutes of driving, my initial impression of Germany was that it wasn't so different from America. The portion of the airport we were in was brand-new and the surrounding buildings were contemporary as well. Except for the German language on the signs, we could have been at home.

Then I got on the freeway heading east and nearly got mowed down by the fast-moving cars. All the drivers seemed to be going blindingly fast and I could barely get my Seat to move faster than a sofa. So I got in the far right lane and just tried to stay out of everyone's way.

Thankfully, I didn't have to drive on the freeway for very long. I exited onto a back road that took me into the deeply wooded hills and that's when things began to look very different from the world I knew.

The road narrowed and took us through the center of one ancient storybook village after another. The buildings were two or three stories tall at most. They were made of densely packed stones or half-timbered with exposed structural and decorative wood beams in the walls.

The villages were so well preserved and charming that they looked more like Hollywood sets or theme parks than real places that had existed relatively unchanged for centuries.

This was especially true of Lohr, which I found nestled between a curve in the river Main and the fabled Spessart Forest, where, if you believe the Brothers Grimm and Walt Disney, a runaway Snow White was taken in by the friendly singing dwarfs who worked in the mines.

In the center of town was a stone tower capped by a wooden cabin with a rounded, baroque top. It rose over the steepled roofs, the pointed spires of the three churches, and the turrets of the castle. It was as if some tornado had ripped a cabin off the ground, whisked it into the air, and then dropped it on the tower.

I drove into the town square and parked behind the castle, which was now a museum. There was still a drawbridge leading to the castle but it was only for show. The moat was dry and lined with freshly mowed grass. A banner draped over the drawbridge featured a haggard Snow White and seven rough-featured dwarfs who didn't look like they'd ever whistled while they worked.

Despite this somewhat commercialized acknowledgment of its fabled past, Lohr still had such a fairy-tale quality to it that the cars and the thoroughly modern people talking on their cell phones seemed totally out of place on the cobblestone streets among the medieval buildings.

I spotted the town's tourist center in a lopsided half-timbered building across the square. I glanced at Monk, who was snoring away, and decided to leave him behind in the car while I sought out some information.

I couldn't help smiling as I got out of the car and walked over to the tourist center. Everything around me was so different from where I lived and yet, because it all evoked memories of so many beloved fairy tales, it was warm and familiar to me at the same time.

The tourist center was tiny, the walls filled with maps and brochures about Main-Franconia, the region Lohr was in.

The middle-aged woman behind the counter greeted me with a big smile as I came in.

"Hello," she said. "May I help you?"

I was surprised that she'd instantly pegged my nationality and addressed me in English.

"Am I that obviously American?" I asked.

"Americans have a way of walking," she said.

"What way is that?"

"Confident and bold. Not that Germans are meek, of course. And it's also the way you're dressed. We have the same brands and styles here, but you Americans wear them differently."

"Confidently and boldly," I said.

What she said was probably true for Germans, too. Monk looked silly in lederhosen but I guessed that a German wouldn't because he'd know how to wear them.

"Is there something special you're interested in seeing or learning about in Lohr?" she asked me.

"I'm trying to find a psychiatric conference that's taking place here this week."

"There's only one. It's being held up at the Franziskushohe Hotel." She pointed to a spot behind me. "On the hill."

I turned and looked out the window.

The hotel was a wide, three-story structure of stone and wood nestled high in the forested hills behind Lohr. The old building was so integrated into its surroundings that it seemed like a natural extension of the landscape.

"The Franziskushohe was built in the 1880s as a sanitarium for people with lung diseases, which is why it's so far above the town," she said. "Nobody wanted those sick people near them, and the patients, of course, wanted the clean mountain air to purify their lungs. It became a convent in the 1950s and stayed that way until the last nun died a few years ago. The hotel opened up shortly after."

That was more than I wanted or needed to know, but I suppose it was her job to inject as much history and local color as possible into the answer to every question.

"How do I get up there?"

"Just keep your eyes on the hotel and drive. There's only one road up the hill. You can't miss it."

"Can you recommend somewhere to stay if the hotel is booked up?"

She handed me a map and drew a circle around a building in the center of the old town. "There's a bed-and-breakfast right here. It's been operated as an inn almost continuously for centuries. Tell Heiko and Friderike that Petra sent you."

I was about to thank her when we heard someone outside scream in sheer terror.

There are two instinctive reactions to a sound like that.

One is to take cover so whatever is terrifying the person outside doesn't find you. The other is to go see what is so terrifying and then decide if you should run for your life.

I have a feeling that the old phrase "curiosity killed the cat" comes from that second reaction. And, for all I

knew, the cat was killed here ages ago by whatever was terrifying the person in the street today.

But I walked outside anyway while Petra ducked behind the counter.

Perhaps on some subliminal level I knew who was doing the screaming even before I saw Monk hopping around the square in his lederhosen as if he was walking on hot coals.

People had gathered in a circle around him but were keeping a safe distance as I approached.

"What's wrong, Mr. Monk?"

"What isn't?" he shrieked while continuing to hop around.

The medication had definitely worn off. This was the Adrian Monk I knew.

"Give me the top five," I said.

"I'm naked!"

"No, you're not," I said.

"I'm not wearing pants!"

"You're wearing shorts," I said.

"I'm so ashamed."

"So you thought that jumping out of the car, screaming at the top of your lungs, and drawing a crowd was the best way to hide your shame."

"It was a reflex," Monk said. "Cover me."

I stood in front of him. "Why are you hopping?"

"There's no place to put my feet."

"How about on the ground?"

"Have you seen it?" he said. "There are no two stones that are the same size and shape. There's no pattern whatsoever. It's impossible to stand still. It's treacherous."

"I'm standing still," I said. "So is everyone who is staring at you."

Monk look past me and blanched. "Oh God, here come the police."

I turned to see a big man in a green uniform and a brown leather jacket approaching us warily. He said something to us in German.

"I'm sorry," I said to the officer, "but we don't speak German."

"What is all the screaming about?" he asked. "Have you been robbed?"

"Only of my dignity," Monk said. "Are you going to arrest me for indecent exposure?"

He shook his head. "This is Germany."

"You'll have to excuse my friend. He doesn't adjust well to new environments or shorts," I said. "I could use some help carrying him back to the car."

"Is he injured?"

"In a manner of speaking," I said. "He can't walk on uneven, irregular cobblestones."

"It's chaos," Monk said, hopping from stone to stone. "You can't stand on chaos."

The officer glanced at me. "I'll take him. You hold open the car door for me."

Before Monk could protest, the officer effortlessly lifted him off his feet, lugged him to the car, and dropped him on the passenger seat.

Monk sighed with relief. "Thank you, Officer."

"We really appreciate your help," I said. "And your understanding."

The officer looked back at me and whispered, "This man needs psychiatric care."

"That's why we're here," I said. "His psychiatrist is staying at the Franziskushohe."

He nodded. "Would you like a police escort?"

"I think we can make it on our own," I said. "But thank you for offering."

I got into the car and started the engine. The officer knocked on my window and I rolled it down.

"Don't stop until you get there," he said.

10

Mr. Monk and the Appointment

I got a little lost finding my way out of the center of town but that wasn't such a bad thing. It gave me a chance to do some sightseeing.

We went down a narrow cobblestone street lined with adorable half-timbered houses that seemed to lean against one another for support. Each house had planter boxes full of blooming flowers under every window. The front doors were so small that it was easy to imagine that hobbits or dwarfs lived inside. I couldn't see how anyone of average height could get in and out of the doors without smacking his head.

I bet the locals could tell who lived in town by their bruised or calloused foreheads.

The road took us through a gateway in what remained of the wall that had encircled the settlement back in the Middle Ages. It was one of the historical facts about Lohr that I'd gleaned from browsing the Germany guidebooks.

Here's another fact: In its heyday, five or six hundred years ago, Lohr was renowned for its glassworks,

producing mirrors so clear that they saw the truth, no doubt inspiring the talking mirror in *Snow White*.

The foothills leading to the hotel were dotted with cottages and duplexes. Many of them appeared to have been cheaply built in recent years and lacked the charm and character of the town below.

"This is a godforsaken place," Monk said as we ventured into the hills.

"I think it's utterly charming."

"It's a rest stop on the road to hell," Monk said. "Have you seen the buildings? The streets? Nothing is straight."

"It's like stepping into a fairy tale," I responded. "This is where the story of Snow White and the Seven Dwarfs actually took place."

"Of course it is," he said.

"You mean because the fable matches the true story of Sophie Margaret von Erthal, the beautiful baroness who lived in the castle?"

Shortly after Sophie's mother died, her father remarried. The evil stepmother owned one of the famous Lohr "speaking mirrors" and was so envious of Sophie's beauty that she ordered the forest warden to kill the young woman. Sophie fled into the woods and took refuge with miners, who had to be very short to work in the cramped tunnels.

"No, that's not it," Monk said.

"Then why do you think the story came from here?"

"Look around, woman. Only a place as hellacious as this could produce a horrific tale like Snow White and the Eight Dwarfs."

"It was a magical fable," I said. "And there were seven dwarfs, not eight."

"There's nothing magical about infectious diseases. Sneezy infected everyone. That's why Dopey was

Dopey, Grumpy was Grumpy, and Sleepy was Sleepy. They were all desperately ill," Monk said. "Happy was deluding himself about the threat. Doc should have had his license to practice medicine revoked for sheer incompetence. And if Bashful had had any backbone at all, he would have run screaming from that cabin."

"What does any of that have to do with an eighth dwarf?"

"Follow the evidence. The eighth dwarf was obviously killed by whatever disease he contracted from Sneezy. That's why he was written out of the story as time went on."

"There is nothing in the story to suggest the existence of an eighth dwarf."

"Read it again. The clues are all there. Besides, nobody would write a story, much less publish one, about seven dwarfs. They might tell a story about six dwarfs, or possibly eight, but never seven. In fact, they say there might have been as many as four other dwarfs in the story."

" 'They' say? Who are 'they'? You keep talking about these people but I've never seen them."

Monk ignored my question and just plowed on.

"The names of the dwarfs were reportedly Burpy, Puffy, Dizzy, and Cranky. They must have been awfully sick, since, like the others, they are only remembered today for the most noticeable symptoms of their infections."

"Walt Disney gave the dwarfs those silly names for the cartoon," I said. "They didn't have names in the original fable by the Brothers Grimm."

"The brothers were grim because they were telling a story about a group of deformed men infected with a highly contagious, terrible disease," Monk said. "Ironically, that poisoned apple probably saved Snow White's life."

"How do you figure that?"

"It got her out of that house before she was infected and into the safety of a hermetically sealed glass coffin," Monk said. "Snow White should have thanked her wicked stepmother instead of killing her. Someone should rewrite that story so it's socially and medically responsible before it's told to any more impressionable children."

The discussion we were having was ridiculous but it served a useful purpose—it distracted Monk from his anxieties for a few moments. While he was busy lecturing me about the seven—excuse me, *eight*—dwarfs, he'd forgotten about his lederhosen, missed the stain on his shirt, and hadn't discovered the dirty tissue in his pocket.

We reached a narrow stone bridge over a trickle of a creek. A sign beside the bridge indicated that we'd arrived at the grounds of the Franziskushohe. We drove over the bridge and followed the road, which wound gently up the steep, manicured hillside to the hotel.

We crossed several hiking trails and passed a system of steps composed of large stones set into the dirt. There were several benches scattered about so people could rest and take in the spectacular view of the town and the meandering river below.

The road ended in a parking lot in front of the hotel, which faced the rising, thickly wooded hillside. The back of the hotel faced the wide-open view.

It was a sunny spring day, but there was something about the sturdy old building that made me think of snowy winters, cable-knit sweaters, hot cider, heavy comforters, and roaring fires. It was a place that seemed to promise warmth and security.

There were rows of wooden lounge chairs behind the hotel and more of them on the hillside above, spread over a long patio covered with a shingled roof. I saw

hammocks strung between the tall trees and a stone fireplace ringed by log benches.

I could already picture myself curled up in one of those hammocks, swaying gently in the breeze and reading a good book. Or crouching beside the crackling fire, roasting marshmallows speared on the ends of branches scavenged from the forest.

As I searched the parking lot for a space, I noticed several trails branching off into the woods. Each trailhead was marked with a sign that featured a map, some writing in German, and black-and-white historical photographs.

A hike into the woods sounded good to me, too.

I parked in front of one of the trail signs and we got out of the car. Monk opened his door slowly and sighed with relief when he saw asphalt instead of cobblestones. This was ground he could stand on.

I took a deep breath. The air was like wine. I could almost taste traces of cedar and berry. I was so glad to be there.

The trail sign was in German, so I couldn't read what it said, but it seemed to offer historical footnotes about the Franziskushohe. The grainy picture on the sign was dated 1901 and showed patients relaxing outside on lounge chairs, sheets over their laps, and being tended by nurses.

I turned so that I blocked the sign from Monk. I didn't need him freaking out right now.

"It's nice here, isn't it?" I said.

Monk grimaced. "There's too much nature."

"What's wrong with nature?"

"It isn't very clean," he said, and headed off towards the entrance to the hotel. I quickly followed after him.

There was a massive stone fireplace, just like what I had imagined, a staircase that looked like it had been carved out of one enormous piece of wood, and a set

of French doors opening out onto the garden and the view.

Monk was stepping up to the registration desk when something outside caught his attention.

I followed his gaze. It was Dr. Kroger, dozing on a chaise longue, a notepad and pen on his lap.

Monk glanced at his watch and smiled: "Perfect timing."

He opened the French doors and marched outside.

I didn't move at first.

To be honest, I was afraid to go outside. I wanted something between me and the explosion that was about to come, even if it was only a pane of glass.

There was an empty chair to the left of Dr. Kroger. Monk turned it at a slight angle, approximating the position of the patient chair in Dr. Kroger's office.

He sat down, laid his arms straight on the armrests, and smiled contentedly. He looked truly relaxed and at peace and, for a moment, I was genuinely happy for him.

I took a deep breath and walked outside, but I stayed close to the door in case I needed to make a quick escape.

Monk glanced at Dr. Kroger, who was still dozing. He rolled his shoulders and glanced at the doctor again and then kicked the chaise longue.

Dr. Kroger jerked awake and looked to his left to see the cause of the rude intrusion into his slumber.

I don't think his brain registered exactly what he was seeing at first. Dr. Kroger saw a man in lederhosen, but something wasn't computing. It took a second before he recognized that the man was Adrian Monk.

The doctor did a horrified double take. It took another second for his mind to reconcile the incongruity of Adrian Monk in Germany wearing lederhosen before he could accept what his eyes were telling him.

All of this played out quite clearly in the exaggerated expressions on Dr. Kroger's face.

I wish I'd taken a picture.

Dr. Kroger sat up straight in slack-jawed astonishment. *"Adrian?"*

Monk shook his head. "You would not believe what I've been through over the last few days."

"What are you doing here?"

"We have an appointment and, boy, do I need it. I think my current troubles can be traced back to the fateful day when my mother passed on to me the responsibility of keeping track of my blinks." Monk motioned to the notepad on Dr. Kroger's lap. "Shouldn't you be writing this down?"

"This is totally inappropriate," Dr. Kroger said tightly. "You can't just follow me to Germany and expect me to treat you."

"That's why I'm so lucky to have Natalie," Monk said, tipping his head towards me. "I couldn't have done it without her."

"Really?" Dr. Kroger turned to look at me and I felt my bowels seize up. I waved meekly.

"It's nice to see you," I said. "You're looking very rested."

Dr. Kroger stood up, grabbed me firmly by the arm, and led me into the lobby.

Monk stayed in his seat.

"I am shocked, Natalie," he said.

"I bet you are," I said.

"What Adrian has done today is a serious breach of the doctor-patient relationship and you enabled him to do it," he said, thrusting his finger at me like a weapon.

"No more than you enabled him to follow me to Hawaii," I said.

"I thought you were an intelligent and responsible

woman, that you were a positive influence on Adrian's emotional and psychological well-being. Obviously I was wrong. You are a deeply disturbed woman."

"My job is to look out for Mr. Monk's best interests and that's exactly what I am doing."

"By helping him to stalk me and invade my private life?" Dr. Kroger declared. "What he has done is a crime and you were his accomplice."

"I don't begrudge you a private life or a vacation. God knows, I'd like to have them, too," I said. "But don't play dumb. You had to know Mr. Monk was going to completely fall apart without you and that there was no way he would ever see a one-armed psychiatrist. But you didn't care. You dumped the problem in my lap and went on your way, leaving me to deal with it."

"And this is your idea of a solution?"

"Take a look at him. Adrian Monk is here, in Germany, a world apart from his own. Imagine the crippling fears he had to overcome just so he could be here in that chair right now. That's how much he needs you. All he asks in return is one hour of your time. One hour of patience, understanding, and advice. Is that so damn hard for you to give?"

Dr. Kroger looked back at Monk, who was sitting peacefully in his chair, then back at me.

"I should call the police and have him removed," Dr. Kroger said.

"And create an embarrassing scene in front of your colleagues from around the world?" I said. "I don't think so."

Dr. Kroger grimaced with frustration. He was in a no-win situation and we both knew it.

"He's not going to be satisfied with just a session," he said. "Adrian will want to cling to me every second that I'm here."

"He'll leave," I said.

"In my professional opinion, you're wrong," Dr. Kroger said. "I know Adrian a lot better than you do."

"Then you should have expected this, shouldn't you?" I said as cuttingly as I could. "You just have your session with him and let me handle the rest."

"What he's done today is very wrong," he said. "I don't know if I can continue seeing him as a patient after this."

"We'll worry about that when we get back to San Francisco," I said. "Right now, you have an appointment and Mr. Monk is waiting. I'll see you in an hour."

And with that, I turned my back on Dr. Kroger and walked away.

11

Mr. Monk Returns

I picked one of the hiking trails at random and just started walking uphill. I wandered past the covered patio and into the woods.

Once I was enveloped by the forest, I might as well have been in my hometown of Monterey, California. The only difference was the sunlight. It was as if there was a filter over the sun. It wasn't as bright or as harsh as I was used to. If I lived in Lohr, I'd save money on sunglasses.

It was also surprisingly quiet. I couldn't hear any cars and it was easy to forget I was only thirty or forty yards from a hotel full of people.

The quiet was really nice. You don't realize just how loud your world is until the volume is suddenly turned down. I became aware of sounds I don't usually hear in my hectic urban life. The breeze rustling through the leaves. Birds chirping. The buzz of insects. The trickle of water washing over rocks in a creek. The crackle of dry brush under my feet. The gentle background noise was like soft music.

I wandered a bit farther and came upon what first ap-

peared to be a tree house. But as I got closer, I could see that it was actually a hunter's blind made of branches and wood and enshrouded with vines. If not for the corrugated metal roof, it would have melded perfectly with the trees.

I climbed up the ladder into the blind and sat on the bench inside for a few minutes. I tried to imagine what it would be like sitting there for hours with my rifle, waiting for a defenseless animal to wander by for me to shoot.

I didn't see the pleasure or the sport in that. But sitting in that blind, I was overwhelmed with childhood memories of playing in the tree house that I'd built with my friends from scrap wood we'd scavenged from a construction site.

They were memories I hadn't tapped in years. It was like channel surfing and stumbling unexpectedly onto a favorite movie that you'd forgotten.

I got so lost in my reverie that forty minutes seemed to pass in a matter of seconds. When I realized the time, I climbed out of the blind and walked back down to the Franziskushohe.

I came into the lobby just as Dr. Kroger and Monk were finishing up their session outside. Dr. Kroger escorted Monk into the lobby as if it was his waiting room in San Francisco. If I'd been sitting on the couch reading *Cosmopolitan* or *Highlights for Children*, the re-creation would have been complete.

Monk was transformed. He appeared settled, almost serene. He was back to his old self again. Except for the lederhosen, that is.

"I think we made some real progress today, Adrian," Dr. Kroger said. His words sounded forced to me.

"The excitement doesn't have to stop now," Monk said. "We can keep right on going."

"Your session is over for today."

"But you don't have any other patients to see. We can spend all of our time together," Monk said. "You're here, Natalie is here. This can be a dream vacation."

His dream, our nightmare.

Dr. Kroger gave me an "I told you so" look. But I was prepared for this. I'd worked out my strategy during the walk back to the hotel.

"We can't stay here, Mr. Monk."

"Of course we can. This is a hotel," Monk said. "The three of us could get adjoining rooms. Wouldn't that be grand?"

"I don't think so, Adrian," Dr. Kroger said.

"Why not?" Monk said.

"Because for seventy years this building was a sanitarium for people with tuberculosis," I said. "And bronchitis, asthma, emphysema, and pneumonia."

"To name a few," Dr. Kroger said, meeting my eye and giving me a slight, appreciative nod.

"A few?" Monk said.

"Think of all the thousands of sick people who've been here," Dr. Kroger said, "and all the coughing and sneezing and wheezing that has occurred within these walls."

"The whole place is probably caked with layers of dried phlegm," I said.

Monk shuddered. "That's not possible."

"See for yourself," I said.

I led them outside and across the parking lot to one of the trailhead signs, which had a reproduction of a vintage photograph showing patients strolling with their nurses outside the hotel.

Monk stared at the picture in disbelief. "And they made this into a hotel? Were they insane?"

"After the sanitarium closed it became a convent," I said. "Maybe they thought it was cleansed by prayer."

"Prayer isn't an antibiotic," he said and held his hand out to me. "Wipe."

I gave him one. He looked at Dr. Kroger as he scrubbed his hands and arms with the moist disinfectant towelette.

"You should leave with us," Monk said. "While you can still breathe."

"I'm staying," Dr. Kroger said. "The conference is here and I have a strong immune system."

"God help you," Monk said, handing me the used wipe and motioning urgently to me for a new one. He started cleaning his legs with the towelette as Dr. Kroger began to walk back to the hotel.

"Good-bye, Adrian," Dr. Kroger said.

"See you the day after tomorrow," Monk said.

Dr. Kroger froze in his tracks and turned slowly to look at us. "You're coming back?"

"For my next appointment." Monk snapped his fingers at me for another wipe. I gave it to him.

"Do you think that's wise, with all the disease and nature around here?" I asked.

"I would walk across hot coals to see Dr. Kroger," Monk said. "That's how much he means to me."

"You can't imagine how that makes me feel," Dr. Kroger said and trudged back to the hotel, his shoulders slumped with misery. He was a beaten man. I knew how he felt.

Monk started wiping his face and neck. "There goes a great man, facing certain death so that he can enhance his knowledge of psychiatry for his patients."

"Do you feel better now?"

"Wonderful." Monk held the wipe over his nose and mouth. "Completely relaxed."

"I can see that," I said.

We went back to the car. He didn't stop breathing through the wipe until we drove back over the little bridge at the bottom of the hill and were heading into town.

"We need to call Captain Stottlemeyer right away," he said.

"What for?"

"I've solved a murder," he said.

"You have?" I said. "Whose?"

"Clarke Trotter's," Monk said.

I'd forgotten all about the cheating husband who was clobbered with a frying pan and I thought that Monk had, too. Monk hadn't seemed to be paying attention to anything at the crime scene except his own misery.

But apparently I was wrong. On some level, he was unconsciously picking up details the whole time, despite his emotional and psychological meltdown. It was like he had a split personality, one that was freakishly unstable and another that concentrated unwaveringly on details and was impervious to distraction.

"What makes you think that Captain Stottlemeyer hasn't already closed the case?" I asked.

"He would have called."

"Why would he do that?"

"Professional courtesy," Monk said. "He wouldn't want me concentrating on the mystery for nothing."

"He didn't think that you were concentrating on it at all," I said.

"Of course he did," Monk said. "He was relying on me."

"He couldn't rely on you," I said. "That's why you were fired from the case."

"I don't recall things that way," he said.

"That's because you have a selective memory," I said. "You remember every single detail except the ones that don't fit your worldview."

"Everything fits in my worldview," Monk said.

We parked in the town square again. I scrounged around in my purse for my cell phone and called the captain.

"What's the emergency?" he asked groggily. I'd obviously awakened him.

"Shouldn't you be at work?"

"It's my day off," he said.

Oops. I checked my watch. It was about seven a.m. in San Francisco.

"Sorry," I said. "We're nine hours ahead."

"What are you talking about?"

"We're in Germany," I said.

"Who is?"

"I am," I said. "With Mr. Monk."

"You've got to be kidding," he said. "Monk has to be sedated just to cross the bay into Oakland."

"I'd tell you all about it but this call has probably cost me more than my mortgage payment already. Mr. Monk has solved a murder."

"In Germany?"

"In San Francisco." I put the phone on the speaker setting and held it up between Monk and me. "He knows who killed Clarke Trotter."

"It pains me to say this," Monk said. "The murderer is Betty, his mother-in-law."

"How do you know that?"

"She confessed," Monk said.

"I was in her house with you and I didn't hear any confession," Stottlemeyer said.

"She didn't confess there," Monk said. "She confessed to us at Trotter's apartment."

"She wasn't with us in Trotter's apartment," Stottlemeyer said, his voice strained with irritation.

"But she left her confession behind," Monk said. "It was the kitchen."

"The kitchen was her confession?" Stottlemeyer said.

"You've got it," Monk said.

"I don't have anything," Stottlemeyer said. "Except an early-morning headache."

"Here's what happened," Monk said. "Betty went over to Clarke's apartment to talk with him. We'll never know why he let her in, but he did. It was a fatal mistake. Something he said or did pushed her over the edge. She grabbed the frying pan from the stove and hit him with it. Then she went back to the kitchen, intending to clean the pan and cover up her crime. But when she saw all the filthy dishes, the dirty counters, and the complete disorganization, she couldn't stop there. She had to wash all the dishes and clean the entire kitchen. The mess was too much for her to ignore."

"It's hard to imagine anyone being that compulsive," I said. "Isn't it?"

"She was only human, Natalie," Monk said. "No decent, civilized human being could walk away from a mess like that."

"No decent, civilized human being could commit a murder," I said.

"I sympathize with her," Monk said. "She's a good woman who was provoked into a violent act by a repugnant human being. She was acting out of love for her daughter and her grandchildren. And I admire her."

"What for?" I said.

"Even after committing a murder, she did the right thing and cleaned up the mess in Trotter's kitchen," Monk said. "That selfless act of decency should go a long way towards convincing the judge to grant her some leniency at sentencing."

"Before this case can ever get to a courtroom, we're going to need proof to back up your theory," Stottlemeyer said. "Where is it?"

"The kitchen is the proof," Monk said.

"Anybody could have cleaned it," Stottlemeyer said.

"It wasn't anybody," Monk said. "It was her. The

items on the counters and the dishes in the cupboards are arranged just like the dishes in her kitchen."

"You didn't see inside the cabinets," Stottlemeyer said.

"I didn't have to," Monk said. "I saw how she arranged the items on her counters and how things were organized on Trotter's. And I saw Trotter's dish towels. They were folded and ironed, just like the towels and cloth napkins in her home."

"They were?" I said.

"You could see that?" Stottlemeyer said.

"She probably wore dish gloves while she cleaned the kitchen," Monk said, "but I wouldn't be surprised if she took them off to iron the towels. You'll find her fingerprints on the iron."

"So his tidy kitchen was as good as a signed confession," I said.

"It's better than one," Monk said.

"I'll look into it," Stottlemeyer said. "It's good to have you back, Monk."

"I'm in Germany," Monk said.

"And still solving more murders in San Francisco than I am," Stottlemeyer said. "It's rough for my ego but I'll live with it. Catch you later. Try not to get into too much trouble over there."

We said our good-byes and I put the phone back in my purse.

Monk looked at me. "Promise me you'll never tell the captain about this."

"About what?"

Monk gestured to his lederhosen. "If word got out that I was running naked through the streets of Germany, it could ruin my career. Dr. Kroger is bound to secrecy by doctor-patient privilege, but you aren't."

"It's springtime, Mr. Monk. You're on vacation in a

foreign country. It's okay to wear shorts. All the tourists are doing it," I said. "Besides, you have nice legs."

"What are you doing looking at my legs?" he said. "Look away."

I did, stifling a smile.

"This can only lead to trouble," he said.

"What kind of trouble could it lead to?"

"Promise me you'll never say a word about this," he said. "Not even to me."

"Your secret is safe," I said. "At least until I write my memoirs."

"You're writing a book?" he asked, a touch of panic in his voice.

"Not yet," I said. "But someday I might."

12

Mr. Monk and the New Experience

The Schmidts were a physically mismatched couple in their sixties who gladly welcomed us to their bed-and-breakfast in the heart of Lohr.

Heiko was at least six feet tall, his body curled like a question mark, perhaps from decades of walking hunched over so he wouldn't hit his head on the exposed beams that supported the low, wavy ceilings of their bed-and-breakfast.

Friderike was short and as round as a bowling ball. Her hair was pulled back in a tight bun and she wore her flowered apron as if it was her skin.

What they had in common was an easy smile and a natural hospitality.

Friderike showed us up to our rooms on her own, sparing her tall husband a potential head-bruising, though neither Monk nor I was so lucky. We both managed to bang our heads, me while climbing on the uneven staircase and Monk while walking down the corridor.

"If you need some ice, you just let me know," she said. "A cup of hot mint tea helps, too."

She took a long, old-fashioned key out of her apron pocket and opened the door to one of the rooms.

"This was my room when I was a child," she said. "And now it's yours."

I peeked inside. It was snug, only a little larger than the iron bed in the center of the room. Thick wooden beams stretched across the low, bowed ceiling. The floor seemed to slope towards the stone fireplace, where another thick slab of smooth wood served as a mantelpiece and supported a row of books. There were candles everywhere and a small, square window covered with hand-sewn drapes.

"I love it," I said.

"But it isn't level," Monk said.

"It looks very cozy to me," I said.

"It is," Friderike said. "Warm in the winter and cool in the spring."

She led us down the hall to the next room. It didn't have a fireplace, but otherwise it was the same as mine. Monk shook his head in disapproval.

"These rooms are uninhabitable," Monk said. "And the entire building is crooked. It could tumble down at any moment."

"It's probably leaning a bit, but the house has always looked that way," she said. "That's because it was built without right angles."

Monk gasped. "Why would anyone do that?"

"They believed that the devil sits in right angles," she said.

"My God," Monk said. "Were they living in the Dark Ages?"

"Yes," she said cheerfully, "they were."

"When was your home built?" I asked her.

"In 1440. The walls are made of oak from the Spessart and mud, rocks, and twigs from the banks of the river Main."

"Mud?" Monk said.

"And it's still better-made and sturdier than the homes they build today. I wouldn't want to live in one of those flimsy places."

Friderike was probably right. I doubted that a modern American tract home could endure as long as the buildings in Lohr had against the vagaries of time and war.

What was really amazing to me was that the wooden beams of their buildings had been exposed to the elements for centuries without rotting, and yet, no matter what I did, I had to replace my window frames every few years.

I had to know the secret.

"How did they keep the wood from rotting?" I asked.

"Oh, that's simple. They soaked it in ox blood," she said. "It keeps the worms away."

"And people, too." Monk abruptly turned and marched to the stairs, banging his head on a beam again.

I grabbed him firmly by the arm and turned him around.

"There is nowhere else to stay, Mr. Monk."

"There's the car," he said, rubbing his forehead.

"They don't allow people to sleep in their cars here," I said.

"How do you know?"

"I saw a sign." It was a lie, but I was confident the regulation existed. I looked back at Friderike. "We'll take the rooms."

"We're glad to have you," she said, handing me the keys. "Breakfast is at seven. I'll make you both a cup of tea."

She walked past us down the stairs.

"Natalie, be reasonable," he implored me. "The walls are made of dirt and soaked in ox blood."

"Do you think the walls at home are any healthier? Who knows what chemicals have gone into them?"

"I do," Monk said.

"You mean like asbestos, lead, and formaldehyde?" I said. "I feel a lot safer surrounded by walls made of mud that was taken from the riverbanks centuries before everything was polluted by chemicals and insecticides."

"But infested with sewage and plague," he said.

"That was hundreds of years ago. But think of all the people who have been in that rental car in just the last few weeks," I said. "I can't imagine what germs and bodily fluids they might have left behind."

"I can." Monk put his hand on his forehead again and closed his eyes. "I feel dizzy."

"It's hunger, dehydration, and lack of sleep," I said. "Or a concussion."

I led Monk to his room and told him to rest while I brought up our suitcases. When I returned a few minutes later, I found him rubbing the wall with a disinfectant wipe. There was a cup of hot tea on his nightstand and one on mine, too.

I suggested to Monk that we shower, change, and meet downstairs in an hour for dinner.

"An hour isn't enough time," he said.

"How much time do you need?"

He was quiet for a moment. "Under perfect conditions, and by that I mean if I wasn't occupying a mud hut, cleaning the shower would take only two to three hours. I'm going to need at least eight, but I am being conservative."

"I'm leaving for dinner in an hour," I said. "With or without you."

I went to my room and closed the door. I sat down on the edge of the bed and enjoyed my cup of tea, which was piping hot and had a touch of honey. It

was delicious and, as promised, it seemed to reduce the size of the bump on my head.

I finished my tea, took a shower, and changed into fresh clothes. I felt like a new woman.

I was careful to crouch as I went down the stairs. I wondered if anyone had ever suggested to them that they pad the beams.

Monk was waiting for me in the front room, studying the decorative plates and needlepoint portraits of Lohr that were hanging on the white-plastered walls.

He was dressed in his usual uniform—a 100 percent cotton shirt buttoned up to the neck, a buttoned-up gray sport coat, pleated slacks with eight belt loops instead of the usual seven, and brown Hush Puppies loafers buffed to a brilliant sheen.

Heiko Schmidt sat in a stiff-backed chair, smoking a pipe and studying Monk.

"Is that how folks are dressing in the States now?" he asked.

"They should," Monk said.

Heiko nodded. He wore a checked shirt under a cable-knit cardigan sweater that seemed to be two sizes too large. The ribbed napping of his corduroy pants was nearly smoothed away with wear.

"Very stylish," Heiko said. I think he meant it.

Monk cocked his head from side to side. It wasn't often that he got an unsolicited compliment.

"I think it's going to catch on," he said.

I asked Heiko if he could recommend a place to eat in Lohr.

"The Boar's Head," he said. "Best food in town outside of Mama's own kitchen. It's right down the street."

I thanked him and we headed out to dinner.

Night was a lot darker in Lohr than it was in San Francisco. The cobblestone streets and half-timbered

buildings were softly illuminated in the glow of lamps crafted in the style of old gas lanterns. If there were any parked cars around, I couldn't see them and I was glad for that. The dim light in the deep blackness seemed to erase all the signs of modern times. It was easy and fun to imagine that we were back in the Middle Ages.

Monk didn't notice. He was watching his feet, carefully selecting each stone that he stepped on until he reached a drainage gully that ran down the center of the street.

The stones in the drain were laid down in a consistent pattern, two stones wide. It meant that Monk had to walk with one foot directly in front of the other, like he was on a tightrope, if he wanted to avoid touching the randomly placed stones on either side of the drain.

I slipped my arm around Monk's and he immediately stiffened up.

"What are you doing?" he asked.

"Walking arm in arm with you."

"I know that," he said. "But why?"

"Because we're in an adorable medieval village on a warm spring night and I'm happy to be here with you."

I wasn't aware of it until I'd said it, but it was actually true.

"That doesn't make any sense," he said.

I sighed. "I'm afraid I might trip on one of these uneven stones and I'm holding on to to you for dear life."

"I don't blame you," Monk said. "Whoever laid these stones was deranged."

I felt him relax a bit, which for him was quite a lot.

We walked on in silence, arm in arm. I liked the sound of our feet against the cobblestone. It wasn't a sound I ever heard at home. It was soothing.

"This is nice," I said.

"I'm uncomfortable here," he said.

"You're uncomfortable everywhere."

"I'm not uncomfortable in my apartment," he said.

"But is that how you'd like to live? In total isolation?"

"It's probably not possible," Monk said. "But it doesn't hurt to dream."

The restaurant was in a building every bit as old, lopsided, and charming as the bed-and-breakfast where we were staying, so naturally Monk was reluctant to step inside. But since my arm was entwined with his, I was able to yank him in without much effort.

The walls of the restaurant were adorned with antlers and stuffed birds of all kinds, and above the fireplace in the main dining room there was a giant boar's head topped with a bowler hat crowned with colorful plastic flowers.

Monk wanted to leave immediately but I convinced him that he needed to eat and I reminded him that he didn't bring any food of his own so he was stuck consuming the local fare. He would have tried to bring a year's worth if he hadn't been heavily medicated when he packed.

He shook his head in despair. "This is why you should just say no to drugs."

"Because you could end up eating in a lovely old restaurant in an idyllic small town in Germany?"

"Exactly," Monk said. "Next thing you know, I could be plucking my eyes out with hot pokers."

"I'll try to keep you away from hot pokers," I said.

"Let this be a lesson for your daughter."

"I will be sure to tell her."

We were led to a table for two against the wall. I sat with my back to the wall so Monk had to face only me

and one set of antlers rather than look at the boar's head and the mounted fowl.

The waiter gave us menus in English without being asked. Somehow he'd figured out we were American tourists despite the distinctive Lohr bumps on our heads.

The menu was simple and short, with only a few steak, fish, and salad items. The rib-eye steak was described as "muscle from the zone between the ribs with typical bubbling fat pockets," which might have been accurate but didn't sound too appetizing. The fish entrée was described as "salmontrout on white rice with sauce of mustard and leafy vegetables from the earth." I tried to imagine a hybrid of a salmon and a trout, and what it might taste like.

I opted for a simple garden salad and Monk chose a bowl of white rice. We weren't being very adventurous in our culinary choices, but it was only our first night. I figured I'd ease into it.

It was enough just to be sitting there, regardless of what I was eating.

If someone had predicted only two days earlier that I'd be taking a trip to Europe with Adrian Monk, I never would have believed it. In fact, I would have said it was impossible.

"What we're experiencing now is very special," I said. "I hope you appreciate it."

"I'm trying not to see the antlers," Monk said. "That's the only reason I'm looking deeply into your eyes."

"I wasn't talking about that. I'm talking about being here, halfway across the world. *This* is what's special."

"Special is another way of saying not the norm," he said.

"Exactly," I said.

"I like the norm," Monk said. "Norm is good. I wish I was named Norm."

"But now here you are, in Europe, experiencing an entirely new culture. Isn't it exciting?"

"I wouldn't say that."

"Then how does it feel?"

"Like a deep, penetrating nausea," he said.

"This is a great opportunity, Mr. Monk. You should embrace it."

"I don't embrace," Monk said.

"When was the last time you had a vacation?"

"When we went to Hawaii," he said.

"That wasn't a vacation. We spent the whole time investigating a murder."

"It was fun."

"It was work. A real vacation doesn't include a corpse."

"Then what do you do?"

"Nothing. That's the whole point," I said. "Tomorrow morning you're going to wake up with no commitments to fulfill, no demands on your time, no mysteries to solve, and the whole day in front of you in a place you've never been before. That's a vacation."

Monk groaned. "No wonder I don't have them."

"Open yourself up to the experience," I said. "You might like it."

"I've had experiences," Monk said. "I'm not a fan."

Our food was delivered then, and we ate in silence. By the time we'd finished the meal, the jet lag had caught up with both of us. It was only about eight o'clock, but we were both fighting a losing battle to keep our eyes open.

We went back to the bed-and-breakfast and retired to our separate rooms.

As I slipped between the sheets and rested my head on the fluffy pillow, I thought about the day to come.

Tomorrow wouldn't begin with us standing over the victim of a brutal homicide. We had nothing to do except relax and explore our new surroundings.

I congratulated myself. Going to Germany with Monk had turned out to be a wonderful decision, not just for me but for both of us.

He just didn't realize it yet.

13

Mr. Monk Goes on Vacation

Thanks to the jet lag, I awoke at four a.m. and couldn't get back to sleep. So I used the time difference to my advantage and called home to check on Julie.

I assured my daughter that I was having a miserable time so she wouldn't be jealous. It wasn't a hard sell. She could imagine what traveling with Monk was like. I felt a little guilty having a European vacation without her, but not so much that I was ready to take the next plane home.

Does that make me a selfish person and a bad mom? I hope not.

After the call, I read through the guidebooks for places to see and things to do and skimmed the German-English dictionary for helpful words or phrases for traveling with Monk.

I couldn't find any direct translations for "please excuse my friend, he means no offense" and "do you have any disinfectant?" in German. I made a mental note to ask the Schmidts.

I also wrote a list of nearby places that Monk and I could visit after we exhausted all the possibilities of

Lohr, which, judging by the size of the town, we'd do by early afternoon.

Friderike was hard at work in the kitchen when I came down at seven a.m. She was preparing eggs, sausages, and biscuits, which Heiko then brought out to the butcher-block-style table where Monk and four other guests were waiting.

Monk wasn't eating the hot breakfast, of course. He was having toast, cutting off the crusts and carefully painting the bread with jam.

I sat down across from him and introduced myself to the other guests—a businessman visiting one of the factories, an older German woman who didn't speak English, and a young couple from Belgium who couldn't keep their hands or lips off each other.

Heiko set a bowl in the center of the table. There were a dozen white sausages floating in steaming-hot water. I wasn't sure what we were supposed to do with the sausages, so I waited to see what the others did.

The businessman took one of the sausages out of the bowl with his spoon and set it on his plate. He cut the sausage open at one end, picked it up with his fingers, and sucked the meat out like he was drinking through a straw.

Monk cringed from head to toe and I have to admit I didn't find the sight too appealing myself. The businessman saw me watching him and appeared to be amused by our reaction.

"Weisswurst," he said, indicating the sausage. "Very good."

The old lady took a sausage out of the bowl but she didn't suck the meat out. Instead, she slit the sausage down the middle, and delicately rolled the white meat out of the skin with her fork. She dipped the meat in some kind of mustard and ate it.

That looked more appealing to me than sucking the

meat out of the skin, but I didn't think I could eat anything with mustard in the morning.

Within a few minutes of my arrival, the businessman
went off to his meeting, the old woman was picked up
by relatives, and the young couple hurried back to
their room, probably to finish what they'd started at
the table.

I took a sausage and decided to eat it like the old
woman had, only without the sauce. I was about to put
the meat in my mouth when Monk scowled.

"You know what a sausage is, right?" he said. "It's
minced meat jammed into a pig intestine. And you
know what's in an intestine, right?"

"Yes, I know, thank you," I said. "You ate a sausage
yesterday."

"I doubt that," he said.

"Does that drug you take cause amnesia, too?"

"No, but after it wears off, the things I remember
doing are so outrageous that I don't know how much
was real and what was a nightmare."

"It was all real," I said.

Monk shivered. "God help me."

I ate the sausage. It had an unusual texture, but it
was delicious and had a surprisingly complex favor. I
could taste smoked meat, onion, ginger, and a hint of
lemon. I quickly gobbled down some more.

Friderike joined us and asked what our plans were.
When I told her we didn't have any, she told us the
farmers market was being held in the town square
today. She was going to do some shopping for groceri-
es, and if we wanted to walk with her, she'd be glad to
be our tour guide on the way. I quickly accepted for us
both, though Monk didn't look too excited about it.

She retrieved a big woven basket from the kitchen,
stuffed it with some small burlap bags to carry her gro-
ceries, and off we went.

It was a perfect day, with a mild temperature, a slight breeze, and only a few wisps of cloud in the sky. The air felt clean and light, as if all the pollution had been filtered out as it blew through the Spessart.

Friderike and I walked on either side of Monk, who kept to the gully in the center of the road.

Now that I was up close to the buildings, I noticed that above each tiny doorway was something hand-written in chalk: 20*C+M+B*08. I gestured toward the writing.

"What does that mean?" I asked Friderike.

"It's the year, two crosses, and a blessing on the house," she said. "It's part of a ritual that goes back to the sixteenth century."

"Everything here does," Monk said. "It's time you people modernized."

"January sixth is the Feast of the Three Kings: Caspar, Melchior, and Balthasar. On that day, children go door-to-door dressed as the kings and ring the bell," she explained. "When you open the door, the children declare that the Messiah is born, sing a song, and if you give them some coins for the poor, they write that sign with sanctified chalk."

"And if you don't pay?" Monk asked.

Friderike shrugged. "Everyone pays or you won't be blessed. Things will be very bad for you."

"And the police allow this?"

"Why wouldn't they?" Friderike replied.

"You're paying for protection. If you don't, then these ruffians see to it that something bad happens," Monk said. "It's extortion."

"It's for charity," Friderike said.

"That's what they always say," Monk said. "But it goes straight for hooch and weed. No wonder they are in disguise. It makes it harder for them to be identified."

Friderike looked puzzled. "Hooch and weed?"

"Never mind," I said, waving off Monk's remark as if it was smoke in the air.

Monk motioned to a church we were passing. "The top is missing off that eight."

There was a date etched in stone atop the doorway. Monk was right. It looked like someone had lopped the top off the eight in the date 1387.

"That's a four," Friderike said.

"It's definitely the bottom of an eight," Monk said.

"That's how they wrote fours back then," she said. "As half of an eight."

"And nobody could find the time in the last six hundred and twenty years to fix it?" Monk said. "I'll be glad to do it for you while I am here. Do you have a chisel I can borrow?"

Friderike was so bewildered by Monk's remarks that she stumbled on a cobblestone, but quickly regained her footing.

"You should walk in the pedestrian lane," Monk said.

"The what?" she said.

"The people path," Monk said, motioning to the gully he was in. "It's much safer."

"Oh, no, you shouldn't walk there," Friderike said. "It brings bad luck."

"Whoever said that must have been the same guy who thought carving half an eight is the same as a four," Monk said. "What could possibly be wrong with walking where it's smooth, safe, and orderly?"

"That's where people used to empty their room pots," she said.

"What's a room pot?" Monk asked.

"A medieval toilet," I said. "Basically, a bucket of—"

Monk yelped, leaping out of the gully and practically into my arms.

He looked back accusingly at Friderike. "You dumped sewage into the street?"

"They didn't have indoor plumbing back then," she said. "The streets are sloped so the drains run all the way down to the creek, which feeds into the river."

"Where they drank their water, washed their clothes, and got the mud to build their houses," Monk said.

"It's a big river," she said, "with a strong current."

Monk gave me a grim look. "This entire town is a toxic waste dump. It should be evacuated immediately and quarantined for public safety."

"People haven't used the streets to dump their waste in over a hundred years," I said. "It's clean now."

"Radiation has a half-life of centuries," Monk said, stepping carefully from stone to stone.

"Human waste isn't radioactive," I said.

"Nobody thought atoms were until they started splitting them," Monk said.

"That doesn't make any sense," I said.

"It makes perfect sense," Monk said. "It explains why this place produced so many dwarfs, why Sneezy was Sneezy, and why people thought writing half of an eight was the same as a four."

On some subjects it was pointless to argue with Monk because there was no chance of changing his mind. This was one of those subjects.

"The town square is coming up," Friderike said. "Between 1626 and 1629, over a hundred women were accused of being witches. They were tortured until they confessed and then burned at the stake in the middle of the square."

"And I can guess why," Monk said. "The poor women probably committed the heresy of suggesting that maybe it wasn't such a good idea to have sewage running down the streets because it could make people

very sick, physically and mentally. What was I thinking, coming here?"

"We could go home right now," I said. "If you don't mind missing your next two appointments with Dr. Kroger."

Monk grimaced. "Life is cruel."

The town square was crowded with people wandering amid the tents, tables, and catering trucks selling fruit, vegetables, meat, seafood, and household knickknacks.

There were also jugglers, musicians, glassblowers, painters, and sculptors plying their art and trade among the vendors, giving the market an Old World, party atmosphere that reminded me of the Renaissance fair that used to come to Monterey each summer when I was growing up.

Unlike the fair, though, this was authentic.

We soon lost track of Friderike. She stopped to shop and we got caught up in the flow of the crowd. I let myself be carried along, but Monk fought the current and ended up looking like one of the street performers.

He leapt, and pirouetted, and ducked to avoid physical contact with strangers and to keep his balance on his selected cobblestones. There were small children who actually stopped to watch him. I did my best to ignore him, preferring to let my gaze wander over the butchers and bakers, painters and puppeteers.

I was browsing through a vendor's selection of handmade stuffed animals when, out of the corner of my eye, I saw an extraordinary thing.

Monk stopped his strange dance and began to run into the crowd, pushing through the people.

Something was very wrong. I immediately ran after him.

"Mr. Monk!" I yelled. "Wait!"

But he charged ahead, oblivious to the people he was rudely elbowing and shoving aside.

Monk was so determined in his pursuit that he didn't seem to care at all whether he ran over uneven cobblestones or stepped in the drain.

Whatever had caught his attention was of such great importance that it neutralized his fears and anxieties. I couldn't imagine what he had seen that could have such power over him.

And then he came to such an abrupt, complete stop that I nearly plowed right into his back.

"What is it?" I said, trying to catch my breath. "What's wrong?"

Monk had reached an intersection of several narrow streets and was looking up and down each one of them, his head practically spinning.

I was getting dizzy just looking at him. Or perhaps it was the sudden exertion combined with jet lag.

"What did you see?" I asked. "What were you running after?"

"He's gone," Monk said, the expression on his face tight and forlorn. "I lost him."

"Who?"

Monk took a deep breath and closed his eyes. And when he opened them again there was a steely expression of determination on his face that I'd never seen before.

"The man who killed my wife," he said.

14

Mr. Monk and the Six Fingers

Monk went up one street and down another, looking in every alley, courtyard, and alcove. He was chasing a phantom and I was hurrying to keep up with him.

"How do you know it was him?" I said.

"I know what I saw," Monk said.

"Which was what, exactly?"

"I saw a man in the crowd buying a pastry," Monk said. "He had six fingers on his right hand."

"Are you sure?"

"It's not something you see every day," Monk said. "The man who killed Trudy is here and I let him get away."

I knew only the general details about Trudy's murder. She was a reporter for a small local paper and she was killed by a car bomb that was remotely activated by a cell phone.

Monk suspected that Dale Biederback, a ruthless eight-hundred-pound egomaniac known as Dale the Whale, had something to do with her murder. Trudy had written several unflattering stories about Dale,

who hadn't left his bed in a decade and owned half the real estate in San Francisco.

Dale nearly sued the Monks into poverty before settling, dropping his lawsuit in exchange for their summer home, which he then used to store his extensive porn collection. Obviously he did that just to irritate the Monks even more.

Monk could never prove Dale the Whale's connection to Trudy's murder, but he did put the morbidly obese monster in prison for hiring someone to kill a local judge.

Even so, it was Dale the Whale who gave Monk the vital clue that allowed him to track down Trudy's bomber to a New York hospital, where the cancer-stricken man was on his deathbed.

In a dying declaration, the bomber swore to Monk that he'd been hired to plant the explosive by someone else, a man whose name he didn't know and whose face he never saw, but who had six fingers on his right hand.

Monk and Stottlemeyer had been on the lookout for a six-fingered man ever since but without success.

"You've had a rough week emotionally and psychologically," I said to him. "You're jet-lagged. Maybe your eyes were playing tricks on you."

"My eyes don't do that," Monk said. "I saw a man with eleven fingers."

"Okay," I said. "Maybe you did."

"I did," Monk said firmly.

"But you don't know it was the same man who hired someone to kill Trudy," I said. "It could be another eleven-fingered guy."

"I doubt it," Monk said.

"Why?" I said. "Why would the killer be here, of all places?"

Monk stopped and looked at me. "Think about it. This is the perfect place for him to hide. A small town clear across the world. Not just any small town, but one steeped in death and disease, one that was so horrific that it spawned an enduring nightmare like *Snow White*."

"This is a lovely town," I said. "*Snow White* is a beloved fable."

"Lohr is the last place on earth I would ever look for him or ever visit," Monk said. "He knew that."

"And yet here you are, by sheer coincidence, in the one place on earth he chose to hide."

"It's fate," he said.

"It's ridiculous," I said. "Besides, you don't believe in coincidences, especially when murder is involved."

"I do now," Monk said.

I didn't know whether or not Monk had actually seen a man with six fingers. But I didn't believe for one moment that the man who ordered Trudy Monk's death was hiding out in Lohr, Germany. It was obvious to me what was really happening.

"I have a much more logical explanation for what you saw," I said.

"What could possibly be more logical than what I just told you?"

"You are in a place where you've never been and you have to adapt to a totally different language, culture, and way of life than you are familiar with. It makes you uncomfortable—you said so yourself last night. On top of that, you are facing a day where you have nothing to do. You couldn't deal with it, so in a panic your mind invented something that would completely occupy your thoughts and distract you from all the frightening differences around you."

Monk stared at me for a long moment before saying, "That is the craziest thing I've heard."

"You can't tolerate change and you can't tolerate the idea of having a day off," I said. "So you created a purpose for yourself that couldn't be denied: finding Trudy's killer, even though we are in the least likely place for you to find him."

"Which is exactly why he is here," Monk said. "You have just proven my point."

"You didn't listen to a word I said."

"Yes, I did," Monk said. "But just the words that made sense, which was roughly one out of ten."

"You mean you only listened to what you wanted to hear."

"Of course. Why would I do otherwise? That would be like intentionally eating something that makes you sick."

I couldn't argue with that analogy. It was totally accurate and unintentionally revealing. He couldn't listen to anything that conflicted with his extraordinarily rigid worldview.

"So what do you want to do? A door-to-door search?"

"Good idea," Monk said. "Let's gather those kids who dress up as the Three Kings and get them to do another collection. We can tag along and see who opens the doors."

"That doesn't seem very practical, Mr. Monk. January sixth is a long way off and I don't think anybody will be fooled."

"You're right. We don't have the time to take the subtle approach," Monk said.

"That was subtle?"

"We have to go to the police."

"What can they do?" I said. "There hasn't been a crime."

"My wife was murdered," Monk said.

"I know, Mr. Monk, and I don't mean to deny the pain

and loss that you feel. But she wasn't killed here and there's no evidence that the eleven-fingered man you saw, if you even saw him, was the man who did it."

"That's why we need the police," Monk said. "If we find the man, we'll find the evidence."

"I have a better idea," I said. "Let's hold off doing anything until your appointment with Dr. Kroger tomorrow. Maybe he can help you work through the issues at the heart of all of this."

"Tomorrow could be too late," Monk said. "The killer could be packing up and preparing for his escape right now."

"Okay, let's see Dr. Kroger today."

Dr. Kroger wouldn't be too pleased, but Monk's mental health took precedence as far as I was concerned.

"I don't need a psychiatrist," Monk said. "I need a special unit of trained detectives scouring this godforsaken place for the man who killed my wife."

And with that, Monk marched off in search of the police and I saw my vacation slipping away into madness.

The Lohr police station wasn't much larger than the tourist office and it was occupied by just two people: the female dispatcher and a uniformed officer at the counter, who turned out to be the same guy who'd witnessed Monk's meltdown in the town square and carried him back to the car.

The officer's name was Schust. To say he was unsympathetic to Monk's request would be an understatement.

I could understand that, but I was on Monk's side. Because when it comes down to it, despite whatever reservations I may have, my job is to support and assist Monk in any way I can.

"Perhaps Mr. Monk hasn't made the situation clear," I said. "He is a special consultant to the San Francisco Police Department and he's investigating a murder."

Officer Schust looked skeptically at Monk. "He's a detective?"

"The best in America," I said.

I didn't believe Monk was right, but I had to do whatever I could to help his cause. Besides, I figured the sooner I could prove to him that either he was delusional or the six-fingered man he saw wasn't the killer, the sooner we could get back to enjoying our vacation.

"He's afraid of cobblestones," Schust said.

"If you were smart, you would be, too," Monk said. "One wrong move and you could break your neck. Those streets should be paved."

"We aren't going to pave the streets," Schust said. "And we aren't going to do a door-to-door search for an eleven-fingered man either."

"I want to see whoever is in charge here," I said.

"You'll have to come back another time," Schust said. "Hauptkriminalkommissar Stoffmacher is unavailable."

"We'll wait," Monk said.

"He could be gone all day," the officer said. "He's investigating a homicide."

"Perfect," I said. "Point us to the crime scene so Mr. Monk can solve the murder and the Hauptkriminalkommissar can focus all of his attention on finding our man."

"A crime scene is not a tourist attraction," Schust said. "We're done here, Fräulein Teeger."

The officer turned and went back to his desk. When Monk looked at me, his expression of steely determination was back.

"This isn't such a big town. It shouldn't be too hard

to find the crime scene," Monk said. "We'll just drive around until we find a bunch of police cars."

"They still won't let us cross the police line," I said. "What we need is an introduction. Wait here."

I stepped outside, took out my cell phone, and called Captain Stottlemeyer. I hadn't forgotten that we were nine hours ahead of San Francisco, but this was an emergency.

Stottlemeyer answered groggily. "Yeah."

"It's Natalie, Captain. I need a favor."

"Do you know what time it is here?"

"Let me ask you a question," I said. "Did you arrest that crazy woman for murdering her sleazy son-in-law?"

"Yeah, we did," Stottlemeyer said. "Can I go back to sleep now?"

"I need more details," I said.

"Monk was right. Her fingerprints were all over the iron. When she was confronted with the evidence, she spilled the whole thing. We couldn't shut her up. Satisfied?"

"So you're in Mr. Monk's debt," I said.

"Yeah, I owe him one," Stottlemeyer said. "When he gets back, I'll let him organize my desk."

"That's not going to be enough," I said.

"He gets paid for this," Stottlemeyer said.

"You fired him, remember? He did this out of the kindness of his heart and a deep, abiding sense of public service."

"He did it because he's compulsive and he can't let go of this stuff."

"That doesn't matter. The fact is, you'd still be heading nowhere on this case if he hadn't taken time out of his dream vacation to help you. Now all he's asking for is a small favor in return."

"What did you have in mind?"

"We need you to call the police in Lohr, Germany, and convince them that Mr. Monk is a very important and respected member of the San Francisco Police Department."

"Why do they have to know that?"

"Does it matter?"

"Yeah, because a call like that makes whatever Monk is doing official and a reflection on our department. And second, if you're hesitating to tell me why you need me to vouch for him, it must be something big. Has he stumbled on a dead body already?"

I sighed. "Mr. Monk caught a glimpse of a man in a crowd today and then lost him. We need the police to help us find the guy."

"What has the guy done? Was he missing a button on his shirt? Was he only wearing one earring? Was his shoe untied?"

"He had six fingers on his right hand."

"Oh hell," Stottlemeyer said.

"You see my predicament."

"Do you really believe that's what Monk saw?"

"What's important is that he believes it," I said. "Nothing means more to him than finding Trudy's killer. Even if there's only a one-in-a-billion chance that he's right, we have to support him, no matter what."

"This could end up being a tragic embarrassment for him and for us," Stottlemeyer said.

"I know," I said. "But what choice do we have? We're his friends."

"Where are you again?"

"Lohr, Germany," I said. "Snow White's hometown."

"I thought her hometown was Disneyland."

"It wasn't."

"Next you're going to tell me Sleeping Beauty didn't live there either," Stottlemeyer said. "Give me a few minutes. I have to wake some people up."

I went back into the police station and sat down next to Monk in one of the two chairs in the lobby.

"What did you do?" Monk asked.

"I called Captain Stottlemeyer," I said.

"Is he going to help us?"

I gave Monk a look. "Has he ever let you down?"

A half hour passed. The officer and the dispatcher were clearly annoyed to have us sitting there, but they couldn't really throw us out.

I told Monk that Betty had been arrested, but he just shrugged. He never doubted that she was guilty, no more than he doubted himself about seeing the man with eleven fingers.

The dispatcher's phone rang. She answered it and motioned to Schust to pick up the extension. He did.

The officer listened for a moment, looked over at us with astonishment, hung up, and made another call. He spoke to someone for a few minutes, glancing at us repeatedly as he did, then ended the call and walked over to us.

"I apologize, Mr. Monk, if I offended you in any way," Schust said. "I've been ordered by the leader of the regional police to take you to see Hauptkriminalkommissar Stoffmacher right away. Please come with me."

The officer led us outside to his car. As we followed him, Monk looked at me for an explanation. I shrugged.

"You must have friends in high places," I said.

"I'm afraid of heights," Monk said. "That's why I'm glad I have two friends down here with me that I can always count on."

15

Mr. Monk Sees a Corpse

We'd barely been in Germany for twenty-four hours
and we were about to see a dead body. It's not exactly
on my list of things to do when I go someplace new.
But the same thing happened when Monk followed me
to Hawaii, when we went to a wine tasting in Napa,
and when he was a guest at my brother's wedding.
Wherever Monk goes, you can always count on a dead
body showing up sooner or later.

Maybe that's why he never received invitations to
weddings, anniversaries, birthdays, parties, movie
screenings, time-share presentations, or anything else.
Nothing kills a good time faster than a killing. He attracts more death than Jessica Fletcher and she's practically the Grim Reaper in a housedress.

The crime scene was one of those duplexes built in
the foothills below the forest, right under the shadow
of the Franziskushohe. The duplex was a wide A-frame
with matching front doors and windows. I'm sure that
Monk appreciated the perfect symmetry.

An officer was unfurling red-and-white-striped police
tape and wrapping it around trees and streetlights on the

property to secure it in place. The police tape read: PO-LIZEIABSPERRUNG. The one thing I'd already noticed about the German language was that it seemed to cram entire sentences into one long, incomprehensible word.

Schust lifted the tape up so we could pass under it and then he escorted us into the right-side portion of the duplex.

It was a tiny place, maybe seven hundred square feet, with the living room and kitchen on the first floor and the bedroom on the second. The decor was thrift-shop Euro-seventies, with lots of bright colors.

The victim was a man who appeared to me to be in his early thirties. He was sprawled on his side on the floor, a gun not far from his hand. His hair was matted with blood. This definitely wasn't what I'd had in mind for sightseeing.

There were two men standing over the body. The men were both in off-the-rack suits and ties, which was the same underpaid-plainclothes-cop attire you'd see in America. I guess some things are true everywhere—cops aren't paid enough and people kill.

One of the men had an enormous black mustache that looked like a crow had been caught in an oil slick, tried to fly, and crashed into his face instead. The elaborate mustache completely overpowered his face and, frankly, the entire room.

The other man was younger, with an earnest, puppy-dog expression on his pale, baby face. He gripped his notepad and pen as if they were life preservers.

"Hauptkriminalkommissar Stoffmacher," Schust said to the man with the outrageous mustache, "this is Adrian Monk and his assistant, Natalie Teeger."

Stoffmacher offered Monk his hand.

"Welcome to Lohr, Mr. Monk. Your reputation precedes you," he said and waved Officer Schust away. The officer left.

"You've heard of me?" Monk shook Stoffmacher's hand.

"You were preceded by a phone call by my superiors," Stoffmacher said. "They tell me you are the top detective in San Francisco, perhaps in all of America."

"I am," Monk said.

"They neglected to mention your modesty," Stoffmacher said.

"I am also very tidy," Monk said, trying to shake a bit of white fluff off his shoe.

"Good to know," Stoffmacher said, narrowing his eyes at him. He clearly wasn't sure what to make of Monk. Most people aren't.

The man next to Stoffmacher cleared his throat. Stoffmacher took the hint.

"This is Kommissar Geshir," Stoffmacher said, almost reluctantly.

"I'm always glad to meet another colleague in law enforcement. It so happens that I'm the top detective in this department," Geshir said to Monk as he offered him his hand. Monk shook it.

"Congratulations," Monk said, still wiggling his foot to rid himself of the evil fluff. Finally it flew off.

"You are also the only detective in the department," Stoffmacher said.

"Which puts me at the top," Geshir said.

"Or the bottom," Stoffmacher said. "If you count me."

"You're the boss," Geshir said, "so you don't count."

They were so busy arguing that neither one of them appeared to notice Monk disinfecting his hand with a towelette. Watching the two detectives, I was overwhelmed by a strange sense of déjà vu.

"You're telling me I don't count?" Stoffmacher said. "You might want to consider the implications of that remark."

Geshir shifted his weight nervously. "My English isn't very good. I probably chose the wrong words."

"I'm sure you did," Stoffmacher said.

He turned to Monk, who at this point was already beginning to roam around the room, tipping his head from side to side, doing his Zen-detecting thing.

I found it reassuring to see him at work. It meant that he hadn't totally lost his grip. Maybe now that he had something to occupy his mind and his time, he might be less overwrought about the six-fingered guy he thought he'd seen at the market.

Stoffmacher looked at me. "What is he doing?"

"Solving your homicide," I said, my eyes drawn to Stoffmacher's mustache. I'd never seen anything quite like it. I wondered how many hours he spent waxing it, oiling it, or soaking it in tar.

"That's a nice gesture, but this isn't a murder," Stoffmacher said. "It's suicide. Axel Vigg was despondent. His girlfriend ended their relationship, he was fired from his job at the glass factory, and he was about to be evicted. So he shot himself in the head. Sadly, these things happen."

Monk straightened a painting on the common wall with the duplex next door. It was a still life of a fruit bowl. I'd be tempted to shoot myself, too, if I had to look at a bowl of fruit every day.

"He's been dead at least twelve hours," Monk said. "How was the body discovered?"

Geshir referred to his notes.

"Vigg was supposed to meet some friends last night and didn't show. This morning he didn't answer his phone or his door, so his friends got worried and called his landlord," Geshir said. "The landlord unlocked the door and found the body."

Monk walked over to the front door and examined

the knob and the dead bolt. "Did the landlord unlock both locks?"

"I don't know," Geshir said.

"I'd like to find out," Monk said.

"It doesn't matter," Geshir said. Stoffmacher nudged him. "But I will go outside and ask him."

Geshir stepped past us and went outside. Monk's attention was drawn to something else. He walked over to the bright orange couch, which would have been gaudy even in the seventies, and examined what looked to me like a bullet hole in the thin cushion of the backrest. He scrutinized the rest of the couch, too, as if he'd never seen one before.

"Why did he shoot his couch?" Monk asked.

"Maybe because it's ugly," I said. "Personally, I would have set fire to it instead."

"It was a test shot," Stoffmacher explained, "to make sure the gun was operating properly and wouldn't jam when he did the deed."

Monk pointed through the air, following what I assumed was an imaginary line from the couch to the gun on the floor. He crouched beside the gun and peered at it.

"Did anyone hear the gunshots?" he asked.

"Not that we know of," Stoffmacher said. "If he shot himself during the day, the neighbors were most likely at work. Even if they were home, they probably wouldn't remember hearing a gunshot. It's not unusual to hear gunfire in this neighborhood."

"Really?" I said. "It seems so safe and peaceful here."

"It is," Stoffmacher said. "People don't even lock their doors at night."

"So why would they be accustomed to hearing gunshots?" I asked.

Monk stood in front of the couch and stared at the wall and the sun-bleached outline on the wallpaper of a painting that once had hung there. I know he detested wallpaper. The seams rarely matched up, so the patterns were never properly aligned.

"We are on the edge of the forest and hunting is a popular sport," Stoffmacher said and I remembered the hunting blind I'd sat in yesterday. "I'm not surprised that no one heard this poor man shoot himself."

Monk rolled his shoulders. "This wasn't a suicide."

"You're saying it was murder?" Stoffmacher said.

"It wasn't murder either," Monk said.

"Then what was it?"

"An accident," Monk said.

Stoffmacher stroked the curled end of his mustache. "You think the victim accidentally shot himself in the head?"

"He didn't shoot himself," Monk said. "Someone else shot him."

"So you're saying someone else was holding the gun," Stoffmacher said, "and accidentally pulled the trigger."

"That's not what I am saying at all." Monk turned to the brick fireplace and began counting the bricks on either side to make sure they were even and symmetrical.

"Forgive me. I think we're having a little language problem," Stoffmacher said. "That must be why I am misunderstanding you."

"You're not," I said.

"Then what is he talking about?" Stoffmacher asked me.

That's when Geshir bounded in like a golden retriever coming back with the tennis ball he'd been told to fetch.

"The landlord says he only unlocked the doorknob," Geshir said. "The dead bolt wasn't locked."

"Now it all makes sense," Monk said.

"It doesn't make any sense at all," Stoffmacher said, exasperated.

I had to smile.

They were experiencing pure, unadulterated Monk for the first time. They had no idea how his mind worked. I'm not saying that I did either, but at least I was used to the backwards, sideways, and often inexplicable way he put things together. I had the benefit of knowing it would fit in the end and that it was best just to go with the flow rather than question it.

"It's obvious what happened here," Monk said. "It's right up there on the wall."

Monk pointed to the bleached patch of wallpaper above the couch. Stoffmacher, Geshir, and I looked at the wall.

"There's nothing there," Geshir said.

"There was, but now it's over there." Monk gestured to the painting of the fruit on the opposite wall. "That painting used to be on this wall. It matches the bleached outline on the wallpaper."

"So?" Geshir asked.

"Someone moved it." Monk went over and lifted the painting off the other wall, revealing a hole. "To hide this."

Geshir walked up to the hole and peered through it.

"You can see right into the living room of the other apartment," Geshir said. "I wonder if a really hot woman lives there and if she likes to walk around naked."

Stoffmacher grimaced with pain, but it wasn't physical. "That's a bullet hole, Kommissar. Is there anybody home next door?"

"I don't see anyone," Geshir said.

Stoffmacher grabbed him by the collar and yanked him away from the wall. "I mean, did you knock on the door when we arrived and did anyone answer?"

"No," Geshir said, sounding a bit flustered. "I mean, yes, I knocked, but no, no one answered."

"Get the landlord to open it up," Stoffmacher said.

"Why?"

"Because whoever fired the shot did it from the other apartment," Stoffmacher said. "It's an exit hole."

Geshir went outside to find the landlord.

I decided that Friderike was right. Homes today aren't nearly as well made as homes that were built centuries ago. A bullet certainly wouldn't go through a wall at her house. It wouldn't even scratch it.

I wondered whether it would make more sense to pack some mud and rocks around my windows rather than replace the weather-beaten wooden frames every few years.

Stoffmacher turned to Monk. "How did you know that bullet hole was going to be there?"

"All the clues pointed to it," Monk said.

"What clues?" he asked.

"The bullet hole in the couch, the bleached wallpaper where the painting was, and the little nicks on the handle of the gun."

"There are nicks on the gun handle?" Stoffmacher crouched beside the gun and squinted at it. So did I. We both saw the tiny nicks on the bottom and edge of the handle.

"The shooter used his gun to hammer the nail into the wall," Monk said. "So he could hang the picture over the bullet hole that came from the other apartment."

"How did you see those marks on the handle?" Stoffmacher asked.

"I always see the little things. It's a gift," Monk said. "And a curse."

"I don't get the curse part," Stoffmacher said.

"You will," I said.

"There's also dried dirt on the couch cushions where

the shooter had to stand to remove the painting," Monk said.

Stoffmacher and I looked at the couch. Sure enough, there were bits of dirt as well as some fluff from the stuffing of the back cushion and a pillow feather. He mulled over this latest discovery.

"So the neighbor fired a bullet into his wall and accidentally killed this man," Stoffmacher said, motioning to the corpse on the floor. "The neighbor came in, put a gun in Vigg's hand to make it look like suicide, shot the couch, moved the painting to cover the bullet hole, and then locked the doorknob on his way out to delay the discovery of the body."

He could lock the doorknob without the key, but not the dead bolt, which explained why the question of whether the dead bolt was locked or not was so significant to Monk. Everything seemed to fit, but there was one piece I didn't get.

"Why did he shoot the couch?" I asked.

"To make sure the crime lab would find gunshot residue on Vigg's hand so we would believe he shot himself," Stoffmacher said. "Then the neighbor moved the painting to cover the bullet hole."

"That's one explanation of how things happened," Monk said.

"There's another?" Stoffmacher said.

"It's possible that the man next door isn't the one who fired the bullet that went through the wall and accidentally killed Axel Vigg."

"Then who did it?" I asked.

"Whoever shot and killed the man next door," Monk said.

16

Mr. Monk and the Deal

We went outside and found Geshir talking to the landlord, a flustered little man with a mustache that looked
like a bow tie. Monk examined a feather on the door-
step and then looked up at a group of ducks and their
ducklings crossing the roadway towards the creek on
the other side. I wondered if he was going ask the police to cite them for littering.

Geshir took a set of keys from the landlord and met
us in front of the neighbor's door.

"The apartment is rented, furnished, on a month-to-
month basis by a man named Bruno Leupolz," Geshir
said. "He's only lived here a couple of weeks."

"Where does he work?" Stoffmacher took some
rubber gloves from his pocket, slipped a pair on, and
handed us each a pair, but Monk didn't put them on.

"The landlord doesn't know much about him,"
Geshir said, "except that he came from Berlin and pays
in cash."

Stoffmacher motioned to the door. Geshir put on a
pair of rubber gloves, unlocked the door, and slowly
pushed it open.

The first thing I noticed as we stepped inside was the smell. Or rather the lack of one. It meant that we weren't going to find a decomposing corpse, which was a big relief for me. One was enough for one day.

The layout was like the other one, only in reverse. The place was clean and sparsely furnished and the walls were bare. There was a writing table pressed up against the wall, right below the bullet hole. There was no blood on the walls, the carpet, or the linoleum floor of the kitchenette.

We fanned out into the living room in silence, looking around for signs of I don't know what.

Monk examined the ashes in the fireplace, the pencils and blank paper on the writing table, and the inkjet printer on one of the chairs.

Nothing seemed unusual or out of place to me, but I don't have Monk's eye for detail.

We followed the two cops upstairs, Monk nearly stumbling to avoid a tiny feather on one of the steps. The bedroom was small and had a view of the hotel up on the hill. There was a pair of men's casual shoes, the laces still tied, in front of the half-open closet, the doors scuffed where other shoes the tenant had kicked off his feet had hit them.

I was pleased with myself for noticing that. The only reason I did was because my late husband, Mitch, used to kick off his shoes without untying them all the time. Not only did he scuff up the doors and walls, but he left the shoes all over the floor for me to trip over when I woke up at night to go to the bathroom.

There was a pair of pants and a shirt flung on top of the unmade double bed. Monk rolled his shoulders. I knew how much he hated anything that was unmade. He was probably fighting the urge to tuck in the sheets and fluff the pillow.

Geshir opened the bathroom door and we looked in-

side. There was nothing unusual in there either. Like a corpse, for instance. It appeared that Monk was wrong about a murder having occurred here.

Stoffmacher stroked his mustache. "It looks like Herr Leupolz accidentally shot his neighbor, tried to make it look like a suicide, and then fled."

"But he didn't take any of his clothes," Monk said. "They are still hanging in his closet. His suitcase is still there, too."

"He didn't have time to pack," Stoffmacher said.

Monk tipped his head from side to side, shifted his weight from foot to foot, and rolled his shoulders. Stoffmacher and Geshir stared at him.

"Is something wrong?" Geshir asked.

I could answer that for them. Monk's body language wasn't exactly subtle.

"Everything is wrong," I said.

"Why did he change his clothes before leaving?" Monk asked.

"Maybe those are his clothes from the day before," Stoffmacher said.

"But they are on top of his unmade bed," Monk said, "which suggests to me that he changed his clothes after he awoke. If he slept in the bed with the clothes on top, they wouldn't be lying flat. They would be tangled with the sheets or on the floor."

"If he was fleeing, maybe he simply wanted to be wearing heavier clothes on his journey," Stoffmacher said. "Or something with more pockets. I honestly don't know."

"Neither do I," Monk said. "It's a mystery."

"Not a very interesting one," Stoffmacher said.

"There's more," Monk said and went downstairs. We followed him to the writing table in the living room.

"He's obviously a writer, but where is his writing?" Monk said. "There are pencils and papers on the table,

and a printer, but nothing in the house that actually has writing on it. And why would he take his laptop but leave his charger behind?"

Monk motioned to a charger in the wall. I'd missed that when I looked at the room and I'm sure the two *Kommissars* had, too.

"It's simple," Stoffmacher said. "He was in a hurry. He just grabbed his laptop and his papers, and fled."

"He might have taken his laptop, but he didn't take his papers. They were burned." Monk led us over to the fireplace and squatted in front of it. "There are paper clips, staples, and the spiral rings from notebooks in the ashes. Why would he burn his papers?"

"Maybe Leupolz was suicidal and his journals contained his suicidal rantings," Geshir said. "He burned them because they were incriminating."

"Why would they be incriminating?" Stoffmacher asked.

"Because maybe he was going to shoot himself in the head and, at the last second, had a change of heart," Geshir replied. "His hand twitched and he fired into the wall, accidentally killing Vigg. So he made it look like Vigg killed himself instead. His notes would have tipped us off to what really happened. But I deduced it anyway."

Stoffmacher gave Geshir a withering look. "That certainly explains why you're the top detective in Lohr."

Geshir beamed. "Thank you, sir."

"And not Frankfurt, Stuttgart, Cologne, or any other major city," Stoffmacher said.

"But it could have happened that way," Geshir said.

"No, it couldn't," Stoffmacher said, then looked to Monk for support. "Could it?"

"I don't think so," Monk said while shaking another bit of fluff off his pant leg as if it was corrosive. "If Vigg's death was an accident, why didn't Leupolz just admit it? Why turn it into a crime by running?"

"He would have shot himself instead," Stoffmacher said. "Who could live with the guilt and humiliation?"

"When he tried to kill himself the first time, he discovered the will to live," Geshir said. "He ran because he realized that he loves life and didn't want to spend it with the guilt and embarrassment of this accident hanging over him."

It seemed to me that there was some logic to that argument, but I was sort of rooting for Geshir after Stoffmacher's unnecessarily nasty remark, so maybe I was being overly charitable.

"I don't think that's what happened here," Stoffmacher said.

"Do you have a better explanation?" Geshir asked.

"As a matter of fact, I do," Stoffmacher said. "Maybe Leupolz has nothing to do with the bullet hole or Vigg's death. Maybe he is at work, or his girlfriend's apartment, or on a trip, blissfully unaware of the tragedy that has occurred here in his absence."

"Then what happened?" I asked.

"A very nervous burglar with a gun broke into the house, was startled by a noise next door, and accidentally shot into the wall," Stoffmacher said. "He made the killing look like a suicide and then ran off with Leupolz's valuables."

"That doesn't explain the ashes in the fireplace," Monk said, blowing a tiny pillow feather off the tabletop.

"Maybe Leupolz didn't like what he was writing and burned it himself last night," Stoffmacher said. "I've heard that writers are highly emotional people. He certainly wouldn't be the first frustrated author to burn a manuscript."

Monk shook his head. "We're missing something."

"Bruno Leupolz," Stoffmacher said. "Once we find him, the mystery will be solved."

"I don't think so," Monk said.

"Rest assured," Stoffmacher said, "he will talk."

"Not if he's dead," Monk said.

"Look around," Geshir said. "There's no blood, no signs of a struggle, and no corpse. If you don't include the dead man next door."

"I know, but you said this is a very safe neighborhood and most people leave their doors unlocked," Monk said. "So why would a common burglar come here with a gun?"

"He wouldn't," Stoffmacher said wearily.

"But a killer would," Monk said.

"So why isn't there blood?" Stoffmacher said. "So why isn't there a body? What happened here?"

"I don't know," Monk said. "But there's a pillow missing."

Stoffmacher and Geshir shared a confused look.

"What pillow?" Stoffmacher asked.

"Leupolz has a double bed," Monk said. "But only one pillow. The other one is gone."

"What difference does that make?" Geshir asked. "Pillows aren't valuable."

"But they can make a decent silencer," Monk said. "The shooter used the pillow from Leupolz's bed to muffle his gunshot. That's why no one heard it. He tried to clean up the feathers afterwards, but it's not easy. That's why there's still some Hungarian goose down and feathers here and why he tracked some into Vigg's apartment."

"Why would someone want Leupolz dead?" Stoffmacher asked. "And why wouldn't he leave the body? And why would he bother to disguise the death next door as a suicide? Why not leave both bodies? Why leave Vigg and hide Leupolz?"

"I don't know the answers to those questions," Monk said. "But I will help you figure it out if you help me with something."

Ah, so there it was. Monk hadn't forgotten his goal; he'd simply been setting his hook. I'd never known him to be quite so manipulative.

"What is it you want?" Stoffmacher asked, brushing a bit of down off his sleeve.

"Somewhere in Lohr is a man with six fingers on his right hand. I need you to find him."

"Why?" Geshir asked.

"Because he hired someone to kill my wife."

Monk briefly explained what had happened to Trudy and what led him to believe a man with eleven fingers was responsible for her murder.

"I am deeply sorry for your loss," Stoffmacher said. "But how do you know it's the same man if you haven't actually seen him before yourself?"

"I know he is the same way I knew everything I discovered here today," Monk said.

"Here you had evidence," Stoffmacher said. "Where is your evidence that this eleven-fingered man you saw is the killer you've been seeking?"

Monk tapped his chest, right above his heart. "Do we have an agreement or not?"

Stoffmacher nodded. "I'll have my men start looking for him as soon as we find Bruno Leupolz."

"My wife's killer could be gone by then," Monk said.

"He may be gone already, but this case comes first."

"There's no urgency to find Leupolz," Monk said. "He's dead."

"We don't know that. We don't know anything. If you have any insights, I'd like to hear them. In the meantime, we'll be in touch as soon as we've learned anything new," Stoffmacher said. "I'd tell you to have a pleasant stay, but I don't think that's really possible now."

He had that right.

17

Mr. Monk Makes a Discovery

Stoffmacher was right: We couldn't just go back to the bed-and-breakfast and wait. And I doubted I could work up much enthusiasm for sightseeing after what we'd already seen. This is why I don't recommend hanging around corpses on a vacation.

There weren't a lot of options open to us. Ordinarily we'd go off and start investigating on our own. But that wasn't possible here. We didn't have the authority, we didn't know the town, and we didn't speak German.

I was at a loss as to what to do next. But Monk wasn't.

"Dr. Kroger needs to know about this," Monk said as we stepped outside the duplex of death.

"Can't it wait until your appointment tomorrow?" I said, trying to give Dr. Kroger a little peace, not that he deserved it.

"This is a major development in the investigation of Trudy's murder," Monk said. "He's the only one who truly understands what I have been through because he's been there from the start. He's felt my pain. This is going to mean as much to him as it does to me."

I wasn't so sure about that, but I couldn't think of anywhere else to go or anything else we could do.

"Okay," I said. "Let's go."

I needed some air, so I suggested that we walk up to the hotel. Monk was fine with that.

"Do you want to take the road or one of the trails through the forest?" I asked.

"The road," Monk said. "There's less nature."

"You say that like it's a good thing."

"It is," Monk said.

"What's wrong with nature?"

"It's full of dirt, germs, bugs, and animals," Monk said. "And the things that animals leave behind."

"We all leave things behind, Mr. Monk. It's natural."

"See?" Monk said. "Nature again. We spend most of our lives cleaning up after it."

"*You* do," I said.

"Mother Nature was obviously a very filthy person," Monk said.

The houses in the neighborhood were spaced widely apart and loosely followed the line of the forest. There weren't any fences, though there were a few plants and low rock walls marking property boundaries.

The road got gradually steeper. I wondered if there was a shortcut we could have taken through the woods. But if we'd taken it, I would have missed an oddity. At first I mistook it for a group mailbox atop a post, but as we got closer, I saw it was actually a cigarette vending machine. There were pictures of various brands of cigarettes and a knob under each one to pull after the proper number of coins had been inserted in the slot.

We both stood there staring at the machine as if it was a meteor. I'd never seen a vending machine on a residential street corner, much less one that sold cigarettes, and I'm pretty sure that Monk hadn't either.

"That's odd," I said.

"No odder than anything else in this town," Monk replied.

"I wonder what other vending machines they have in the neighborhood and what they sell."

"I guarantee disinfectant isn't one of the things," Monk said.

"You're probably right," I said.

"I usually am."

We continued walking. We crossed a bridge over a tiny creek and were on the Franziskushohe property.

"Don't you ever doubt yourself?" I asked.

"All the time."

"About what?"

"What shirt to wear," Monk said.

"All your shirts are the same."

"That's what makes the choice so hard," Monk said.

"I mean about big things," I said as we crossed the bridge we'd driven over yesterday. "Decisions you've made about your life, about love, about the future."

"When I make a decision about something, it's based on the facts and how things are supposed to fit together," Monk said. "Facts are immutable and things only fit together one way, so how can I be wrong?"

"Facts can change and things don't always fit the way they should."

"That's heresy," Monk said. "I'd keep your voice down if I were you. They burn women at the stake for that here."

We took the steps up the hillside rather than following the winding road. It was steeper, but seemed like a more direct route to me. Monk followed my lead without comment.

"Look at you and me," I said. "If you consider the facts about us and our lives, we shouldn't fit together at all, and yet we've worked together for years."

"That's a poor example," Monk said. "I made a decision about you, based on the facts and how things are supposed to fit together, and I was right."

"I don't see it," I said, stopping to catch my breath. I needed to get more exercise. "What facts? What fit?"

"My longtime nurse had left, so I was looking for a capable person to protect my interests, anticipate my needs, and keep my life as even as possible."

"Exactly," I said and started up the steps again. "And I wasn't a nurse, a secretary, or a psychic. I was a bartender and a single mother. Those are the facts and it made me a lousy fit for the job."

"You're forgetting that Sharona was a single mother, too," Monk said.

"What does that have to do with anything?"

"You hold your home together, struggle with finances, and face countless small disasters, all while providing a safe, productive, predictable, and nurturing life for your child. Those are facts, and I needed someone with those same skills for me. You fit right into the space left by Sharona. Fact and fit—that's why it's worked."

Before Sharona and me, there had been Trudy, who kept him more than together. From what I've heard, when she was around, he had all his anxieties in check. He was almost normal, and yet still possessed his amazing skills as a detective.

The difference, of course, between her and us was that Monk loved Trudy and she loved him.

We cared for him, and he probably did for us, but there was no love in his life anymore. That was a fact, and a sad one. I don't think he was looking for anyone to fit into his life that way again and maybe he never would. At least not until he could solve her murder and relieve himself of some of the undeserved guilt he carried for her death.

"So you are always right," I said.

"On matters of fact and fit," Monk said, "yes."

"And are there any matters that don't involve fact and fit?"

"Not in an orderly world," he said.

"But we don't live in one," I said.

"I'm working on it," Monk said.

We reached the hotel parking lot and headed for the lobby. Up on the hillside, under the long, covered patio, I could see a dozen people gathered, chatting and holding tall glasses of beer. It was some sort of outdoor buffet. Dr. Kroger was among them. He intercepted a muscular man in gray sweats who jogged in off one of the hiking trails.

"Mr. Monk," I said, "Dr. Kroger is up there."

Monk followed my gaze and smiled. "He's going to be so excited. We've waited so long for this."

He hurried past me, quickly climbing the log steps placed in the dirt. I was right behind him.

As we went up the steps, I could see a middle-aged woman with a camera motioning Dr. Kroger and the man in sweats to pose together for a picture.

"Don't be bashful. This is for the conference collage," she said with a heavy Cockney accent. "Give us a big smile."

"Looking at you, Mildred, how could we have anything less on our faces?" Dr. Kroger said.

"You charmer," she replied.

The man put his arm around Dr. Kroger's shoulder and the two of them smiled for her camera. The man had a rugged, earthy handsomeness, like the Marlboro Man, only without the cigarette dangling from parched lips.

Mildred snapped the picture and her camera flashed just as we reached the patio.

Monk staggered back, letting out a pained cry.

"Blinded by the flash?" I asked.

"I wish," he said, staring at Dr. Kroger, who was just noticing us.

"Adrian?" Dr. Kroger said. "You're not supposed to be here."

Monk kept moving backward, stumbling on the steps and losing his balance. I had to grab him to keep him from falling over.

"Mr. Monk," I said, "what's wrong?"

"It was all a lie," Monk said. He was still staring at Dr. Kroger. "He never wanted to help me."

"What are you talking about?" I asked.

"He kept me from the truth. Nothing was real. My life has been an illusion."

Monk wasn't making any sense, but I was used to that. Whenever he solved a mystery, he saw how the bits and pieces of evidence fit together in a revelatory moment of startling clarity. It took him a minute to process the information so we could see it as clearly as he did.

But those realizations were usually moments of joy and contentment for him. What I heard in his voice and saw in his face now was horror. And what mystery was he solving?

I turned to Dr. Kroger, hoping for some guidance in this situation.

And that's when I realized that it wasn't Dr. Kroger whom Monk was looking at. He was looking at the man who was standing beside Dr. Kroger and had his right arm around the psychiatrist's shoulder.

The man had six fingers on his right hand.

A shiver ran through my whole body like an electric shock. I felt dizzy and sick. And I'm sure my reaction wasn't one tenth of what Monk was feeling.

"Adrian." Dr. Kroger took a step forward, an expression of concern on his face. "I think you need help."

Monk shook his head, turned around, and ran down

the steps. He kept on running until he disappeared from sight below the hotel. I watched him go. There were tears stinging my eyes.

I couldn't imagine the horror and betrayal that Monk was feeling. His whole world had just been turned inside out—and mine along with it.

Dr. Kroger came up behind me. "What has gotten into him, Natalie?"

I read a story once about a man who couldn't get his desktop computer to work properly. After spending three fruitless hours on the phone with customer support, he threw his computer out the window of his tenth-floor apartment. Unfortunately, the computer, the monitor, and the keyboard all landed on the roof of a police car.

When the police officers asked him why he did it, he shrugged and said, "I just snapped."

He threw away thousands of dollars. He could have killed someone on the street. Didn't he consider for one second what he was about to do? I didn't understand it, at least not until that moment in Lohr when I snapped.

I whirled around and punched Dr. Kroger in the face. And as he staggered back, his eyes wide with shock and his nose bloody, I threw myself at him. We landed on the ground with my hands around his throat. I saw stars, but I think it was just the flash of Mildred taking more pictures.

Several men grabbed me by the arms, pulled me off of Dr. Kroger, and dragged me away.

Now, with the benefit of hindsight, I know what happened. I made the same connections that Monk did and lost control. Monk ran. I attacked. We'd both realized that the man Monk had trusted to gain control of his anxieties and phobias may actually have been doing everything he could to exacerbate them.

The man he'd trusted to help him become psychologically stable enough to return to the police force may actually have been working to keep that from ever happening.

The man he'd trusted with his most intimate feelings and fears may have been helping the man who murdered Monk's wife avoid ever being caught.

Thinking about it again made me want to hit Dr. Kroger some more. I lunged for him, but the men held me back.

Dr. Kroger looked at me like I was some kind of wild animal, which, at the moment, I guess I was.

The man with eleven fingers helped Dr. Kroger to his feet and handed him a napkin to hold under his bloody nose.

"What is going on, Charles?" the man asked. He had a deep baritone voice that embodied authority and an undefined European accent. "Who are these people?"

"As if you didn't know," I said to him, struggling against the men who held me. I wanted to hit that guy, too.

Monk was right. The man who hired someone to put a bomb in Trudy's car had fled to the last place on earth Monk would ever visit. But then Dr. Kroger made the mistake of going there, leading Monk directly to his wife's murderer.

"The man is Adrian Monk, one of my patients," Dr. Kroger said, clutching the napkin to his nose. "This is Natalie Teeger, his assistant."

"They stalked you all the way to Germany?" the man said. Everyone turned and looked at me with disbelief. "I'm calling the police."

"That won't be necessary," Dr. Kroger said.

"The hell it isn't," I said. "Call them. If you don't, I will."

Dr. Kroger approached me slowly, with his head

cocked. I wasn't sure if he was doing that to stop the bleeding or to regard me with curiosity.

"I'm not going to press charges," Dr. Kroger said. "But I would like to understand why you attacked me."

"How can you look me in the eye and ask me that question after what you have done?" I said. "You might as well have killed Trudy Monk yourself."

"Have you lost your mind?" Dr. Kroger asked.

"You tell me, Doctor," I said and nodded towards the man next to him. "Does he have six fingers on his right hand or am I hallucinating?"

Dr. Kroger looked back at the man, then again at me. There was an expression of horrified realization on his face as the full impact of what was happening sank in.

"Oh my God," he said.

"The charade is over," I said. "And you're both going to prison."

18

Mr. Monk and the Perfect Storm

A hush fell over the patio. All the people there, with the possible exception of Dr. Kroger and Trudy's murderer, were stunned. It's not often you see a woman attack someone and accuse him of murder.

"What is she talking about?" asked the man with eleven fingers.

"A terrible misunderstanding," Dr. Kroger said.

"You can both stop pretending," I said. "It's all over now."

Dr. Kroger faced the two men who were holding me. "You can let her go."

"She could hurt you or herself," said one of the men who held me.

"Natalie won't hurt anyone," Dr. Kroger said.

"Don't count on it," I said.

"This woman is clearly violent and unstable," said the other man who held me. "She should be restrained and sedated."

"I respect your opinions, doctors, but considering the situation, her reaction was entirely understandable and justified," Dr. Kroger said. "She believes I be-

trayed her friend in a profound and deeply disturbing manner."

"You did," I said.

"I can see how it would appear that way," Dr. Kroger said and then gestured to the man with eleven fingers. "But he is not the man you think he is and I haven't done what you think I have done. I can explain everything."

The two men let me go but stood warily at my side, ready to grab me again if I suddenly went for Dr. Kroger's throat. That was wise of them, because that was exactly what I intended to do.

"Come with me, Natalie," he said. "We'll go somewhere quiet and talk this out."

"How about a jail cell?" I said. "I hear that they are very quiet."

"You have nothing to lose by hearing me out," Dr. Kroger said. "I am not going anywhere and neither is Dr. Rahner."

"Who is Dr. Rahner?"

"That would be me." The man behind Dr. Kroger raised his six-fingered hand and waved it at me. "The one you just accused of murder."

"You're all witnesses," I said to everyone else on the patio. "You know what you saw and what you heard. Remember that if anything happens to me before the police get here."

"You are perfectly safe," Dr. Kroger said. "Nothing is going to happen to you."

I marched away from the covered patio and down the steps to the parking lot. Dr. Kroger followed me, holding the napkin to his nose. I could see the people up on the patio watching us.

"This is as far as we go," I said. "I am staying out in the open where we can be seen."

"Do you really think that I would harm you?" Dr. Kroger said.

"I know from experience that murderers will do just about anything when they are cornered and exposed."

"I am not a murderer, Natalie."

"No, you just help them get away with it," I said. "What I don't understand is why."

"I don't blame you or Adrian for making all the wrong assumptions," Dr. Kroger said. "This is a perfect storm of coincidences."

"Mr. Monk doesn't believe in coincidences," I said.

"They happen," Dr. Kroger said.

"Not like this," I said.

"That's why I called it a perfect storm," Dr. Kroger said. "You think that Dr. Rahner is the man who arranged for Trudy's murder and, because you've seen us together, that we're involved in a conspiracy together to deceive Adrian. You believe I have been keeping Adrian incapacitated and off the force to protect Trudy's killer."

"Prove me wrong," I said.

"It's preposterous," Dr. Kroger said. "Surely you can see that."

"What I see is you with a man who has six fingers on his right hand, just like the killer Mr. Monk has been pursuing for years. What are the odds of that happening if it's not a conspiracy?"

"Astronomical," Dr. Kroger said. "But think about it. Why would I risk my freedom, my practice, and my reputation to help a killer get away with murder?"

"Money? Blackmail? I don't know. You tell me."

"I came here to attend a psychiatric conference. Dr. Rahner is a world-renowned psychiatrist and the conference organizer. He specializes in studying the psychological, social, and emotional impacts of physical abnormalities on the individuals who have them and on the greater society that they live in. That's what this conference is about and why I am here, along with

three dozen other psychiatrists from around the world. There is nothing sinister about it and it certainly has nothing to do with Adrian or his wife."

"Why should I believe you?"

"Because you are a rational person." Dr. Kroger examined the bloody napkin. "Usually. Think about it, Natalie. If I was involved in such a vast conspiracy, would I really be stupid enough to be seen in public, even half a world away, with the killer?"

I was torn.

When I saw Dr. Kroger and Dr. Rahner together, I made the same connections that Monk did. Monk and I didn't usually think alike, but this time we reached the same immediate, unavoidable, and visceral conclusion: Trudy's killer was here and Dr. Kroger was helping him. Everything fit together and made sickening sense.

But Dr. Kroger made a compelling argument. Why would he get involved in such a complex conspiracy? Why would he allow himself to be seen openly and publicly with a man who matched the description of Trudy Monk's murderer? Could Dr. Kroger be both that coldly manipulative and that unbelievably careless?

If it was, as Dr. Kroger suggested, a perfect storm of coincidences, then it was a cruel cosmic joke on Monk.

But if it wasn't, then Dr. Kroger was shrewd, evil, and very dangerous.

"I don't know what to believe right now," I said. "But I'm not the one who has to be convinced."

"The truth is not going to be easy for Adrian to accept," Dr. Kroger said. "I will need your help."

That put me in a lovely position. Either an innocent man was enlisting my aid or an accomplice to a killer was trying to make me part of his conspiracy to play with Monk's mind.

I wasn't going to make that decision on my own.

"I'm going to call Captain Stottlemeyer right now and let him know what's happened," I said. "He'll look into your story and find out the truth."

"I think that's a good idea," Dr. Kroger said. "Adrian trusts Captain Stottlemeyer."

"Mr. Monk trusted you, too."

"He still can," Dr. Kroger said.

"We'll see about that," I said, turning my back to him and walking away.

As I went down the hill, I took out my cell phone and called Captain Stottlemeyer. I didn't care what time it was in San Francisco. This was more important than a good night's sleep.

"Yeah?" Stottlemeyer grumbled groggily.

"It's me again," I said.

"You do understand that there is a time difference between San Francisco and Germany, right?"

"We found the man with eleven fingers," I said. "His name is Dr. Martin Rahner."

"Is he the guy who killed Trudy?"

"We don't know," I said.

"So why are you calling me? I'm sure the police over there can handle it."

"Because we found him having his picture taken with Dr. Kroger. It turns out they know each other."

"I still don't know what you want from me."

"Don't you see the significance?"

"I'm not even sure I am having this conversation," Stottlemeyer said.

"If Dr. Rahner is the one who killed Trudy Monk, then he could have been using Dr. Kroger to keep Mr. Monk too messed up to ever solve the case."

"That's pretty far-fetched," Stottlemeyer said.

"Or if they aren't in cahoots, it's the biggest coincidence in the history of coincidences."

"Did you just say 'cahoots'?"

"Whether it's a conspiracy or a coincidence, it's still hard to believe. That's why we need you to run a background check on Dr. Rahner to see if he has any connection to Dr. Kroger, Mr. Monk, and Trudy Monk."

"Would you like me to also stop by your house, maybe water your plants, collect your newspapers, or wash your car?"

"I know that I'm intruding on your sleep—"

"Again," he interrupted.

"—and that what I'm asking is an imposition—"

"Again," he interrupted.

"But think of what it means to Mr. Monk."

"You've already used that as leverage with me before tonight," Stottlemeyer said.

"Did it work?"

"I'll call you when I have something," Stottlemeyer said. "No matter what time it is."

"You just want to get even by waking me up, too."

"Brilliant deduction," he said as he hung up.

I put my phone back in my purse and that was when I spotted Monk, huddled under a tree, hugging his knees to his chest. He looked like a frightened child.

I sat down next to him and put my hand on the back of his head.

"Are you okay?" I asked.

"I just found out that my psychiatrist has been conspiring with the man who killed my wife to keep me off the police force," Monk said. "I'm dandy."

"What if it's all just a cruel coincidence?"

"And dogs can talk, the earth is flat, and granola won't kill you."

"Granola isn't dangerous," I said.

"The last few years of my life have been a complete illusion," Monk said. "I may not be who I think I am."

"You are still Adrian Monk," I said.

"But I might not have any psychological problems

at all. I could be the most together person in San Francisco," Monk said. "We've only got Dr. Kroger's word that I need counseling. Maybe I don't need any help at all."

"Maybe you don't," I said. "What do you think?"

"I don't know," Monk said. "I can't concentrate."

"Because you don't know what to believe anymore or who to trust."

"Because of that rock wall over there," he said. "Not a single rock is the same shape. Who can think with all of that going on?"

I followed his gaze. There was a low rock wall along one end of the hotel property made up of hundreds of different stones. They weren't making any kind of ruckus that I could hear.

"So stop looking at it," I said.

"I can still feel them," Monk said.

"Then let's go somewhere else," I suggested.

"You can't run from something like that," he said. "It haunts you."

I think that statement pretty much answered the question of whether or not Monk still needed psychological counseling, but I let it go. Instead, I shared with Monk everything that Dr. Kroger had told me about Dr. Rahner and the "perfect storm" of coincidences.

"Dr. Kroger insists that there's no connection between this eleven-fingered guy and the one responsible for Trudy's murder," I said. "I don't know what to believe."

"Neither do I," Monk said. "About Dr. Kroger or about myself."

"I called Captain Stottlemeyer and asked him to look into Dr. Kroger's story. Whatever he digs up should help us determine the truth," I said. "But what you believe about yourself is entirely up to you, Mr. Monk. It always has been. You decide who you are. No one else has that power."

"Ever since Trudy was killed, I've been told that I'm not psychologically or emotionally capable of functioning on my own or being a police officer anymore. I believed what they told me."

"You think it's a self-fulfilling prophecy," I said. "They tell you that you're a certain person and you become that person."

"It could be a conspiracy to make me think I'm crazy when, in fact, I'm the epitome of sanity."

"I wouldn't go that far," I said.

"It was Dr. Kroger who said I couldn't take care of myself, who said I needed a nurse," Monk said. "What if Sharona was in on it, too? That way they could brainwash me day and night."

"Sharona would never do anything to hurt you," I said. "She cares about you, just like I do."

Monk looked at me, scrambled to his feet, and backed a good three feet away from me as if I was contagious. I knew what was coming next.

"Maybe you're in on it, too," he said, pointing his finger accusingly.

"You found me, Mr. Monk. Remember?"

"No, Captain Stottlemeyer did," Monk said. "Come to think of it, he also won't support my reinstatement. Maybe he's in on this, too. Maybe you all are."

"Okay, now you're just being paranoid," I said.

"Am I?" Monk said. "Did Dr. Kroger tell you to say that? Does he want to add paranoia to the crippling self-image he's crafted for me?"

"Mr. Monk, listen to yourself," I said. "You're becoming unhinged."

"I've solved every murder I've ever investigated except the killing of my wife. And now I know why. Everyone has been working against me, clouding my mind with lies and illusions so I wouldn't see the truth."

"If I am in cahoots with Dr. Kroger, why did I help you to come to Germany?" I said. "Why would I risk exposing our conspiracy? I'd have to be incompetent to do that."

Monk mulled that over for a moment. "You've got a point."

"And you would have asked yourself those same questions if you'd given it one moment of thought," I said. "You have to calm down and think things through."

"If you were part of it, you would have found a way to stop me from getting on that plane," Monk said. "At the very least, you would have tipped Dr. Rahner off that I was coming so he wouldn't be here when I arrived."

"That's right. Now think about Captain Stottlemeyer," I said. "If he was on their side, would he have hired you as a consultant to the police, let you build up your confidence, hone your skills, and reestablish your reputation and credibility as a detective?"

Monk nodded. "No, he wouldn't. He would have shut me out and made me think I'd lost my mojo."

"I agree with you that something very strange is going on here, Mr. Monk, but you can't let paranoia cloud your judgment."

"I have to clear my mind and concentrate only on the facts."

"Now you're talking," I said.

"Because if I give in to paranoia, they win."

"They?" I asked.

"Everyone who is out to get me," he said.

19

Mr. Monk and the Stakeout

We trudged back down the hill to Vigg's house. The police were gone but they'd left the property surrounded by the single strip of crime scene tape. It was the only sign that a double murder might have taken place on that quiet street.

We continued on towards the center of the village, using the church spires and the watchtower to guide us.

"So what's the plan?" I asked.

"I'm going to ask Hauptkriminalkommissar Stoffmacher to arrest Dr. Rahner and send him to San Francisco to stand trial for murder," Monk said.

"Don't you think they're going to need more evidence than his extra finger and the word of a dead bomber?"

"It's obvious that he's guilty of something," Monk said.

"Because you say so?"

"Because he has eleven fingers," Monk said. "All you have to do is look at him to see that he's unbalanced."

"It's a physical abnormality," I said. "It doesn't mean anything."

"Who knows what other ways he might also be unbalanced?"

"His finger isn't a physical manifestation of deeper
problems."

"Of course it is. It's nature's way of warning you,"
Monk said. "Would you eat a chicken that had two
heads or a fish with three eyes?"

"Probably not," I said. "But we're talking about a
person's character, not edibility. You can't judge somebody on the basis of a physical defect. That's unfair
and insensitive."

"You know what they say. If you wouldn't eat a person, you shouldn't trust them."

"Who says that?"

"My new neighbor," Monk said.

"You've only spoken to him once, and I was there," I
said. "He didn't say that."

"It's common cannibal wisdom."

"Since when are you an expert on cannibals?"

"Since one of them moved into my building," he
said.

Even if there was a conspiracy against Monk, I was
fairly certain that Dr. Kroger's diagnosis of his mental
health was absolutely accurate.

We found Stoffmacher at his desk in the police station,
holding a mirror up to his face and examining his mustache, touching it up with a tiny comb. He didn't seem
too pleased to see us standing at the front counter.

"I have no news to share," Stoffmacher said without
getting up from his desk. "We haven't found Bruno
Leupolz or your eleven-fingered suspect."

"We have," Monk said. "He's at the hotel on the
hill."

"Leupolz?"

"The other guy," I said.

Monk said, "His name is Dr. Martin Rahner and he's attending the same seminar as my psychiatrist. What do you think of that?"

"It's not uncommon for psychiatrists to attend psychiatric conferences," Stoffmacher said. "Regardless of how many fingers they have."

"I think it's a conspiracy," Monk said. "My shrink has been helping my wife's killer evade capture all of these years."

Stoffmacher set down his mirror and his comb. "That sounds crazy."

"That's exactly what my psychiatrist wants you to think," Monk said.

"Especially coming from a patient who followed his psychiatrist here from the United States," Stoffmacher said.

"That's the beauty of it," Monk said. "Who would believe me?"

"It's a convincing argument," Stoffmacher said.

"His or mine?"

"His," Stoffmacher said. "And he hasn't even made it yet."

"But you aren't falling for it," Monk said. "Because I've already proven to you at the Leupolz crime scene that I'm thoughtful, intelligent, and rational."

"Do you expect me to arrest them?" Stoffmacher asked.

"That would be nice," Monk said.

"Do you have evidence of their guilt or any outstanding warrants for their arrest?"

"Are those necessary in Germany?" Monk asked.

"We follow the rule of law here," Stoffmacher said. "We are a civilized country."

"If that were true, you wouldn't have cobblestone streets," Monk said.

"What?" Stoffmacher said.

I spoke up quickly before Monk could make himself look any crazier. "Mr. Monk would appreciate it if you would do a background check on Dr. Rahner and keep an eye on him."

"I'll see what I can do," Stoffmacher said. "But I'm afraid the homicide investigation is taxing our resources as it is. All my officers are occupied right now looking for Bruno Leupolz."

"I understand," I said.

"I don't," Monk said. "Leupolz is dead."

"We don't know that," Stoffmacher said.

"I do," Monk said. "Don't worry—bodies have a way of turning up. So you can investigate Dr. Rahner and watch his every move until someone finds the corpse."

"If there is a corpse to be found, we'd like to be the ones to do it," Stoffmacher said. "Good day, Mr. Monk."

"The hell it is," Monk said and walked out.

I followed after him.

Monk stepped carefully from stone to stone, almost as if he was playing hopscotch.

"Do you really think it's a good idea to irritate Stoffmacher?" I said. "We need his help."

"He's hiding something," Monk said.

"His irritation," I said.

"What if he's in on it too?"

"I thought you weren't going to let paranoia overwhelm you," I said.

"I'm not," Monk said. "But this entire town is twisted. Look around."

"Good idea," I said.

"What is?"

"Let's look around," I said. "We can't do anything until we hear from the police in San Francisco or the police here. We might as well get a sense of the place in the meantime."

"I have the sense," Monk said. "It's nausea."

"So do you have a better idea?"

Monk motioned to the hills. "I've spent years look-ing for my wife's killer. He may be up in that hotel right now. I am not letting him get away."

"What are you going to do?" I said.

"I'm going to keep watch outside the hotel," Monk said. "If he tries to leave, I'll be on him like his shadow, if his shadow had ten fingers instead of eleven."

I couldn't go sightseeing while he maintained his vigil, so I reluctantly went along with him. We walked up the road to the Franziskushohe, stopping at the bridge that crossed the tiny stream. The low walls on either side of the bridge gave us a place to sit.

"This is the only way to drive into or out of the prop-erty," Monk said.

"Actually, it's not," I said. "There's a logging road at the far end of the parking lot and a dozen hiking trails. If he wanted to leave, we'd never know it."

"How do you know?"

"There are maps and historical markers along the trails," I said. "I looked at one of them."

"We're going to need more men," Monk said. "But in the meantime you'll have to go on patrol."

"What does that mean?"

"I'll stay here," Monk said. "You walk the trails."

"I can't be on all the trails at once," I said.

"It's the best we can do," Monk said.

"We?" I said. "I'm the one who has to do all the walk-ing. Why don't you go on patrol?"

"I might encounter nature," Monk said.

When he put it that way, the idea of an afternoon spent walking through the woods in peace seemed a lot more attractive than sitting on the bridge with him.

"Okay," I said. "I'll do it."

"Check back with me hourly," Monk said. "Let's synchronize our watches."

That was easier said than done. It took us twenty minutes to synchronize our watches to the exact second, and another two minutes on top of that just to confirm they were ticking at the same rate.

Once we were done, I went up the hill to check whether Dr. Rahner was still at the hotel and to get a map of the trails.

The woman at the front desk informed me that Dr. Rahner was delivering a lecture in the ground-floor conference room. She gave me a trail map. It was in German but the illustrations were easy enough to follow.

Before heading off on patrol, I walked around the hotel looking in windows until I saw a ground-floor room full of people. I crept up close, ducked behind a bush, and peeked inside the window as inconspicuously as I could. I was worried that if anyone saw me—the crazy woman who'd tried to kill one of the attendees—they might call the police. It wouldn't help our cause if Stoffmacher thought I was nuts, too.

I could see Dr. Rahner behind a podium, giving a PowerPoint presentation. Dr. Kroger was in the audience, taking notes. His nose was swollen. I felt a little twinge of guilt. I don't usually go around socking people. If Dr. Kroger turned out to be innocent, I was going to have to get him a fruit basket or something.

Now that I'd established that our target was still there, I slipped away, picked a trail at random, and started wandering. Within a few minutes, I was swallowed up by the dense forest and the temperature seemed to drop a good ten degrees. Since my mission was to patrol possible avenues of escape, I chose paths that allowed me to circle the property.

It was a waste of time, but I found it relaxing. The

only sounds I heard were birdsong, the wind rustling through the trees, and my own footsteps on the dry leaves and dirt. There was nobody there but me.

I didn't see anything but trees and brush. There were no storefronts full of things to buy and no advertisements trying to seduce me into spending my money.

The air was fresh and rich with the scents of pine, flowers, and moist earth. It was so nice to take a breath and not smell exhaust fumes, cigarette smoke, or something being fried.

But I did smell something familiar, something that reminded me of home, and not in a pleasant way. I sniffed again and followed the scent.

I didn't have to go far. The trail led to a clearing with a muddy pond surrounded by weeds. There was a persistent buzz in the air, but it wasn't from an electrical line.

It was from the flies, the ones drawn to the body of a man lying facedown on the trail. He was wearing jogging shorts, a T-shirt, and a bright white pair of new running shoes.

I didn't have to take his pulse to know that he was dead.

20

Mr. Monk Meets Nature

I had a cell phone, but I didn't know if I had reception. And even if I did, I didn't have the number for the police station or know how to call information to get it.

I had no choice but to leave the body where it was, mark its location on my trail map, and go back to the hotel and ask the woman at the front desk to call the police.

So that's what I did.

The woman at the front desk, the same one who gave me the trail map, looked at me with confusion after I told her what I wanted her to do.

"I'm not sure I understand," she said.

"I'd like you to call Hauptkriminalkommissar Stoffmacher at the Lohr police station and tell him that I found a dead body on one of the trails."

"A dead body of what?"

"A person," I said. "A man."

She was already pale, but she seemed to get even paler. If she lost any more color, someone might mistake her for a corpse, too.

"You saw a dead man?"

That's what happens when you travel with Adrian Monk. He doesn't even have to be with you.

"Yes, I did," I said. "That's why I'm asking you to call the police."

"Was it one of our guests?" she asked.

"Does it matter?" I said. "Tell Stoffmacher I will meet him at the bridge."

I walked out and headed down the hill. I could see Monk pacing, looking at his watch and glancing up at me. I didn't have to see his face to feel his disapproval. I was late for my hourly check-in, but I thought I had a good excuse.

"We synchronized our watches," Monk said as I approached. "So you know you're twenty minutes late with your report."

"Dr. Rahner is still at the hotel," I said. "And either I found Bruno Leupolz or the homicide rate in this town is skyrocketing."

"What are you talking about?"

It was nice not to be the one asking that question for a change.

"I found a dead man on the trail," I said.

"You left it there?"

"What else was I supposed to do?" I said.

"Stay with the body and send a passerby back to notify the police."

"It's a wilderness trail," I said. "There was nobody else around."

Monk scowled. "That's why they should have security cameras out there. And lights, paved roads, and sidewalks."

"Then it wouldn't be a wilderness trail anymore," I said.

"It would be an orderliness trail," Monk said, "which is always better."

Two silver-and-blue police cruisers came up the road

and stopped at the bridge. Officer Schust and another cop I recognized from outside the Vigg house were in one car, Geshir and Stoffmacher in the other.

Stoffmacher and Geshir got out of their car and approached us.

"I understand that you discovered a corpse?" Stoffmacher said.

I nodded.

"Are you sure?" Geshir asked. "Maybe he was just napping."

"I know a dead body when I see one." I took out my map and pointed to the spot. "He's right here, on the trail beside a shallow pond. You can't miss it."

"Why don't you show us?" Stoffmacher said.

I started for the car with the two detectives but then noticed that Monk wasn't joining us. I looked back to see him still standing on the bridge.

"Aren't you coming?" I asked.

"I can't abandon my post," Monk said.

"What post?" Stoffmacher said.

"He's standing watch," I said, "making sure Dr. Rahner doesn't leave the hotel."

Stoffmacher motioned to the police car with the two officers inside. "That's why they are here. I'm locking this area down. Nobody will come or go without my authorization."

"Who is watching the trails?" Monk asked.

"No one. I don't have enough men for that," Stoffmacher said. "But I will station an officer at the hotel to make sure that nobody leaves the property."

"But the building has several entrances and exits," Monk said.

"And there are security cameras at all of them, which my officer can monitor from his position in the lobby," Stoffmacher said. "Satisfied?"

"I can live with that," Monk said.

"I'm so relieved," Stoffmacher said.

Geshir drove the four of us up to the hotel parking lot. We got out of the car, found the trailhead, and started walking.

"Be careful," Monk said. "There's nature everywhere."

He sank his head into his shoulders and drew his arms in as close to his body as he could so he wouldn't brush against anything as he stepped gingerly down the trail.

"I understand that you don't believe in coincidences," Stoffmacher said. "So perhaps you can explain why our first homicide in five years happened on the day that you arrived."

"Bad luck," Monk said.

"And then when someone goes missing who you presume is dead, it happens to be your assistant who stumbles on the body and proves you right."

"Worse luck," I said.

"Attention, more nature," Monk cried out. "Take evasive action!"

"Why?" Geshir said. "There's nothing that can hurt us."

"Oh really?" Monk pointed to something in the dirt along the edge of the trail. "What do you call that?"

"Rabbit droppings," Geshir said.

"Perhaps now you won't be so cavalier about our safety," Monk said and then pointed to a low-lying branch. "Leaf alert! Leaf alert!"

Monk ducked far lower than necessary to avoid the leaves and then looked back as if he was afraid they might give chase.

Stoffmacher turned to me. "Isn't 'bad luck' just another way of saying 'coincidence'?"

"Not really," I said. "Maybe it is in German."

I turned my head away, as if my attention was

caught by something, but really I didn't want him to detect the lie all over my face. I need not have bothered. At that same moment Monk let out an agonized shriek and started hopping around on one foot, which got everyone's attention.

"What is it?" I asked.

"Please, God, get it out." Monk grabbed Geshir for support and lifted up his foot to me. "Hurry."

I squatted and examined the bottom of his shoe, expecting to see his foot impaled on a nail or a railroad spike. But there wasn't even a thorn.

"I don't see anything," I said.

Stoffmacher leaned down next to me. "Neither do I."

"Are you both blind?" Monk shrieked. "It's right in the middle of my foot!"

I squinted and made out a pebble only slightly larger than a grain of sand stuck in one of the treads of his shoe.

"You mean that tiny pebble?" I said and used my fingernail to flick it out.

Monk sagged with relief. "Thank you."

Stoffmacher regarded Monk in disbelief. "You could feel that?"

"If someone plucked your eyeball out with a fork, would you feel that?" Monk said.

"Of course I would."

"Then don't ask stupid questions," Monk said and began limping along. "How much farther is this body?"

"Not far," I said.

"Good," Monk said. "Because if we have to go much farther, the four of us could end up just like him."

"We could step on rabbit droppings and die," Geshir said with a grin.

"If I step on rabbit droppings, don't wait for nature to take its merciless course," Monk said. "Just shoot me."

Stoffmacher leaned towards me and whispered, "I wouldn't take your job for all the money in the world."

"And I get paid considerably less than that," I said.

"Then why do you do it?" he asked.

"To visit exotic places," I said.

That's when we began to smell the body. We came upon the actual corpse a few moments later. Monk saw it first and held out his arms to stop us from going farther. His hand brushed a leaf and he yanked it back as if it had been burned.

"Wipe!" Monk motioned to me frantically. I fished a wipe out of my purse and gave it to him.

He cleaned his hands, gave me the used wipe, and took two cautious steps forward. Stoffmacher slipped on rubber gloves and asked Geshir to call the coroner and the forensic unit. Geshir nodded, took out his cell phone, and made the call.

Monk cocked his head and held his hands out in front of him, as if feeling for heat rising off the ground as he walked.

Stoffmacher reached into his pockets and produced two little shoe covers that looked like blue shower caps. He put them over his shoes, then took two more out of his pocket and handed them to me.

"What is he doing?" Stoffmacher asked.

"I call it Monk Zen," I said as I slipped the covers on my shoes. "I think he's trying to sense what's out of place."

Monk stopped, looked at his feet, and started to whimper.

Stoffmacher glanced at me. "Is that normal?"

"That's a flexible concept when it comes to Mr. Monk," I said and started towards him.

"Stand back!" Monk yelled, holding up his hand in a halting gesture. "Nobody move!"

"What is it?" Geshir asked. "Are you standing on a land mine?"

Stoffmacher gave Geshir a withering look. "A land mine? Why would there be a land mine here?"

"I don't know." Geshir motioned to Monk. "Ask him."

"This is worse." Monk spoke very slowly. "At least with a land mine the hot kiss of death comes quickly."

"What could be worse than a land mine?" Geshir said.

"The ground around me looks dry, but it's actually moist," Monk said. "I have mud on my shoes. It's too late for me, but not for you. Go. Save yourselves while you still can."

Stoffmacher muttered something in German that I'm pretty sure was profane, marched past Monk, and crouched beside the body. Geshir joined him.

Monk remained frozen in place, wincing. I stayed with my boss like the loyal assistant that I am. Plus, I had no desire to lean over a smelly corpse.

The dead guy appeared to be in his late forties. He had two days' worth of stubble on his fleshy cheeks and was pale-skinned, but maybe that was just because he was dead. His head was turned to one side, his eyes and mouth wide open.

"He's in exercise clothes and wearing running shoes," Stoffmacher said. "He must have been jogging through the forest when he died."

"He was murdered," Monk said.

Geshir searched the man's pockets with his gloved hands and pulled out a thin wallet. He sorted through it.

"It's Bruno Leupolz," Geshir said. "His credit cards are still in his wallet. There's also about sixty euros in cash."

"I don't see any blood or signs of violence," Stoffmacher said. "No cuts, not even a bruise."

Geshir looked back at Monk. "You were wrong. He wasn't shot."

"Maybe he was poisoned," I said.

"Whether he was poisoned or not," Stoffmacher said, "this doesn't fit with Monk's theory of what happened in the house at all."

"It fits mine," Geshir said.

"That Leupolz accidentally killed Vigg while trying to shoot himself," Stoffmacher said.

Geshir nodded. "Leupolz was so distraught over what he'd done that he ran into the woods and poisoned himself."

"Why not do it in his apartment?" I asked.

"He was trying to distance himself from what he'd done," Geshir said. "That's why he made it look like Vigg killed himself. Leupolz didn't want to die a murderer."

Stoffmacher nodded approvingly. "You may be on to something."

"The only thing he's on is a feather," Monk said.

"What?" Geshir said.

"Lift up your left foot," Monk said. Geshir did. There was a feather in the mud. "That feather is the same as the ones we found in Leupolz's apartment."

"So what?" Stoffmacher said. "It makes sense that he might track things with him from his own apartment."

"The pillow exploded when the killer used it as a silencer," Monk said. "That's why there were feathers all over the apartment. That feather proves I was right."

"But there weren't feathers all over the apartment," Geshir said.

"Because the killer cleaned most of them up," Monk said.

"But Leupolz wasn't shot," Stoffmacher said. "So there was no killer, no silencer, and no exploded pillow. This body proves that you were wrong."

Monk shook his head. "We're missing something."

"What's missing is a coherent explanation for these two deaths," Stoffmacher said. "We need to go back to the beginning and rethink all of our assumptions."

"You mean *his* assumptions." Geshir gestured to Monk.

"Yours, too," Stoffmacher said. "Mine as well."

"You have assumptions?" Geshir said.

"I do, occasionally, think about the investigations I am conducting," Stoffmacher said. "I just don't feel the need to share with you everything that runs through my head."

"You are both getting lost in irrelevant details," Monk said. "You need to step back and concentrate on what's truly important here."

"And what would that be?" Stoffmacher asked.

"My shoes," Monk said. "They are covered with mud."

"There is a dead body in front of us," Stoffmacher snapped. "Your dirty shoes don't matter!"

"What about his?" Monk said, motioning to Leupolz. "How did he get up here without getting a speck of dirt on them?"

We looked at Leupolz's running shoes. They were bright white and perfectly clean, the laces tied in a neat double bow.

That certainly complicated things.

21

Mr. Monk Gets Some News

Geshir rubbed his chin. Stoffmacher curled the end of his enormous mustache. And I swatted at the flies that were buzzing around me while we considered the implications of Monk's observation.

Leupolz didn't walk there.

So how did he get on the trail? If he didn't float there, then it meant he was carried somehow. And the odds are he wasn't alive when that happened.

But that explanation raised even more questions.

Why not leave him at his house? Why dump his body on a hiking trail? How did he die? Why weren't there any signs of violence? How was his death connected, if at all, to the violent end of Axel Vigg? Or was it just one more bizarre coincidence in a day filled with a record-breaking number of them?

Those were just a few of the questions going through my mind and were probably among the ones that Stoffmacher and Geshir were thinking about, too.

"There's more," Monk said.

Stoffmacher sighed. "Of course there is."

"Look at how his laces are tied. The starting knot and

finishing bow are perfectly balanced. It's a textbook example of the Norwegian Reef Knot. But, as I am sure you recall, the shoes he kicked off in his bedroom were tied with sloppy Granny Knots."

I remembered the shoes, but not the knots. I don't pay attention to the things that Monk does. I also couldn't tell you how many parking meters there are on Market Street, how many sesame seeds there are on a hamburger bun, or if there are any hangers in my closet that aren't facing the same direction.

"You're suggesting that someone else put on his shoes," Stoffmacher said.

"And dressed him in that jogging outfit," Monk said. "It was probably the same person who dumped his body here. This whole scene has been staged."

"To tell us what?" Geshir said.

"I don't know yet," Monk said. "But it was improvised in a hurry. If the killer had planned this in advance, he wouldn't have been so sloppy."

"You keep saying 'the killer,'" Stoffmacher said. "But there is no indication yet that Leupolz was murdered."

"He was," Monk said.

I heard the sounds of people approaching. I turned and saw a dozen people in matching yellow plastic overalls marching up the trail. They carried metal cases, cameras, a body bag, and a stretcher. I assumed that they were the coroner and the first wave of crime scene technicians.

"You should dredge that pond," Monk said, tipping his head towards the muddy brown watering hole a few yards from the trail.

"What for?" Geshir said. "We aren't looking for anything."

"There's the missing laptop," Monk said. "My guess is that's where the killer tossed it, in a vacuum cleaner

bag stuffed with feathers and a pillowcase, after removing the hard drive."

The technicians began to take pictures and set up shop around the body. A man I took to be the coroner squatted beside Stoffmacher and began to examine the body.

"I think we can take it from here," Stoffmacher said to Monk. "We appreciate all the advice you've given us."

"What about my problem?" Monk said.

"We'll contact you at your bed-and-breakfast if we have any developments in our investigations," Stoffmacher said.

"That's easy for you to say," Monk said. "How am I supposed to get there?"

Stoffmacher looked confused, so I explained things to him.

"Mr. Monk is referring to his muddy shoes," I said. "If he takes a step, he risks getting even muddier."

Stoffmacher sighed and said something in German to the two men with the stretcher. They brought the stretcher over to Monk.

"They'll take you back to the car," Stoffmacher said.

The two men held up the stretcher and Monk carefully eased himself onto it.

"I knew this was how I would be leaving here," Monk said miserably. "At least I'm not in the body bag."

Monk had to change his shoes the moment we returned to the bed-and-breakfast. He came out of his room a few minutes later wearing an identical pair of Hush Puppies, his dirty pair in a sealed plastic bag that he held at arm's length.

"You're throwing out your shoes?" I said.

"What other choice do I have?"

"You could clean them."

"There's only one thing that will clean these shoes."

Monk handed the bag to Heiko Schmidt on our way out. "Incinerate this immediately."

We headed out for an early dinner at the same place we'd visited the night before. This time I was a bit more daring. I ordered the Wienerschnitzel and was pleasantly surprised when they didn't deliver a hot dog to the table.

When I was growing up in Monterey, there was a chain of fast-food places in California called Der Wienerschnitzel that served a wide array of lousy hot dogs that looked even worse than they tasted.

I assumed, like every other ignorant Californian, that Wienerschnitzel was the German term for hot dog. But no, it's not. It's actually a lightly battered and fried veal cutlet that's similar to a country-fried steak, only a lot more light and tasty.

So why would somebody call a hot dog stand the Fried Veal? It would be like calling a hamburger place the Chow Mein.

It made no sense.

Trying to understand the logic behind Der Wienerschnitzel was the depth of intellectual thought I was capable of after the long day that I'd had.

As tasty as dinner was, it took all the willpower I had not to fall asleep at the table. Monk was fighting fatigue, too. We left the instant we finished eating.

I was back in my room and in bed by eight p.m. I was so exhausted, I was certain that I would sleep through until breakfast. But jet lag was still messing with my internal clock and I woke up, refreshed and fully alert, at three a.m.

I was lying in bed, trying to decide what to do with myself for the three or four hours until breakfast, when my cell phone rang. I answered it, grateful for something to do.

"That's a surprisingly energetic and cheerful greet-

ing for someone who was rudely awakened from a deep sleep," Stottlemeyer said to me.

"That's because I was wide-awake," I said.

"It is three a.m. there, right?"

"Yep," I said.

"And you're awake," he said.

"Sorry to disappoint you, Captain."

"Are you kidding? I'm relieved," Stottlemeyer said unconvincingly. "The last thing I want to do is disturb your rest."

"Were you able to find out anything about Dr. Martin Rahner?"

"I was," Stottlemeyer said. "Is Monk awake?"

"How would I know?" I said. "We aren't sharing a room."

"Find out," Stottlemeyer said. "If he's asleep, you'd better wake him up."

"Can't whatever you have to say wait until morning?"

"He's waited too long already," Stottlemeyer said.

"It's that big?"

"It's that big," he said.

I put on a bathrobe and, carrying my cell phone, went down the hall to Monk's room. I knocked on the door and hoped I was loud enough to wake him but not the rest of the guests.

He answered the door in his pajamas. His eyes were closed. He might have even been sleepwalking.

"What is it?" he asked groggily.

"The captain has some information about Dr. Rahner," I said.

Monk motioned me inside and closed the door. We sat down side by side on the edge of his bed; I put Stottlemeyer on the speaker and held the phone up between us.

"We're both here, Captain," I said.

"How are you holding up, Monk?" Stottlemeyer asked.

"The whole world is conspiring against me," Monk said. "With the possible exception of you, Natalie, and Randy Disher."

"*Possible* exception?" I said.

"I like to keep an open mind," Monk said.

"That's what you are famous for," Stottlemeyer said, his sarcasm completely lost on Monk. "Here's what I've learned. Dr. Rahner is a respected psychiatrist and author in Germany who has lectured at several colleges in the United States over the years, including UC Berkeley."

"When was he in the Bay Area?" Monk asked.

There was a long pause. For a moment I thought we'd lost our connection.

"The two weeks before Trudy was killed," Stottlemeyer said.

Monk took the news stoically, nodding slightly, as if Stottlemeyer was only confirming what he already knew.

"What was he doing there?" Monk asked.

"He delivered a couple of lectures," Stottlemeyer said. "They were underwritten by a grant from Dale Biederback."

Dale the Whale. The obscenely obese madman who tried to ruin the Monks after Trudy wrote a series of unflattering investigative reports about his business dealings.

The significance of the news nearly knocked me off the bed, but once again Monk took it all with astonishing calmness. He just nodded.

"Did you find any connections between Dr. Rahner, Dr. Kroger, and Dale?" Monk asked.

"Not so far, but we haven't dug very deep," Stot-

tlemeyer said. "We'll need lots of search warrants for that."

"So get them," Monk said.

"We don't have any evidence of a crime."

"You know where Trudy is buried," Monk said.

It was like a slap. There was a long silence on the phone. For a moment I wondered if maybe Stottlemeyer had hung up. I wouldn't have blamed him if he had. Monk didn't appreciate how hard his friends worked for him. Or if he did, he rarely showed it.

"That's not fair," Stottlemeyer said softly.

"Neither was her murder," Monk replied, without a trace of remorse for his cutting remark.

"I want to get the sonofabitch who killed Trudy and I'll do whatever is within my power to do. But I can't convince a judge to give me search warrants based on what we've got. It's all circumstantial and adds up to nothing."

"It adds up to me," Monk said.

"Lots of things add up to you that don't to anybody else," Stottlemeyer said.

"But they do in the end," Monk said.

"Okay, then maybe you can tell me what Dr. Rahner's motive was for hiring someone to plant a bomb in Trudy's car."

"Maybe he doesn't have one," Monk said.

"If you want to commit a random murder, you don't seek out a bomber and hire him to do it," Stottlemeyer said. "You do it yourself, fast and simple."

"What I meant was that maybe he did it for Dale," Monk said. "The same way that Dale's doctor murdered a judge for him."

"You think that Dale blackmailed Dr. Rahner into it?" I asked. "And also blackmailed Dr. Kroger into playing with your mind to keep you off the police force?"

"That's one possibility," Monk said.

"You haven't got any evidence," Stottlemeyer said.

"That's what we need the search warrants for," Monk said.

"A judge is going to want a lot more than possibilities before he'll give us warrants to rummage through everyone's phone, travel, and bank records," Stottlemeyer said. "All I can tell a judge now is that Dr. Rahner was in San Francisco in the weeks preceding Trudy's death, giving a lecture that was sponsored by Dale the Whale, and that your shrink might have attended. There's nothing even remotely criminal about that."

"It suggests a conspiracy," Monk said.

"To you," Stottlemeyer said.

"And me," I said.

"But it won't convince a judge," Stottlemeyer told us.

"The bomber who killed Trudy said in a deathbed confession that the man who hired him had six fingers on his right hand," I said. "So does Dr. Rahner."

"The last time I checked," Stottlemeyer said, "having an extra finger isn't a criminal offense."

"You checked?" Monk said.

"I was being facetious, Monk. I didn't check."

"Maybe you should."

"I didn't check because I know it's not a crime and so do you," Stottlemeyer said. "Maybe it is in Germany. Ask the cops over there."

"I will," Monk said.

"Let me know how things go. I'm here if you need any more help," Stottlemeyer said. "Within reason."

I spoke up. "Could you find out why those hot dog places in America are called Der Wienerschnitzel when in German the words actually mean 'fried and breaded veal cutlet'?"

"I believe I said 'within reason,' " Stottlemeyer said.

"That's what I am looking for," I said. "The reason. And it better be a good one."

"I must have a bad connection," Stottlemeyer said. "Is that Natalie Teeger talking or Adrian Monk?"

"Adrian Monk here," Monk said.

"I thought so," Stottlemeyer said.

"No, the ridiculous request was Natalie's. Here's mine: I want to talk to Dale Biederback."

"I liked her request better. It made more sense."

"He knows the truth," Monk said.

"You don't want to do this, Monk. Dale is a monster. He's just going to toy with you and take pleasure in your pain. He's got nothing better to do."

"Can you arrange the call or not?" Monk insisted.

Stottlemeyer sighed wearily. "I'll talk to the warden and see what I can do. Now get some sleep. You both sound like you need it."

We said our good-byes and then we sat there in silence. There was a lot for us to think about.

Was this another perfect storm of coincidences? Or were Dale the Whale, Dr. Rahner, and Dr. Kroger involved in Trudy's death and a plot to keep Monk off the police force?

If so, why?

I looked at Monk. He appeared numb. Neither one of us was going to get any sleep now.

"How are you feeling?" I asked him.

He sighed, his shoulders sagging with the weight of all that he'd learned.

"I'm glad that I've got an appointment with my psychiatrist tomorrow," he said. "I really need it."

"But he could be involved in all this," I said.

"So it will be a very productive session," Monk said. "One way or another."

"I wish I could be there," I said.

"You will be," he said.

"Really?" I said. "Why?"

"I need someone there I can trust," Monk said. "And the way I'm feeling right now, I'm not sure I can even trust myself."

In a way, it was the nicest thing he'd ever said to me. I gave him a kiss on the cheek and left his room before he could ruin the moment by asking me for a wipe.

22

Mr. Monk and Dr. Kroger

After breakfast, I called the Franziskushohe and asked the receptionist to connect me to Dr. Kroger's room. I could tell from his sleepy voice when he answered that I'd awakened him. It seemed like I couldn't call anyone lately without disturbing their rest.

"You have an appointment with Mr. Monk today," I said.

"I haven't forgotten. Frankly, I'm relieved that Adrian still wants to see me," Dr. Kroger said. "It means he's open to resolving the misunderstandings that came up yesterday through positive interaction."

Rather than getting punched in the nose by Monk's lovely assistant, though I wasn't ruling out that approach again.

"I don't want to make him uncomfortable by asking him to meet me here," Dr. Kroger continued, "considering this hotel's history as a sanitarium for people with lung diseases."

"And you'd rather not take a chance that we'll cause another embarrassing scene in front of your colleagues."

"That too," Dr. Kroger admitted.

At least he was honest about that, though it could have been a trick. Maybe he thought if he was honest on the small things, we'd be convinced that his candor extended to the big things, too.

I gave him directions to our bed-and-breakfast and told him to be there in an hour. I expected an argument but I didn't get one.

Monk used the time to rearrange his room into a rough approximation of Dr. Kroger's office. We moved the bed and angled two chairs in front of the window in the same position as the doctor and patient chairs.

That was the intention anyway. Actually accomplishing it was an exasperating experience. Monk kept sitting down in his chair and getting up again to make subtle adjustments in its position right up until the moment Heiko called to say that Dr. Kroger had arrived.

I went downstairs to find Dr. Kroger standing awkwardly in the entry hall, clearly self-conscious about the way he looked, which was awful. His nose was swollen and the bruising had spread to his eyes. It didn't help that Heiko was staring at him.

"It looks worse than it is," Dr. Kroger said.

I don't know whether he was trying to downplay his injury to appear tougher or if it was a gesture to relieve my guilt, not that I felt any. Either way, the comment was wasted on me.

"I float like a butterfly and sting like a bee," I said and then glanced at Heiko. He was wearing Monk's old shoes, cleaned and buffed. "Very stylish."

Heiko beamed. "Danke."

I led Dr. Kroger upstairs.

"Those looked like the shoes that Adrian wears," he said.

"Mr. Monk has always been a trendsetter," I said.

We'd climbed only a few steps when Dr. Kroger

smacked his head against one of the low beams. He cursed and clutched his forehead. That had to hurt.

"Watch your head," I said.

"Thanks," he said, glaring at me. "I haven't done anything to deserve this."

"We'll see," I said.

Monk was sitting straight in his seat, his arms on the armrests, when we came in. His eyes widened when he saw Dr. Kroger's face.

"What happened to your face?" Monk asked.

"Natalie hit me," Dr. Kroger said like a child ratting out a sibling to a parent.

Monk looked at me. "You did?"

"I did," I said proudly.

Monk smiled a little. I think he was flattered.

"But I've forgiven her," Dr. Kroger said, taking his customary seat to Monk's right. "I'm glad you wanted to see me, Adrian."

"I've never missed an appointment," Monk said.

"That's true. You haven't."

"Though now I'm not so sure I needed them as much as I thought," Monk said.

"I'm glad to hear that. I've felt for some time that you could see me just once a week, but you're the one who has insisted on seeing me more often, daily if possible. You even followed me here for sessions."

Dr. Kroger glanced at me as I took a seat on the edge of the bed. If he had any questions about me being here, he kept them to himself.

"You must be so pleased," Monk said.

"Why would that make me happy, Adrian?"

"Hasn't it always been part of your plan to keep me dependent on you?"

"My goal is to help you control your anxieties so that you can become as self-sufficient as possible and enjoy a normal life."

"And return to the police force," Monk said.

"If that's what you want," Dr. Kroger said.

"But you don't," Monk said.

"That's not true. I'd like to see you become a homicide detective again."

"And yet you haven't written a report to the police that declares me fit for duty and recommends my reinstatement."

"Because I don't think you're ready yet," Dr. Kroger said. "But I am confident that you will be soon."

"What does Dr. Rahner think?" Monk asked.

"I haven't discussed your therapy with Dr. Rahner," he said.

"How about Dale Biederback?" Monk asked.

"I haven't discussed your therapy with anyone, Adrian. What goes on between us is private and I won't talk about it without your consent."

"How long have you known Dr. Rahner?"

"I've been aware of his work for over a decade," Dr. Kroger said, "but I met him for the first time a few years ago at one of his lectures."

"In Berkeley," Monk said.

"Captain Stottlemeyer has been working overtime," Dr. Kroger said, shifting his position in his seat. "Yes, it was in Berkeley."

"Two weeks before Trudy's murder," Monk said.

Dr. Kroger looked at me. I glared right back at him. I think he was checking to see if I was about to hit him again.

"I was not aware of that," Dr. Kroger said softly.

"I suppose that you also weren't aware that Dr. Rahner's visit to the Bay Area was underwritten by Dale Biederback," Monk said.

"Oh God, this keeps getting worse and worse," Dr. Kroger said. He closed his eyes for a moment and when

he opened them again he spoke in a calm and measured voice. "Things aren't what they appear to be."

"That much I know," Monk said.

"I didn't mean it that way, Adrian."

"Why did you do it?" Monk demanded, leaning forward in his seat. "What leverage could Dale possibly have against you that would make you do this to me?"

"I haven't betrayed your trust and you aren't the victim of a conspiracy," Dr. Kroger said. "Contrary to the way things appear, nothing nefarious has occurred. Everything can be explained."

"I'm listening," Monk said.

"I've never met Dale Biederback and I had no idea he financed Dr. Rahner's lecture series," Dr. Kroger said. "But I'm not surprised that he did."

"Why not?" Monk asked.

"Biederback was an extraordinarily wealthy and influential man with a tremendous ego and lust for power. Before he went to prison, he underwrote hundreds of social, cultural, and educational programs and construction projects in the Bay Area. You could theoretically connect him to thousands of people just through the events they attended that he supported. Some of them are bound to be people you've met, even Natalie."

I didn't like him using me as part of his defense, so I spoke up.

"But this wasn't just any event. This one happened right before Trudy Monk's murder. And it brought together an eleven-fingered man, who matches the description of the person who arranged the murder, and you, the psychiatrist who would later treat Mr. Monk."

"It's a cruel trick of fate," Dr. Kroger said. "That's all."

"I agree that it was a cruel trick," Monk said. "But I am not ready to blame fate for it just yet."

"I wouldn't either if I were you," Dr. Kroger said. "There's only one way you will ever accept it. You have to do what you do best."

"Sit alone in the dark in abject misery?"

"Investigate," Dr. Kroger said. "You'll get to the truth, as you always do. You should start by getting Dr. Rahner to answer your questions."

"What makes you think he'll talk to me?" Monk asked.

"Because he's a psychiatrist and he's devoted his life to helping people," Dr. Kroger said. "Which is why he's waiting for you right now at the café across the street."

Dr. Rahner was sitting at a tiny table in front of the café, sipping an espresso and picking at a piece of streusel. He smiled and gestured to us to sit with a sweep of his six-fingered hand.

"Thank you for coming, Martin," Dr. Kroger said as we took our seats.

"It's the least I can do," Dr. Rahner said, and turned to Monk, who sat directly across from him. "Charles has filled me in on the unfortunate series of coincidences and what they mean to you. I'd like to help ease your pain in any way I can. Feel free to ask me anything."

"Do you know Dale Biederback?" Monk asked.

"Yes," Dr. Rahner said, "I do."

"You do?" Dr. Kroger said, unable to hide his surprise.

"Of course. He underwrote my lecture series in Berkeley and invited me to his home for dinner."

"Whenever you visit Dale, it's dinnertime," Monk said. "The man never stops eating."

"That's why I was eager to meet him. I'd heard that he was so obese that he couldn't leave his bed. His physical condition fascinated me."

"Most people are disgusted," I said.

"That's what made him so compelling. I study people with physical anomalies and how they interact with a society that considers them outsiders and 'freaks.' He was a very special case because he was so rich and powerful. I was especially interested in how he treated others."

"With enormous cruelty," Monk said. "That's how."

"Which, sadly, is also the way most people with physical anomalies are treated by society. But Biederback amassed the wealth, power, and influence to strike back."

"By ruining lives and killing people," Monk said.

"He is a horrible person. I am in no way condoning what he did. But as a psychiatrist and researcher, I can understand the psychological and societal forces that made him who he is. He was born abnormally overweight, and as he grew, he got fatter and fatter. You can imagine the cruelty he endured, and I believe that's what drove him to become so rich."

"So Dale was just a benefactor and a research subject to you," Monk said.

"He wasn't my direct benefactor; his money went to the university that invited me to speak. But otherwise, yes, I'd say that's a fair assessment."

"I think you're lying," Monk said. "I think Dale had you hire the bomber who killed my wife."

If Dr. Rahner was offended by Monk's accusation, he didn't show it. He just took a sip of his coffee and dabbed his lips with his napkin, using his six-fingered hand to do it, of course.

Monk couldn't take his eyes off that hand and Dr. Rahner knew it.

"You think that I'm a liar and a murderer just because I was born with an extra finger," Dr. Rahner said, wiggling the extra finger for emphasis.

"The bomber was hired by a man with six fingers," Monk said. "How many people could there be who match that description?"

"One hundred and two in the United States that I know of," Dr. Rahner said. "There are probably many, many more."

"How many of them knew Dale Biederback?" Monk said.

"Do you know for certain it was Dale Biederback and not someone else who killed your wife?" Dr. Rahner asked. "Aren't you only making that assumption because you saw Dr. Kroger and me here together?"

"It was Dale who led me to the bomber," Monk said, "and it was the bomber who told me about the man with the extra finger."

"And you've been looking for this elusive eleven-fingered man ever since," Dr. Rahner said. "Now you think you've found him."

"Haven't I?"

"I'm merely the first person you've encountered with an extra finger," Dr. Rahner replied. "But there are many of us out there. Two out of every one thousand children are born with extra fingers or toes."

"I've never seen any of them before," Monk said.

"That's because extra appendages are usually surgically removed at birth by overprotective parents acting on the advice of narrow-minded doctors," Dr. Rahner said. "It's barbaric and inhuman. I've devoted my career to encouraging the acceptance of physical differences. I've also spoken out against surgeries that force people to conform to a perfect body image, whether it's removing webbed toes or adding breast implants. We should embrace diversity."

" 'Diversity' is just another word for things that don't match," Monk said. "It's unnatural."

"Not everything has to match, Adrian," Dr. Kroger said.

"That's just what Dale the Whale would like me to think," Monk said.

Dr. Kroger sighed and shook his head.

"In some ancient civilizations, physical anomalies were considered signs of divine power," Dr. Rahner said. "Lord Chan-Bahlum, ruler of the Mayan city of Palenque in 683 A.D., had six fingers on his right hand and six toes on his right foot."

"Now you know why the Mayans aren't around anymore," Monk said.

"Pope Sixtus II had six fingers on his right hand," Dr. Rahner said. "And the Catholic Church has endured."

"Barely," Monk said.

"I founded Sicherer Hafen, a private resort outside of Lohr where people with physical anomalies can be themselves and experience true freedom without facing scorn, ridicule, or stares," Dr. Rahner said. "I'm giving some of the attendees of the conference a tour this morning and I'd like you to join us."

"Why would I want to go with you?" Monk said.

"It will give you some insight into who I am and how I think so you can judge my sincerity," Dr. Rahner said. "And I have an ulterior motive. I'm hoping that after you meet the people there you'll be less suspicious of the next man you meet with an extra finger."

"What have you got to lose, Adrian?" Dr. Kroger asked. "You might even gain some insights into yourself."

Monk got up and motioned to me to join him. We stepped a few feet away, out of earshot of the others.

"What do you think?" Monk whispered to me.

"You don't have any evidence against Dr. Rahner

now," I said. "If he did kill Trudy, the more time you spend with him, the more opportunities you will have to catch him in a lie."

"Good point," Monk said, and returned to the table. "Okay, let's go to Freakville."

23

Mr. Monk Visits Freakville

Monk and I followed Dr. Rahner's van in our rental car along a winding road that went deep into Spessart Forest. The deeper we got into the woods, the more uncomfortable Monk became.

"There are a lot of trees," Monk said, hugging himself.

"I think it's nice," I said.

"Trees scare me."

"A tree can't hurt you," I said.

"You obviously didn't see *The Wizard of Oz*," he said.

"You mean the scene where the trees come alive?"

Monk shuddered. "It was terrifying. I had nightmares for years."

"It was make-believe. Trees don't really talk and throw apples at you."

"I know that," Monk said. "But they are big and dark and surround you. They are rough and sticky and sharp. They block out the light and have strange creatures living in their branches."

"Like birds," I said.

"And snakes, spiders, ants, bees, and things in co-coons," Monk said. "The only thing scarier than a tree is a cocoon."

"What can a cocoon do to you?"

"You could get trapped in one," Monk said.

"It's not the cocoon you should be afraid of," I told him. "It's the caterpillar big enough to make one that you could get caught in."

"It could be out there," Monk said, looking into the trees.

"No, it couldn't," I said. "Caterpillars that big don't exist."

"Dwarfs have lived in these woods for centuries. Who knows what other freakish creatures are living here, too?" Monk said. "Speaking of which, there's no way Dr. Rahner could have established his colony of freaks without Hauptkriminalkommissar Stoffmacher knowing about it."

That hadn't occurred to me.

"So the police knew who the eleven-fingered man was that we were looking for from the get-go and they didn't say a word," I said. "They were protecting him."

"Unless there are a lot of men with eleven fingers in Lohr, which, given its history, is entirely possible."

We came to a curve and a sign on the road that an-nounced Sicherer Hafen. We passed the sign and al-most immediately came upon the purely decorative wooden gates of the resort, which opened onto a gravel courtyard in front of a picturesque main house.

The entrance to the resort brought back long-forgotten memories from my childhood of my parents taking me to Santa's Village, an amusement park in the Santa Cruz Mountains.

The entrance to Santa's Village was a log-cabin lodge that was covered year-round with fake snow and ici-

cles. Once inside the park, you could meet Santa Claus at the lollipop tree, visit the enchanted forest on a candy cane sleigh pulled by real reindeer, see Santa's elves at work in the toy factory, eat sugarplums in Mrs. Claus's cozy kitchen, and ride the glimmering ornaments on an enormous rotating Christmas tree.

There weren't any reindeer or candy canes at Sicherer Hafen, but the resort had the same woodsy, warm, storybook feel as Santa's Village. The buildings weren't as fanciful and there were satellite dishes mounted on the roofs, but I still expected to hear the sound of sleigh bells wafting from the trees and Christmas music playing from hidden speakers as I stepped out of the car.

We joined Dr. Rahner, Dr. Kroger, and a dozen other shrinks outside the main house.

"We don't usually welcome visitors, but this is a special occasion," Dr. Rahner said. "Please do not take pictures or stare at the guests. Remember that this is a vacation community, a place where our residents and guests can relax and be themselves. That fragile peace is very important to all of us here at Sicherer Hafen and I would appreciate it if you didn't do anything to disturb it."

Monk screamed and pointed at the trees.

"Grizzly bear! Run for your lives!" Monk ran to hide behind our car.

I looked toward the trees and at first had the same instinctive reaction as Monk until I noticed that this bear was wearing cutoffs and holding a volleyball under his hairy arm.

It wasn't a bear but a shirtless man with an unbelievably thick coat of fur over his entire body. I'd never seen anyone like him and, despite Dr. Rahner's request, I couldn't stop staring.

"That is not a bear," Dr. Rahner said. "That's Franco Tozza, our activities director."

"The first activity he should consider is a haircut," Monk said, rising from his hiding spot.

"That is just the kind of ignorance and heartlessness that people come here to escape," Dr. Rahner said. "Franco was born with hypertrichosis, a genetic condition that causes excessive hair growth. It can be a source of great embarrassment and shame in mainstream society. But here it's not. Here he can walk with pride. That is the beauty of Sicherer Hafen."

Franco stopped in front of Monk and smiled. "It's okay. You don't have to be embarrassed."

"I know," Monk said. "But you do."

There were gasps at Monk's inappropriate comment, but Franco didn't seem offended, though I have to admit it's hard to read the expression on someone's face when he looks like Chewbacca.

"He's right. Ordinarily, I'm the one who has to be ashamed, who has to hide his body and try to fit in. But not at Sicherer Hafen. That's what makes this place that Dr. Rahner founded so special." Franco spoke with a strong Italian accent that made him a bit difficult to understand. That, and the hair over his mouth. "People come from across Europe to stay here. We offer all the amenities and activities that other time-share resorts do and something more: true freedom to be yourself."

"I know you are all feeling uncomfortable right now," Dr. Rahner said to the group.

"That's an understatement," Monk said in a whiny voice.

"But what you're feeling is an absolutely normal, instinctive reaction to encountering other humans with physical anomalies."

"What would running away screaming be?" Monk said.

"An overreaction," Dr. Rahner said sternly. "Think about how you are feeling at this moment. Now

imagine how we feel every day, walking among all of you."

"I've got a thick skin," Franco said lightheartedly.

"I bet you do," Monk said.

If I had been next to Monk, I would have jabbed him with my elbow. Instead, I tried to send him a jabbing look. I don't think I succeeded.

"The team is waiting for me on the volleyball court," Franco said, spinning the ball on his finger. "I hope you learn something from your visit. If you get a chance, stop by and watch us play."

He walked away and at that same moment a young woman emerged from the main building. She was dressed in shorts and a tank top and greeted us with a stewardess smile.

"I'm Katie, the sales director," she said. "It's an honor to have you all here with us today. I'm going to give you the grand tour. Please don't hesitate to ask me any questions along the way."

Monk raised his hand. "I have a question."

"Yes, sir?" she said.

"Will you be handing out blindfolds?"

Katie laughed. "Our community is exclusive and unique, but it's not a secret. We want you to see all that we have to offer."

She led us into the main building. It was like a ski lodge, with a grand stone fireplace and a bar. There were several people in resort wear sitting around, reading books, sipping drinks, and quietly talking among themselves.

I saw female Siamese twins, one engaged in conversation with a hunchbacked man, the other reading the German translation of a James Patterson novel. A bearded woman played cards with a dwarf and a man with huge ears. I didn't let my eyes linger on anyone for very long.

"This is our clubhouse common room, where everyone can gather to relax and get to know one another," Katie said. "Every night we have a cocktail party with free food and entertainment. We also have a full library, a billiard room, a computer room, a state-of-the-art theater, and a restaurant."

Monk looked up at the high wood-beamed ceiling. "I wish they had blindfolds. They really, really need blindfolds."

"What are the criteria a person has to meet to be a guest here?" Dr. Kroger asked Katie.

"Isn't it obvious?" Monk said, practically shrieking.

"You have to have been born with a physical anomaly," Katie said, ignoring Monk's comment, "and you must be recommended by Dr. Rahner or a current resident. After that, you have to pass an interview with our residents' council."

"What about to work here?" someone asked.

"Our guests do all the cooking, cleaning, and maintenance of the property," she said. "It's one of the things that create the vibrant sense of community you feel everywhere you go here. Everyone has to chip in and help out."

She led us outside. The condominium buildings were similar in design to the main house and were arranged in a loose half-circle around a large swimming pool and a picnic area, where a barbecue was going on. A man with a tiny head on a disproportionately normal body grilled chicken, spareribs, and steaks and doled out servings to a line of people that included a midget, a woman with an adult body and two tiny arms, and a man with a tail sticking out of a hole cut in the back of his swim trunks.

I glanced at a table and saw a young woman licking barbecue sauce off her lips with a forked tongue. Another man chewed at a sparerib with his fangs. He

met my eyes and I quickly shifted my gaze to the pool, where a woman with a face like an ape made a perfect dive. Another woman did the backstroke across the pool, kicking at the water with her webbed feet. I saw a man with four nipples sunning himself on a chaise longue. He whispered something to the woman on the chaise next to him. She laughed and wiggled her twelve toes in delight.

I turned to see how Monk was taking all this. "This place is unbelievable," I said.

"It certainly is." Monk was looking down and holding his hand against his brow as if he was protecting himself from the glare of the sun.

"Are you covering your eyes?" I whispered.

"Hell yes," he replied.

"Do most of the residents live here full-time?" someone asked.

She shook her head. "Franco and I are the only full-time residents. Everyone else here is a member-guest."

"What does it cost?" asked another shrink.

Dr. Rahner answered. "Each person pays a five-thousand-euro entrance fee, six hundred euros in monthly dues, and about thirty-five thousand euros to purchase a time-share apartment, depending on the size of the unit."

"Freedom isn't cheap," I said.

"It never is," Dr. Rahner said. "That's the sad truth."

"But you're making money," I said. Call me cynical.

"It all goes back into the community," he said. "I do it for them."

"How many apartments are there?" Dr. Kroger asked. I think he just wanted to change the subject.

"Two hundred and twenty," Dr. Rahner said.

"My God," Monk said. "That's a lot of freaks."

I hate to admit it, but I was thinking the same thing.

The place reminded me of the alien cantina scene in *Star Wars*. The one person who didn't seem to fit was Katie.

During the tour, I'd given her the once-over a few times, looking for abnormalities, but as far as I could see she had ten fingers and everything else about her body seemed perfect, even enviably so.

"Forgive me if the question I am about to raise is an indelicate one," I began.

"It can't be more indelicate than his last comment." Katie glowered at Monk.

"You said that only people with physical anomalies are allowed to stay here," I said.

"That's our one ironclad rule," she said, "so we can maintain our unique atmosphere."

"Of horror," Monk mumbled.

"But you live here full-time," I said, "and yet you appear to be, for lack of a better term, physically normal."

"That's why you should never judge people on appearances," she said, "but on their character."

"You're the only normal person in this place," Monk said.

She smiled. "I'm a hermaphrodite."

Monk squeaked and turned his eyes skyward again. I also looked away, because I was afraid my eyes might inadvertently drift to places they shouldn't, looking for signs to confirm her declaration.

I didn't want to imagine what her resident's interview was like. But I did anyway. I almost squeaked, too.

As Katie started to lead the group away, Dr. Rahner pulled Monk aside. Dr. Kroger and I followed.

"Excuse me, Mr. Monk. Here comes someone I'd like you to meet." Dr. Rahner gestured to a man who was walking by, carrying a plate of meat from the barbecue. "This is Hubert Bock, a lawyer from Munich. Hu-

bert, this is Adrian Monk, a famous detective from San Francisco."

"That's a very lovely city." Bock reached out for a handshake. He had six fingers on his right hand.

Monk shoved both of his hands into his pockets. "Yes, it is. Everything is so symmetrical."

"I've been there a lot," Bock said, "but I've never noticed that."

"You've been there?" Monk said.

"Probably a dozen times in the last ten years. I'm in-house counsel for a German pharmaceutical company that has offices there," he said. "I think it may be the most European city in America. What sort of detective work do you do?"

Monk glanced at Dr. Rahner, who bent over to tie his shoe and gave him a smug smile. The doctor had made his point.

"I catch murderers," Monk said.

"That's great," Bock said with a forced smile. "Well, I hope you enjoy your visit to Germany and that you find some symmetry here, too. It was nice meeting you."

Bock went to a table and sat down.

"You see, Mr. Monk, polydactylism is far more common than you thought," Dr. Rahner said, straightening up again. "Maybe Hubert is the man you have been looking for."

"Maybe he is," Monk said.

I was as surprised by the admission as Dr. Rahner and Dr. Kroger appeared to be.

"I'm proud of you, Adrian," Dr. Kroger said. "I had my doubts about you being able to see past your own preconceptions, but you proved me wrong. This is a significant step forward."

"I think it is, too," Monk said, and turned to Dr. Rahner. "I let myself become blinded by what I saw in my

head rather than observing what was right in front of my eyes. But after what I have seen here today, I am certain of one thing."

Dr. Rahner looked pleased with himself and added, "That not all men with six fingers on their right hand are murderers."

"They aren't," Monk said. "But you are."

"I'm confused," Dr. Rahner said. "I thought that I'd just successfully demonstrated that Hubert or any one of hundreds of other men with an extra finger on their right hand could have arranged your wife's murder."

"You did," Monk said.

"Now I'm very confused," Dr. Rahner said.

"Let me make it clear for you." Monk took a step forward and looked Dr. Rahner right in the eye.

I'd seen that expression on Monk's face before and I knew exactly what it meant.

It was the outward reflection of the inner peace that Monk found only when the chaos of facts swirling around in his mind coalesced into perfect order.

He'd solved the mystery. But which one?

When Monk spoke again, it was in a low voice that only Dr. Rahner, Dr. Kroger, and I could hear.

"I don't know whether you were involved in my wife's murder or not," Monk said, "but you killed Bruno Leupolz, and I'll get you for it."

24

Mr. Monk and the Guy

Monk didn't stick around to explain himself or to hear whatever Dr. Rahner had to say. He simply turned and walked back to the car. I lingered a bit out of curiosity. I wanted to see the effect Monk's surprising accusation had on Dr. Rahner.

There was a moment, lasting not much longer than the time it takes to blink, when Dr. Rahner looked as if he'd been doused with ice water.

It happened so fast that maybe I didn't see it at all. Maybe I imagined it.

But I knew I didn't.

Then Dr. Rahner turned to me, frowning with befuddlement, and asked, "Who is Bruno Leupolz?"

Dr. Rahner knew who Bruno Leupolz was. Because Dr. Rahner killed him. I was sure of it. Dr. Rahner could see that as clearly on my face as I'd seen the truth on his.

What I didn't know was how Monk had figured it out or why Dr. Rahner had done it.

I shook my head and glanced at Dr. Kroger, who seemed truly baffled.

"Would somebody please tell me what's going on?" Dr. Kroger said.

"Mr. Monk just solved a murder," I said. "And Dr. Rahner is going to prison."

"You're delusional and so is Monk," Dr. Rahner said.

"I have treated Adrian for years and he most certainly is not delusional," Dr. Kroger said.

"He is now," Dr. Rahner said. "Lucky you."

Dr. Rahner walked away. Dr. Kroger looked at me for answers. I had none to give him, so I walked away, too.

I found Monk waiting in the car for me.

As I got in, Monk said, "He's the guy."

I nodded. "How did you figure it out?"

"His shoes," Monk said. "He ties his laces using the Norwegian Reef Knot."

"I'm sure a lot of Norwegians do, too," I said. "What makes you certain it was Rahner who tied Leupolz's running shoes?"

"The bows were identical," Monk said.

"What else have you got?" I asked.

"That's all," Monk said.

"Oh boy," I said and started the car.

Stoffmacher and Geshir were standing over a table covered with files and evidence bags as we came into the police station.

"Mr. Monk," Stoffmacher said, waving us to join him behind the counter. "I was just about to call you. There have been some interesting new developments in our investigation."

The Baggies on the table contained the gun, some pillow feathers, Leupolz's running shoes, the scorched notebook rings, and a misshapen bullet that I assumed had been extracted from Axel Vigg's head.

"It's solved," Monk said.

"I wish that it was," Stoffmacher said. "If anything, the mystery has become even more perplexing."

"No, it hasn't," Monk said. "It's all over. I know who did it."

"Did what?" Stoffmacher asked.

"I know who murdered Bruno Leupolz and Axel Vigg," Monk said.

"Leupolz wasn't murdered," Stoffmacher said. "The coroner says the journalist died of a heart attack. There were no signs of foul play and his toxicology test came back clean."

Monk's eyes widened. "Leupolz was a reporter?"

"He was a freelance writer for *Im Fadenkreuz*, a news-magazine in Berlin," Geshir said.

"What story was he working on in Lohr?" Monk asked.

"What does it matter?" Geshir said. "He died of natural causes."

"My wife was a reporter," Monk said.

"I don't see what any of this has to do with the murder of your wife," Stoffmacher said.

"It's the second reporter he's killed," Monk said.

"Who?" Stoffmacher said.

"Dr. Martin Rahner," Monk said. "The man you have been protecting. The man you are covering up for now."

"You always knew that Dr. Rahner was the eleven-fingered man Mr. Monk was looking for," I said to the detectives. "But you kept quiet."

"Of course we did," Stoffmacher said. "Dr. Rahner is a respected member of our community. He has been for years. I didn't want him to be harassed simply because he was born with an extra finger."

"He's a murderer," Monk said, his gaze drifting over the evidence bags on the table.

Geshir snorted. "According to a tourist with extreme psychological problems who followed his psychiatrist to Germany."

"Mr. Monk may have a few personal issues," I said, "but he has solved more homicides than all the detectives in Germany combined."

I didn't know if that statistic was even remotely true, but it sounded impressive and I was pissed off. I don't like it when people snort at me or Monk. Snorting is extremely rude.

"However, he's also a man who was dismissed by the San Francisco Police Department because he was psychologically unfit, who has been under the care of a psychiatrist for years," Stoffmacher said, "and who has just accused Dr. Rahner of murdering a man who died of natural causes."

"You're right," Monk said.

"He is?" I said. I expected the police to challenge my arguments but I didn't expect the man I was defending to contradict me.

"Everything he says about me is true and Bruno Leupolz died of natural causes."

"At least he is beginning to see reason," Stoffmacher said pointedly to me, "even if you are not."

"But it was still murder," Monk said. "And Dr. Rahner did it."

"That doesn't make any sense at all," Geshir said.

"Here's what happened," Monk said. "Leupolz was going to write an unflattering article about Dr. Rahner. I don't know what Leupolz discovered, but whatever it was, it was damaging enough to force Dr. Rahner to take extreme measures."

Monk explained that Dr. Rahner slipped into Leupolz's apartment two nights ago to go through the reporter's notes and discover what he'd uncovered. When Leupolz returned, Dr. Rahner tried to scare the

reporter off the story. Dr. Rahner fired a gun into the wall to prove he was serious. It worked. He scared Leupolz to death.

"The reporter had a heart attack and, if that wasn't bad enough, the bullet that Dr. Rahner fired into the wall killed the unfortunate man who lived next door," Monk said. "Things had gone very, very wrong for Dr. Rahner and now he had to quickly improvise a way out of it. It wasn't easy. He had to remove any hint of a crime and any connection between the two deaths so that, at most, it looked like a tragic coincidence."

The first thing Dr. Rahner had to do, Monk explained, was clean up the crime scene and remove anything that tied Leupolz to him. So he vacuumed up the pillow stuffing, burned all the reporter's notes, and stole his laptop.

Dr. Rahner's next task was to make Vigg's death look like a suicide.

He covered the bullet hole in the wall between the two apartments. He put the gun in Vigg's hand and shot the couch to make sure the victim had gunpowder residue on him. And he locked the door on his way out to delay discovery of the body as long as possible.

All that remained now was to dispose of Leupolz's body and create a believable scenario for his death. Dr. Rahner dressed Leupolz in sweats and running shoes and then hid his body in the woods.

"The next morning, Dr. Rahner went for a jog," Monk said. "But what he really did was move the corpse from hiding and onto the trail, so it would appear that Leupolz died of a heart attack while hiking."

There was a long moment of silence while Stoffmacher and Geshir digested Monk's story.

"Or Vigg committed suicide and Leupolz died of a heart attack while hiking," Geshir said.

"The evidence says otherwise," Monk said.

"What evidence?" Stoffmacher asked.

"The bullet hole in Vigg's couch, the hidden bullet hole in the wall between the two apartments, and the locked door in Vigg's apartment, for starters," Monk said, and then motioned to the Baggies on the table. "There's also the feathers, the burned notes, the missing laptop, and Leupolz's clean shoes."

"I could argue that Vigg committed suicide over the loss of his job and his girlfriend, and that he fired the bullet into the couch as a test shot," Stoffmacher said. "The hole in the wall was covered because Vigg used that to secretly observe the previous tenant of the adjacent apartment."

"Who was one hot babe," Geshir said, seeming to enjoy the words. "She was a stewardess for Lufthansa. I bet she walked around her apartment naked and took lots of lovers and that's why he watched."

"Thank you, Kommissar, for that very important insight into Axel Vigg's motivations," Stoffmacher said.

"I believe the Americans call it 'profiling,'" Geshir said. "The detectives who do it are known as 'mind-hunters.'"

"You've lost your mind," Stoffmacher said.

"That's not the meaning in English," Geshir said.

"It's what I mean," Stoffmacher said, turning back to us. "We've learned that Leupolz was a struggling writer who couldn't hold a job and was barely scraping by on freelance assignments. He probably burned his notes and threw out his laptop in frustration. We'll never know for sure, because he went jogging in the hills and died of a heart attack."

"How do you explain the feathers?" I asked.

Stoffmacher shrugged. "Maybe he tore up a pillow in anger. It doesn't matter."

"And what about his clean shoes?"

"There was a light drizzle in the morning," Stoff-macher said. "Perhaps that washed the dirt away."

Monk spoke up. "Did you dredge the pond?"

"No, but even if we did and found the laptop and feathers, it wouldn't prove your theory," Stoffmacher said. "From the moment you arrived in Lohr, you have been intent on twisting everything you see into evidence of murder or a conspiracy about you."

"The evidence speaks for itself," Monk said.

"All right, let's say that you're right and everything happened the way you say it did," Stoffmacher said. "What proof do you have that Dr. Rahner is responsible for the deaths of Bruno Leupolz and Axel Vigg?"

"The shoelaces." Monk picked up the bag containing Leupolz's running shoes. "These are tied with a Norwegian Reef Knot. But the rest of Leupolz's shoes are tied with a Granny Knot."

"So what?" Geshir said.

"Dr. Rahner ties his shoes with a Norwegian Reef Knot," Monk said. "His bows are in the exact same proportion as these. It's as good as a fingerprint."

"Not in Germany," Stoffmacher said.

25

Mr. Monk and the Friendly Skies

It was obvious that the Lohr police were not going to rush out and arrest Dr. Rahner for murder and, to be honest, I didn't blame them. I felt Dr. Rahner was guilty, but that belief was based more on gut instinct than evidence.

Monk left the police station and headed straight for our car. He was so determined to nail Dr. Rahner that he forgot that he was walking on a cobblestone street and didn't hop from stone to stone. Either Monk was completely caught up in his quest or he was suicidal.

"Stoffmacher is going to call Dr. Rahner and let him know that we are on to him," Monk said.

"I think Dr. Rahner might have figured that out for himself when you told him that he was a murderer and that you were going to get him."

"But I didn't tell him our theory about the crime or the evidence we have to support it," Monk said. "Stoffmacher will. Dr. Rahner will start retracing his steps, cleaning up any evidence he might have left behind that we don't already know about. Time is of the essence."

"What can we do?"

"We have to go to Berlin right away and talk to Leupolz's editor at *Im Fadenkreuz*," Monk said. "We need to know what Leupolz was working on."

I'd read about Berlin in my guidebooks and I was excited about going there, if only for an afternoon, but I wasn't sure Monk realized how far away it was.

"Berlin isn't around the corner," I said. "It's at least a five-hour drive."

"And by plane?"

"Maybe an hour or so," I said.

"Book us a flight today," Monk said.

I unlocked the car and we got inside. The prospect of going on even a short flight with Monk or his drugged, obnoxious alter ego the Monkster didn't wow me.

"If you take your pill, the flight will go easy for you," I said, "but how effective will you be at detecting once we land?"

"Totally ineffective," Monk said. "Which is why I've decided not to take the drug for this trip."

"What about your fear of flying? If you freak out on the plane, you could be the one who ends up in jail, not Dr. Rahner."

"I'll just have to draw on my vast untapped reserves of inner strength."

I gave him a look. "What have you been saving them for?"

"This."

My cell phone rang. I dug around in my purse for it, hoping whoever was calling was patient. I finally found it and answered.

"You must be Adrian's nubile assistant, Natalie Teeger."

It was a man's voice that I didn't recognize. He spoke with an almost theatrical pomposity and yet also seemed to be struggling for each breath.

"I am not nubile," I said, but when I realized the alternative, it was too late to take it back.

"That's a pity. Sharona certainly was. In abundance, though I doubt Adrian appreciated it. I did."

"You're a pig," I said.

"Guilty as charged," he said. "That's the first time I've pleaded guilty to anything and yet here I am in prison. Where is the justice in that?"

Once he said that, I knew who I was speaking to.

"You're Dale the Whale," I said.

"Do you really want to insult a man who is using his precious ration of phone time to return your request for a call?"

I wasn't pleased to discover that the police were giving my personal cell phone number to convicted killers. What was Captain Stottlemeyer thinking? He was going to catch hell from me as soon as I got home.

I gave the phone to Monk and immediately wanted to clean my hands afterwards with one of his disinfectant wipes. I knew it was an irrational reaction, but I get that way when I get calls from killers.

Monk kindly put the phone on speaker and held it between us so I could hear both sides of the conversation.

"Hello, Dale," Monk said.

"Adrian Monk, as I live and eat!"

"It's 'live and breathe,' " Monk said.

"I eat far more than I breathe," Dale said. "What are you doing in the Fatherland?"

"I've solved Trudy's murder."

"Oh goodie," Dale said. "I can finally sleep soundly at night again. How did you do it?"

"I found Dr. Rahner, the man you used to hire the bomber."

"Martin Rahner? Now there's a blast from the past,"

Dale said. "Oops, that was a poor choice of words, wasn't it? Forgive me."

Insincerity dripped from Dale's words like bacon grease.

"I know you conspired with him and Dr. Kroger to keep me off the force," Monk said. "What I don't know is what you had on the doctors to make them do your bidding."

"Do you really expect me to tell you?" Dale asked.

"Why not?" Monk said. "You're already doing life in prison. What have you got to lose?"

"What have I got to gain?"

"A clear conscience," Monk said.

Dale laughed, his uproarious guffawing quickly turning into gagging and choking. I was afraid for a moment that he might die during the call and then I would have to throw the phone out.

Yes, I know that was another irrational reaction, but keeping the phone after Dale's demise would have been like sleeping in a bed someone had died in. I couldn't do it. Fortunately, Dale the Whale didn't die and, more importantly, I didn't have to toss out my phone.

Dale finally caught his breath. When he spoke again, though, he'd lost a little of his slimy frivolity.

"Sociopaths don't have a conscience. Thanks to you, I am doubly imprisoned, more so than anyone else in this hellhole. I am doomed to never leave my concrete cell, to never feel the sun on my skin, to always breathe fetid air."

I'm sure that "fetid" was an understatement.

"You have no one to blame but yourself for being a prisoner of both your body and the California penal system," Monk said.

"The prison I made, my magnificent corpulence, I can live with," Dale said. "The one you put me in I

cannot. What harm would it have done to leave me where I was, in my own home? I couldn't have escaped, could I?"

"It wouldn't have been punishment," Monk said. "You are a murderer. You don't deserve any pleasure or comfort in your life."

"Neither do you, Adrian Monk," he said. "As long as you don't know the truth about your sweet wife's fate, you will be as much a prisoner as I am."

Dale started to laugh again. Monk hung up on him and handed me the phone. I still felt like I should disinfect it.

"You might want to change your phone number when we get home," Monk said.

"Gee, do you think?" I asked.

One of the great things I discovered about Germany was that just about everyone there spoke English. It makes it ridiculously easy for us arrogant and lazy Americans not to acknowledge the existence of any other language but our own. Thank God for that. I was able to call Air Berlin and book our flight without any problem.

We arrived at the Frankfurt airport just in time to board our plane. Monk was so nervous, and shaking so much, that I thought he might scream and run back to the car. And that was before we even reached the terminal.

Somehow he managed to hold himself together at the ticket counter, through the security checkpoint, and even down the jetway to the Airbus plane.

There was a table at the end of the passageway covered with stacks of free German newspapers and magazines, including *Im Fadenkreuz*, which I gratefully snagged so we'd have the address of the office and the name of the editor.

I was surprised to see that one of the freebies on the table was *Playboy*. There weren't any headlines or women on the cover, just a suggestive shot of a pair of snowy mountain peaks poking through a sea of clouds. I figured that it must be some kind of abridged edition without the nude photos. Perhaps there were men in Germany who could actually say that they read *Playboy* only for the articles. But I didn't pick one up to find out.

Monk took a big breath before stepping onto the plane and then froze when he looked down the aisle.

"Oh my God," he said. "Are they insane?"

I peered over his shoulder. I couldn't see anything unusual, so I looked for the usual that might drive Monk batty. But I still couldn't see the problem.

"What is it?" I said.

"There are three seats in each row."

He was right. I didn't know how I'd missed that. Not that it would have changed anything. It was what it was.

"The row actually has six seats, which is an even number, but there's an aisle that goes right down the middle," I said. "Look at it that way."

"We are going to crash," Monk said. "Look at it that way."

"Keep your voice down," I hissed into his ear. "We are not going to crash."

"The plane isn't evenly balanced," Monk said. "How can we possibly remain airborne?"

"There are three seats on each side of the plane," I said. "It's balanced and it's symmetrical. You should be thrilled."

"Three is not an even number," Monk said. "The entire plane is uneven. That can't be safe. Do you think the pilot is aware of what's going on back here?"

"Dividing the row in two sets of three is the only way you can divide six in half," I said.

"They should have had four seats across, divided the rows into twos, and saved lives."

A stewardess came up behind me. "Is there a problem?"

"The first cloud we hit we are going to be goners," Monk said.

"Goners?" she said. "What is a goner?"

"Someone who is eager to be gone on their trip," I said with a smile. "We can't wait for that first cloud, because then we know we're really gone. Up, up, and away, that's where we want to be."

She nodded. "Please take your seats."

I gave Monk a shove and practically pushed him all the way to our seats in row twelve. I had the window and he had the middle seat. A businessman with a *Playboy* tucked under his arm took the aisle seat.

Monk pulled the airsickness bag from the seat pocket in front of him and began to breathe into it. The businessman pretended like he didn't notice.

Once everyone was seated, the stewardess went down the aisle passing out more magazines. It seemed like every man in the plane took a *Playboy*. Monk held up his hand as she passed our aisle.

"Would you like something to read, sir?" she asked.

"Yes," Monk said. "Could I get a manual for surviving a crash landing?"

"Information on our emergency landing procedures is printed on the laminated card in the seatback in front of you," she said in the same robotic voice American stewardesses use. I guess stewardess-speak is universal, regardless of your native language.

"I was hoping for something more detailed," Monk said.

"I'm sorry," she said. "That's all we have."

"Okay," Monk said. "How about the Holy Bible?"

"We don't have that either," she said. "How about an *International Herald Tribune*?"

I quickly spoke up. "That will be fine."

She handed me the newspaper and walked on. I swatted Monk in the chest with it and dropped it on his lap.

"What's the matter with you?" I said. "You aren't religious."

"If I am going to meet God today, I want to be holding his bestseller."

"It won't help," I said. "Do you think he's forgotten that you tried to throw out the bowl of holy water at Mission Dolores during Sunday Mass and replace it with hand sanitizer?"

We began to taxi away from the gate. As we did, the stewardesses started their usual safety lecture about how to use the seat belts, where to find the exits, how to operate the oxygen masks, and when to inflate the flotation devices that were stowed under our seats.

Monk bent over and started searching under his seat for something.

"What are you doing?" I said.

"Getting ready," he answered and pulled out the uninflated bright yellow life preserver and slipped it over his head, elbowing me and the businessman in our sides as he reached around to snap all of his straps.

The businessman leaned forward to glare at Monk and our eyes met.

"He can't swim," I explained.

"We aren't in the water," the man said.

"Yet," Monk said.

A stewardess came down the aisle to check that everyone's seat belts were fastened and stopped when she saw Monk wearing his life vest.

"Could I have my oxygen mask now?" Monk said. "It will save time later."

She just shook her head and walked on. I elbowed Monk in the side, just hard enough to get his attention.

"Stop it," I said. "You're going to get us thrown off the plane."

"If it happens over water, at least one of us will be floating," Monk said.

We reached the runway. The stewardesses took their seats and Monk assumed the crash position: bending forward, placing his arms over his head, and pleading for his mother.

The plane sped up and lifted off, the roaring of the engines failing to cover the wailing of a few infants and Adrian Monk.

Once we achieved cruising altitude, Monk tentatively sat up and looked around. That was when the businessman beside him decided to open up his *Playboy*.

It wasn't abridged.

Monk let out a squeal and immediately tried to avert his gaze to something safe.

He looked straight ahead.

But the man in the seat directly in front of him chose that moment to hold up his *Playboy* to better examine the full centerfold.

In fact, just about everyone on board, men and women, young and old, seemed to be interested in seeing what makes women different from men.

We definitely weren't in America anymore.

Monk turned to me in horror. "Oh God, we're on the porno-plane. What do we do when the orgies start?"

26

Mr. Monk Goes to Berlin

We managed to arrive at Berlin-Tegel Airport with our virtue intact and my sanity only slightly frayed at the edges.

A stewardess stood at the door of the plane, smiling and offering the departing passengers a silver platter covered with heart-shaped chocolates wrapped in red foil.

Playboys and chocolate. When it came to the Friendly Skies, the Germans couldn't be beat. I wondered if the lucky folks in first class got lobster and hot-oil massages.

I took two chocolates since I knew Monk wasn't going to take his and started unwrapping one as I deplaned.

Monk staggered off the jet as if he'd been gored by a bull, tossed off a cliff, and then hit by a bus.

"Am I bleeding from every orifice?" he rasped.

"I can't see every orifice, thank God." But the thought was enough to kill my appetite for the chocolate. I tossed it in the trash can at the end of the jetway.

On our descent into Berlin-Tegel, we flew right over

the city center and I got a great view of all the landmarks that the tourist guides say you're supposed to see.

But from the sky, the Brandenburg Gate, the Television Tower, the Gendamenmarkt, the Reichstag and gleaming glass tent over the Sony Center at Potsdamer Platz weren't nearly as fascinating as the sprawling, monolithic apartment blocks that looked like concrete labyrinths. They were monuments to the former East Germany's boom in the mass production of enormous prefabricated slab concrete housing during the 1960s. I didn't have to know exactly where the Berlin Wall once stood to pick out some parts of the city that were once in the German Democratic Republic.

I'd expected that; it fit with my preconceived image of Berlin. What I wasn't expecting was the lush green of the Tiergarten, the former royal hunting grounds, and the vivid blue of the river Spree, which wove through the city like a bright ribbon.

In my mind, Berlin was gray, bleak, and oppressive. But from above, it looked vibrant, colorful, and exciting.

Monk missed it all, spending the descent bent over in the crash position and pleading with God to spare his life. He would have liked that the airport was a big hexagon and that the design theme was carried on inside, from the shape of the pillars to the designs on the floor.

"Did you feel those G's?" Monk said as we crossed the terminal. "They nearly flayed the flesh right off our bones."

"I didn't feel the G's," I said.

"Maybe you're paralyzed," Monk said.

"I'm walking, Mr. Monk," I said. "I think we can rule out paralysis."

"It's posttraumatic stress paralysis," Monk said.

"You're in so much pain that your mind is blocking it to protect you."

"That condition doesn't exist," I said.

"I've just discovered it," Monk said.

His mood improved considerably once we were outside and he saw the hexagonal concrete benches on the hexagonal-patterned sidewalk and the row of identical beige Mercedes taxis lined up at the curb.

"Order," he said, taking a deep breath.

"You can smell it?"

"Can't you?" he asked.

We got into the backseat of the taxi and I gave the driver the copy of *Im Fadenkreuz*, which I'd opened to the page that listed the editorial staff. I pointed to the address at the bottom.

"We'd like to go there, please," I said.

The driver nodded and off we went. I don't know whether he took us on the scenic route to shake every last euro out of us, but we didn't mind. Monk got a chance to see a lot of the sights that he'd missed from the sky.

We drove down a grand, tree-lined boulevard that ran through the middle of the Tiergarten and ended triumphantly at the Brandenburg Gate. It helped that we had our own sound track. There was a marching band performing in front of the gate, and whatever they were playing was big, brassy, and dramatic. I wondered if the tourist office kept them there 24/7 just for the effect.

For twenty-eight years, the gate had stood decaying in the barren no-man's-land between the walls of East and West Germany as a sad and powerful symbol of all the things that divided the country and its people. Now it once again stood for the city, its rebirth, and, in its own way, for restoration of order.

I don't usually think in such a historical perspective, but the music was working on me big time.

The gate had been restored to its former glory, its symmetry matched by the pair of new, identical, four-story neoclassical-style buildings that flanked it. The buildings managed to look old and new at the same time. Beyond it, I could see Parizer Platz and the tree-lined Unter den Linden.

Monk leaned out of the taxi window like a golden retriever to get a better look at the gate as we passed.

"Isn't that beautiful?" he said when he'd settled back in his seat. "Every city should have one."

"Maybe every city should have a Golden Gate Bridge, an Eiffel Tower, and a Big Ben, too. We wouldn't have to go anywhere to see the world."

"Sounds good to me," Monk said.

We made a few turns and found ourselves on Friedrichstrasse, the center of what was now a high-end shopping district. It had once been the administrative center of Hitler's government and, later, of the GDR. But no amount of neon, glass, and travertine could soften the intimidating institutional coldness of the buildings or the rigid order they were designed to convey.

And that was intentional.

The city planners were strictly enforcing the architectural principle of "critical reconstruction," which mandated that buildings had to maintain the same historical shapes, style, and alignment of the past.

The result was that the monumental style of National Socialist architecture, which Hitler referred to as "Words of Stone," and the cold, intimidating power of the GDR had survived, buffed up with shopping mall gloss and the sterilized Disney gleam.

All the buildings were exactly the same height and blockish shape, with smooth, unadorned, symmetrical facades of polished stone and glass that were practically flush with one another.

Each building had a two-story ground floor for restaurants or businesses, followed by four uniform stories of office space or apartments, topped by three terraced stories, creating an unbroken roofline down the entire street.

The flat conformity of the building facades was rarely broken by bay windows or other architectural features. The only things that set the buildings apart from each other were their stone cladding and the shape of their windows, which were evenly aligned in long, symmetrical rows.

Because there were no gaps between the buildings, except where the blocks were broken by other streets, the effect was like driving between two immense walls of stone and glass.

Monk gaped in amazement and pleasure at the buildings as we passed them.

"We have found paradise," he said.

"There's no charm or character to these buildings," I said. "They are so functional."

"You say that like those are bad things," Monk said. "All the buildings fit together perfectly."

"That's the problem," I said. "You can hardly tell one apart from the other."

"All cities should look like this," Monk said.

"What about individuality?"

"I'm all for individuality, as long as it doesn't stand out," he said.

"You like conformity."

"There are valid artistic and practical reasons for maintaining a uniform height for buildings."

"What's artistic about sameness?"

"It assures that the domes and spires of churches, as well as the towers of official government buildings, stand out over everything else. It draws attention to them, underscoring their beauty, their omnipresence,

and the religious or state power that they represent. That's the cunning reason why Friedrich the Great created the eaves-height law in the eighteenth century. It's one of the things that made him great."

I regarded Monk in a new light. "You've done some reading."

"I'm not illiterate," Monk said.

"I meant that you've been reading about Germany."

"I've had trouble sleeping," Monk said, "so I read some of the guidebooks the Schmidts have downstairs."

While he was talking, I'd realized something else. I hadn't seen a single tree or even a leaf since my passing glance at Unter den Linden.

"There aren't any plants on these streets," I said. "Not even so much as a bush or a flower."

"Wonderful, isn't it?" Monk said.

"I think it's weird," I said.

"Nature belongs in the woods, not in the city."

"Nature is a part of life," I said. "It would be nice to see some here."

"Nature muddies things up," Monk said, "and attracts wild animals."

"Is that another example of the thinking that made Friedrich great? Did he outlaw trees, too?"

Two blocks ahead, in the middle of the street, I could see a simple white guard shack with sandbags in front of it, marking the spot where Checkpoint Charlie, the border crossing between East and West, once stood. The shack was a replica and looked like it was more of a photo op for tourists than a meaningful historical marker or a memorial to those who'd died trying to escape to the West.

The taxi driver turned onto a side street and parked in front of a blockish building with a facade of mottled green granite. I paid him and asked for a receipt. I in-

tended to get reimbursed by Monk for every euro I was spending. I should have insisted on a per diem, too.

We got out and I immediately noticed a single narrow strip of red cobblestones running through the asphalt and around the next corner. I took a few steps and saw a plaque embedded in the stone. I felt a shiver when I read it.

"Mr. Monk, do you know where I am standing?"

"In the middle of the street," he said. "If you don't move, you're going to get hit by a bus."

"This was where the Berlin Wall once stood," I said. "I'm standing on history."

"Be sure to wipe your feet," he said. "I'm sure they won't appreciate it if you track history into the lobby."

And with that comment Monk went inside the building.

The logo of *Im Fadenkreuz* was the crosshairs of a sniper's rifle scope. "Crosshairs," I learned from Ernestine Kahn, the managing editor, was the English translation of the name of the magazine.

"What we like to put in our crosshairs is corruption," she said. "We reveal the bribery, the dishonesty, and the greed of public officials and business leaders."

"You'll never run out of stories to tell," I said.

"Not in Germany," she said. "It's the sad truth, but it's great for our magazine and our circulation. People love it when we bring down the rich, the mighty, and the sanctimonious."

It wasn't hard for us to get an audience with Ernestine. I told the front desk that Monk was a homicide consultant with the San Francisco Police Department and that we were investigating the death of Bruno Leupolz. We were immediately invited up to her fourth-floor office, which looked out on a golden office building that stood alone on its own plot of land and

rose above everything else on the street. Friedrich the Great wouldn't have been pleased.

"What is that?" I gestured to the golden monolith.

"A symbol of journalistic freedom and the reason our magazine is in this building," she said.

Ernestine's black hair, pale skin, black pants, and loose white blouse blended seamlessly into the white walls and black furniture of her office, which was as crisp, immaculate, and monochrome as she was. Or vice versa. She must have been practically invisible whenever she sat behind her desk. Perhaps it was a survival technique against predators in the corporate jungle.

I suddenly felt very vulnerable and garishly colorful in my red scoop-neck shirt and blue jeans.

"The Berlin Wall used to be right in front of this building and when it was, all these windows were sealed with bricks and concrete so that no one could see life on the other side or try to escape to it," she said. "Axel Springer was a newspaper publisher. He built that skyscraper so that everyone in the East, where I grew up, could see the wealth, freedom, and opportunity that the West offered. The GDR responded by building six apartment towers just to block people from seeing his building. It made me want to become a journalist."

"Every day you look out that window, you must be reminded of your childhood."

"It reinvigorates me and reinforces why I do what I do, a job that wasn't possible before the wall fell," she said. "So what's your interest in Bruno Leupolz?"

"We think he was murdered," Monk said.

"'We' meaning the two of you," she said.

"For now," Monk said.

"The police say he died of natural causes," she said. "What makes you think that it's something more sinister?"

"Why do I get the feeling that we're being interviewed?" I said.

"You're talking to a reporter," Ernestine said. "I don't talk to anybody unless I think there might be a story in it. Is there one here?"

"There's the story Leupolz was working on for you," Monk said.

"He wasn't on assignment for us. He just liked to use our name," she said. "It opened doors that would otherwise be slammed in his face."

"You didn't mind?" I asked.

She shrugged. "If he lucked into something hot, which was rare, he'd come to us with it first."

"But you knew what he was working on," Monk prodded.

Ernestine grimaced as if the knowledge was causing her physical pain. "He was investigating some psychiatrist who helps people with physical deformities."

"Dr. Martin Rahner," Monk said.

She nodded. "Bruno was convinced the guy was a fraud and a swindler."

"You weren't?" I asked.

"I didn't care one way or the other," she said. "He was just a psychiatrist, though if you believed Bruno, he wasn't even that."

"What do you mean?" Monk said.

"Bruno told me that the doctor's credentials were false, that he'd lied about some degree or plagiarized some paper or something like that," she said. "I didn't pay much attention, to be honest."

"Why not?" Monk said. "Doesn't your magazine expose criminals?"

"We expose people in positions of authority who have abused their power for money or sex, preferably both," she said. "A possibly fake psychiatrist who may

be tricking people with webbed feet into telling him their troubles isn't a story for our audience."

"So why wouldn't Leupolz let it go?" I asked. "Why did he go down to Lohr and keep investigating Dr. Rahner?"

"Bruno's girlfriend was one of Dr. Rahner's patients," Ernestine said. "She dumped Bruno and invested every penny she had in the doctor's resort, and then moved in there."

I knew of only two people who lived at the resort full-time, and only one of them was a woman. Well, mostly a woman. I cringed at the thought at the same moment that Monk did, too.

Ernestine eyed us both. "So you heard about Katie's problem."

"You knew?" Monk said.

"I'm a reporter and I wanted to know why Bruno was so obsessed with this psychiatrist to the point that he would turn down paying assignments to pursue the man," she said. "There was no story. It was entirely personal. He desperately wanted Dr. Rahner to be guilty of something so he could get Katie back, which was why I was so skeptical about Bruno's latest angle."

"Leupolz discovered something else about Dr. Rahner?" Monk asked.

"Bruno claimed that the doctor's time-share resort was actually a huge financial scam, that the money Dr. Rahner convinced his patients and their families to invest in his real estate development business, presumably to build similar resorts elsewhere, was actually going into his own pocket. Bruno said that he'd discovered the doctor had gambled that money on higher-risk investments and lost, so he was now using the cash he'd connived from new investors to pay back the old ones."

"A classic Ponzi scheme, using the money from the new suckers to mollify the old ones," I said. "Would a

shrink abusing the trust of his patients to get them to invest in a real estate scam be a story for you?"

"Only if there was a huge amount of money involved, so Bruno naturally said that there was—tens of millions of euros, including his ex-girlfriend's meager life savings. But he'd say anything to get me to run a story on the psychiatrist. That's why I insisted that Bruno show me lots of hard evidence to support his charges. He said he would."

"But you didn't see it," Monk said.

"That's because it probably didn't exist," she said.

"It doesn't now," Monk said. "His notes were burned and his laptop is missing."

She shrugged. "I was pretty hard on him when we spoke. I told him that he was losing what little journalistic credibility he still had left, and that if he didn't wise up soon, nobody would ever hire him as a reporter again. Maybe burning the notes and tossing the laptop was his way of finally coming to his senses and giving up on a lost cause."

"Or maybe Dr. Rahner murdered him," Monk suggested.

"That would be a story," she said. "What evidence do you have to back it up?"

I was afraid she'd ask that. I was even more afraid that Monk would answer it.

"I've seen the way Dr. Rahner ties his shoes," Monk said.

She raised an eyebrow. "*That's* your evidence?"

"There's more, much more. There's the suicide of Axel Vigg, which wasn't a suicide at all. The hole in his wall wasn't for looking at stewardesses and he didn't shoot his couch. Who would do that? There's also the pillow feathers on the carpet and the clean shoes that should have been dirty but weren't."

It sounded like the rambling of a lunatic to me and I

actually knew what he was talking about. I could only imagine what it sounded like to her.

"I don't understand any of that," Ernestine said, "or how it proves that Bruno's heart attack was a murder, or that Dr. Rahner was responsible."

"Oh, he was," Monk said. "I've seen lots of murderers and he's definitely one. I knew it the instant I saw those six fingers."

"You're going after him because of his extra finger?"

"I know he killed Bruno Leupolz and he could also be the man who hired a bomber to blow up my wife's car. She was a reporter, too."

"I see." She escorted us to her door and held it open. "I thought Bruno was blinded by obsession, Mr. Monk, but you're much worse."

"It's not going to get any better," he said and we left the office.

27

Mr. Monk Hits a Wall

I led us towards Checkpoint Charlie. I figured I could find a souvenir there for Julie and a taxi to take us back to the airport.

Monk frowned with frustration, his hands balled into fists, like a petulant child.

"I know how Dr. Rahner killed Bruno Leupolz and Axel Vigg, I know how he covered up his crimes, and I even know what his motives were," Monk said. "The only thing I don't know is how to prove any of it."

"Do you really think Dr. Rahner is the man who arranged Trudy's murder?"

"I'd like him to be," Monk said.

"But do you *believe* that he is?"

"He's got six fingers on his right hand, he was in San Francisco around the time she was killed, and he's a murderer," Monk said. "It's more likely than not that he is."

"But he might not be," I said.

He looked at me. "You don't think it's him."

"It's possible that Dale the Whale could have found out that Dr. Rahner fudged his credentials long before

Bruno did and blackmailed him into arranging Trudy's murder," I said. "But I don't think Dr. Kroger was involved."

"You think it's just a coincidence that Dr. Kroger and Dr. Rahner know each other."

"Yes, I do," I said. Up until that moment, I hadn't realized that I felt that way. "And if that part is a coincidence, then I have to wonder if maybe the rest of it is, too."

"The killing Trudy part," Monk said.

I nodded. "So what do we do now?"

"We go back to Lohr and see this through to the bitter end," Monk said. "But this time I'm taking one of my pills."

"For a one-hour flight?"

It seemed like overkill. The effects of the medication lasted about twelve hours.

"I also need it for what we're doing when we get back to Lohr," Monk said. "I want to go back into the woods and see if we can find where Dr. Rahner hid Leupolz's body."

Monk would definitely have an easier time dealing with all that nature if he was drugged up.

I wasn't sure that I would, though.

At the corner, the turbulent and violent history of the Berlin Wall was displayed in photographs on a wooden wall that had been erected around a vacant lot where a portion of the GDR's border-crossing complex had once stood.

I paused to look at the pictures and read some of the captions. They didn't tell me much that I hadn't learned in high school, but standing in that spot, I could feel the history. It was still recent enough that people like Ernestine, who didn't seem any older than I was, had been witnesses to it.

The pictorial felt cheap and perfunctory. I thought

it would have been much better to have a few Berlin residents who'd lived with the wall in their lives standing around on the corner. They could have talked to us informally about how the wall had affected their lives and shaped who they were today.

That's not to say there weren't some people there for the tourists. There were a couple of guys wearing old U.S. and Russian military uniforms and posing with tourists in front of the guard shack in return for some spare change. It was the Berlin version of having your picture taken with Mickey Mouse and Dopey and just as meaningful.

There was a souvenir shop a few doors down from the guard shack. I went inside, hoping to find something more authentic and interesting than a T-shirt, key chain, refrigerator magnet, or mug with a picture of the Brandenburg Gate on it.

On the back wall of the store, the shelves were covered with chunks of painted concrete glued to plastic stands. As I got closer, I realized they were pieces of the Berlin Wall, sold by size, from a pebble to a huge slab with rebar poking out of it.

Monk examined a chunk and then started rearranging the pieces that were on the shelf in front of him.

I picked up a blue-green painted bit of rubble about the size of a Ping-Pong ball. It cost nine euros, which was cheaper than a mug and something I couldn't buy anywhere else but Berlin—assuming it was genuine, of course. Even if it wasn't, it was still the perfect souvenir.

"Put that back," Monk said, still moving the pieces around.

"It's okay. They're for sale," I said.

"They shouldn't be," Monk said. "What if someone wants to put it back together?"

"They won't," I said.

"But what if they change their minds? They'll never be able to do it if the pieces are scattered all over the globe."

"Good," I said.

Monk sorted the pieces by size and tried to match them up. It was futile.

"None of these pieces fit," he said with irritation.

"The wall was broken into millions of little pieces, Mr. Monk. You can't honestly expect the bits of rubble on these shelves to snap together like puzzle pieces."

"They could," Monk said. "All we have to do is find all the pieces that are missing."

"You want us to reassemble the Berlin Wall," I said.

"They'll thank us later," Monk said.

"No, they won't," I said. "Besides, it would take us years."

"You should have thought of that before you brought us in here," Monk said miserably. "We're committed now."

I left Monk at the shelves, went up to the counter, and whispered a question to the female cashier. "Do they sell pieces of the Berlin Wall at the airport?"

"Yes," the cashier said, "but they are much more expensive there and they don't have nearly as wide a selection of colors and sizes as we do."

"Thanks," I said.

It might be pricier buying the piece at the airport, but it was the only way I was leaving Berlin with the souvenir. By then, Monk would be under the influence of his wonder drug and wouldn't care about devoting his life and mine to recovering every piece of the Berlin Wall.

I went back to Monk, who was becoming increasingly frustrated at his inability to fit any of the pieces of the wall together.

"This is a living hell," Monk said.

"You'd better take your pill now if we're going to make our flight."

"But what about this?" Monk said. "We can't just walk away and leave chaos behind."

"We'll come back later," I said.

"When?"

"When we have more pieces," I said.

"Good idea," he said and I gave him his pill.

Thirty minutes later, we were at Berlin-Tegel and all was forgotten.

I bought my piece of the wall at the airport gift shop and stowed it deep inside my purse where I hoped Monk would never see it.

Monk, meanwhile, settled in at an airport café, where he was sampling as many different German pastries as he possibly could, including at least four different kinds of streusel.

He wore many of those pastries on his shirt by the time we got on the plane, where he helped himself to a copy of each of the free magazines.

"You can't read German," I said.

"They're free," Monk said. Even on drugs, he was a cheapskate.

The plane wasn't as crowded as our earlier flight. I took a window seat and Monk took the aisle, leaving the seat between us empty.

Before we took off, a stewardess came down the aisle, checking to see if our seat belts were fastened. It was the same stewardess who'd been on our last flight. She seemed shocked by the change in Monk, who was studying the *Playboy* centerfold.

"What do you think?" Monk tipped his head to the naked woman in the magazine. "Real or fake?"

"I'm not an expert," she said.

"If you're not," Monk said, "who is?"

She ignored him and moved on. Monk showed the centerfold to me.

"You're familiar with these," he said. "What do you think?"

I yanked the magazine from his hands and shoved it into the seat pocket in front of me.

"Behave yourself," I said.

The man sitting across the aisle from Monk leaned towards him.

"They're real," he said, nodding to underscore his certainty.

"If those are real," the woman next to him said, "then I'm a man."

"Are you?" Monk asked.

"That's my wife you're talking to!" the man said, his face reddening fast.

Monk shrugged. "This is Germany."

The passenger in front of Monk peered over the top of his seat at him. "What is that supposed to mean?"

Before Monk could reply and things could escalate into a fistfight, the woman in the seat behind Monk tapped his arm.

"They're fake," she said.

"Real," said someone else.

"Fake," said someone else.

"One is real," someone else said. "The other is fake."

And so it went, up and down the plane. By the time we landed in Frankfurt, Monk had managed to poll all the passengers and the crew on this vital question, but they were evenly split on the issue. Most of the men, though, believed the centerfold's breasts were real. Or wanted to.

What a shock.

28

Mr. Monk Takes a Walk in the Woods

It was dark when we got out of our car in the Franziskushohe parking lot. Monk turned on one of the two flashlights that we'd bought on our way back to Lohr and aimed it into the woods, letting the beam play on the trees.

"Ready to go?" he asked me.

"It's dark," I said.

"That's why we've got flashlights," he said. "But the moon is so bright we hardly need them."

"Maybe we should do this in the morning," I said.

"This is the perfect time to do it."

"You're not going to be able to see anything."

"But this is probably what it was like when Dr. Rahner was out there, looking for a place to hide the body until morning. We'll see things the way he did."

"You're on drugs," I said.

"You're scared," Monk said, grinning.

"I am not," I lied.

Monk shined the light under his chin, giving him a ghostly look. "You think the boogeyman is going to get you?"

"I'm being cautious. What if you trip over something?"

"Uh-huh." Monk reached into his pocket and came out with his prescription bottle. "Maybe you'd like one of my pills."

I didn't like being the crazy person in our relationship. So what if I got mauled by a bear or fell off a cliff? I decided that would be better than him getting to be smug and superior.

"The trail is over here." I turned on my flashlight and marched past him. "Follow me."

It didn't take us long to get to the spot beside the muddy pond where I'd found Leupolz's body. Remembering the corpse while standing there in the dark made me very nervous.

Monk aimed his flashlight into the bushes, then out over the pond. Something in the trees at the far edge of the pond reflected the light.

I'd seen a dog's eyes reflect light at night. What if Monk's beam had just passed over a wolf?

"What's that?" Monk asked.

"A beer can, maybe?" I said. "Or a pack of slavering wolves."

"Slavering?" He swept the trees again with his light and caught another glimmer.

"Wolves slaver," I said. "Especially when they are rabid and hungry."

"Let's go see," he said and started walking, not waiting for my reply.

We followed the perimeter of the pond. I shifted my gaze and the beam of my light back and forth, between the woods and the brown water.

Was the pond full of leeches lusting for a taste of my blood? Which was a worse way to go? Feasted on by slavering wolves or bloodthirsty leeches?

Beyond the trees, a few yards from the pond, we

found a weedy clearing where a rotting wooden shack stood. It blended so well with the trees that we hadn't seen it yesterday. On one side of the shack there was a pile of firewood where seemingly a thousand spiders lived. They, too, probably hungered for my sweet flesh.

Monk aimed his flashlight at the shack, the beam slicing through the gaps between the boards to illuminate a pile of rusty paint cans inside, creating the reflection that had drawn him here like a fish to a lure.

And I knew what happened to fishes lured by lures. They ended up scaled, gutted, and grilled.

"This looks like a good place to hide a corpse to me," Monk said, which is exactly what you don't want someone to say in the middle of the woods at night, not when you're already so scared that you find the thought of grilled fish frightening.

"Great," I said. "We can come back in the morning and check it out."

But Monk was already opening the door and going inside.

"I'll wait here," I said.

That was when I heard a twig snap in the woods behind me.

I whirled around, letting my beam play out over the trees and the murky water. I didn't see anything.

It was a relief. It was also terrifying. I went inside the shack and slammed the door shut behind me, just as I thought I heard another twig snap.

Monk was crouched in the far corner, examining something.

"Look at this," he said.

I walked up behind him. There were some white feathers on the ground at his feet.

"Pillow feathers," he said. "Bruno Leupolz was here."

"But we can't prove that Dr. Rahner was," I said.

"Those paint cans are rusted through and leaking," Monk said, motioning to the cans behind me. "You're standing in a puddle of dry paint on the ground. I bet we can find some of it on Dr. Rahner's shoes, maybe even his socks or pant legs."

"Don't you think he would have washed them or thrown them out by now?"

"Oh," Monk said. "I hadn't thought of that. Maybe there's something else in here that will be his undoing."

"We'll have better luck seeing it in daylight," I said.

"But we're here now," he said. He sniffed. "Do you smell gasoline?"

I sniffed. "It could be the turpentine."

"Is there turpentine?"

"I don't know," I said. "But if there's paint around, there's probably some turpentine, too."

"Maybe we can find that on his shoes," Monk said, going over to examine a rotting bag on the ground, its contents of white granules spilled on the floor. "What's this?"

"Looks like fertilizer to me," I said. "Not that I am any kind of expert."

"Maybe we can find some of these granules in the treads of his shoes."

We were crouching to examine the bag when the wall beside us burst into flames in a loud, crackling *whoosh*.

The heat, the sound, and the sudden light made us scramble back in shock and terror. Instinctively, we both went for the door.

But it wouldn't budge. We slammed our bodies against it to no avail. It was jammed tight.

"Were you smoking?" Monk asked me.

"I don't smoke," I said.

"Then how did the fire start?"

I remembered the smell of gasoline. Someone wanted to kill us.

Another wall ignited, the dry wood catching fire remarkably fast, the flames licking out for us like the tongues of ravenous monsters.

I glanced at the paint, the turpentine, and the fertilizer and knew what they would soon become.

A bomb.

In a few seconds we would be dead.

The heat was unbearable—each breath felt like a knife jammed down my throat. I looked around, and through the flames and disintegrating wood consuming one wall I could make out the muddy pond several yards away.

Without thinking, I grabbed Monk's hand, closed my eyes, and ran screaming into the wall.

The wood seemed to shatter like glass. I felt a thousand white-hot stings and knew that my clothes were on fire. I ran blindly, tripped in the muck, and fell face-first into the thick water of the pond, losing my grip on Monk.

It was like falling into pudding. I had to fight to get up, the weight of the mud and my clothes pushing me down into the shallow pond.

When I came up for air, I was standing in water up to my chest, sludge dripping off my scorched clothes and singed hair.

Monk emerged beside me, sputtering and coughing, draped in weeds like a swamp monster. His lapels were blackened from the flames and it looked like a dozen people had tried putting out their cigarettes on his jacket.

We both turned to look at the shack as it exploded, sending canisters shooting up into the air like fireworks, trailing embers. The explosion seemed to suck

the air out of the fire. The shack collapsed on itself and became a big bonfire that lit up the pond. I could feel the hot air against my face.

"Whoo-wee!" Monk shrieked happily, wiping muck from his brow. "That was a rush."

I stared at him. I'd never heard him say "whoo-wee" or anything remotely like it. I couldn't believe he was happy, standing there waist-deep in sludge, his hair still smoking from the fire. I could only imagine how I must have looked, but I knew how I felt.

"Someone just tried to murder us," I said.

"It was fun," he said with a smile.

"Fun? We were nearly burned alive! We're about to be attacked by bloodsucking leeches!"

"Now we know we're on the right track," Monk said.

I wanted to wipe that dopey smile off his face and make him as miserable and angry as I was. And I wasn't beyond rubbing salt in his wounds to do it.

"But any evidence that might have connected Dr. Rahner to Bruno Leupolz's murder has literally gone up in smoke."

"Wrong," Monk said.

"You can't prove the body was hidden in the shack or that Dr. Rahner was ever there because"—I pointed to the fire—"*the shack is gone.*"

"Who cares?" Monk said.

"You do!" I shouted. "Dr. Rahner is going to get away with murder."

"Bullpucky."

"Did you just say 'bullpucky'?"

"This is our lucky night," he said. "If we hadn't been on fire, we never would have found this."

He reached into the muck with both hands and pulled up a big black trash bag that was cinched tight, the yellow plastic drawstrings tied in a neat double bow.

"I present the missing stuff from Bruno Leupolz's apartment," Monk said.

"Or somebody else's trash," I said. "Who knows how many people have ditched their garbage in here?"

"This is a Norwegian Reef Knot, is it not?" He tipped his head towards the drawstrings and began to giggle. "Knot, not. Get it? Knot, not. Who's there? The Monkster, that's who!"

I was starting to regret saving his life. I might have corrected that error then and there if not for the sound of approaching sirens and the possibility of getting caught in the act.

Fire trucks roared up a logging road on the hillside above us and a few minutes later a dozen firefighters spilled down on the clearing carrying shovels and fire extinguishers.

While they doused the bonfire with foam and shoveled dirt on the embers, we slogged out of the pond and sat on a log to await the arrival of the police.

Mosquitoes drawn by the lights buzzed by my ears. I swatted at them and searched my body for leeches as best I could without stripping entirely.

Monk gazed up at the stars and sighed contentedly. "This is nice," he said.

I paused for a moment to stare at him. "We're breathing smoke, soot, and toxic chemicals. We're being bled dry by mosquitoes and leeches. We're soaking wet, covered in mud, and smell like we died yesterday. And you think this is nice?"

"I wish we had some marshmallows," Monk said. "We could put them on sticks and roast them over the embers. Wouldn't that be tasty?"

Stoffmacher and Geshir approached us. I didn't even notice their arrival on the scene.

"When I heard where this fire was, I had a feeling

we'd find you here," Stoffmacher said. "Would you like to tell us what happened?"

"We went to Berlin and found out why Dr. Rahner murdered Bruno Leupolz," Monk said. "The reporter discovered that the doctor isn't a doctor and that he's swindling the investors in his resort."

"Here." Stoffmacher thrust his finger in the direction of the firefighters. "I want to know what happened *here*."

"We found out where Dr. Rahner hid Bruno Leupolz's body before dumping it on the trail," Monk said. "It's that shack over there."

"It was," I said. "Now it's ashes."

"Dr. Rahner must have seen us park at the Franziskushohe tonight and guessed what we were after," Monk said. "So he followed us down here with a gasoline can and a match."

"What evidence do you have to back up your accusations?" Stoffmacher demanded.

Monk looked at me. "Why does everybody keep asking me that question?"

"They're detectives," I said.

"That's no excuse for repetition," Monk said. "It's tiresome."

"So are these encounters with you, Mr. Monk," Stoffmacher said. "If you don't show me some proof right now, I will arrest you for arson."

"You think that we burned down the shack and did this to ourselves?" I said. "That's insane."

"Stranger things have happened," Stoffmacher said. "Mostly since you both arrived in Lohr."

"We have this," Monk said, motioning to the big trash bag. "You'll notice that it's tied in a Norwegian Reef Knot, the same knot Dr. Rahner uses to tie his shoes and the shoes of people he kills and dumps on hiking trails."

"Oh God." Stoffmacher groaned. "Not the knots again."

"Knot, not," Monk said to me with a giggle. "Get it?"

Stoffmacher glared at him. "I don't see anything funny about this. We're lucky the entire forest didn't go up in flames."

"Oh, relax," Monk said. "Don't get yourself all twisted in a tizzy."

"What's a tizzy?" Geshir asked.

"If you'll give us a ride up to the Franziskushohe we can wrap this whole case up tonight," Monk said.

"Can't it wait until morning?" I said. All I wanted to do was get in a hot shower for about two hours and check my body for leeches.

"Why wait?" Monk said.

"Because if you could see yourself right now, you'd die," I said.

"I can see myself," Monk said.

"Tomorrow you'll die," I said.

"All the more reason to do it now." Monk picked up the bag, rose to his feet, and faced Stoffmacher. "Where's the car?"

Baffled, Stoffmacher looked at me. "Is he on drugs?"

"Yes," I said.

The bluntness of my answer seemed to surprise him.

Stoffmacher looked back to Monk. "We'll go to the hotel and I'll allow you to confront Dr. Rahner if you will promise me that no matter what happens, you're done. You won't pursue your investigation any further or trouble Dr. Rahner ever again."

"Deal," Monk said.

"He can't make a deal," I said. "He's on mind-altering drugs."

"Then maybe we should arrest him," Stoffmacher said pointedly.

We were screwed no matter what. Monk was going to have a lot to regret in the morning.

"We'll take the deal," I said.

"Wise decision," Stoffmacher said.

"Great," Monk said. "Who's driving?"

"I am, but you're walking," Stoffmacher said and handed him his flashlight. "You aren't stinking up my car."

Stoffmacher and Geshir turned their backs to us and walked away.

"We were almost killed tonight," I yelled after them. "Is this how you treat victims of violent crime around here?"

They ignored me. I made a very unladylike gesture with my hand in their wake. I'm sure they would have understood its meaning if they'd seen it.

I turned and saw Monk squinting at me.

"What?" I said, daring him to criticize my actions.

"Is that a leech on your neck?" Monk asked.

I grabbed at my neck, but there was nothing there.

"Gotcha." Monk laughed, turned away from me, and headed jauntily towards the trail with a skip in his step.

I thought that was cruel and unfair. I never made fun of his plethora of phobias, not that what I was experiencing was anything less than sensible, rational, and totally reasonable.

I vowed to myself that I would make him pay for this. Dearly.

Mr. Monk Has a Brand-new Bag

Mildred, the woman who had taken the picture of Dr. Kroger and Dr. Rahner, was setting up her collage of conference photographs on an easel in the center of the lobby as we came in dripping sludge.

She let out a shocked little squeak when she saw us. I don't know whether she reacted that way because we looked and smelled like two corpses who'd risen from a bog to eat human flesh or because she was afraid I'd come back to beat up on a few more shrinks. Either way, I didn't hold her reaction against her.

Stoffmacher and Geshir stood at the front desk, talking to the lady behind the counter. She sucked in her cheeks in disapproval and glowered at us.

"They can't go any farther than the lobby," she said to the detectives loudly so that we'd be sure to hear it. "I don't want them tracking mud and spreading that stench all over the hotel."

"That's fine," Stoffmacher said. "Could you call Dr. Rahner's room and ask him to join us, please?"

"Could you ask Dr. Kroger to come down, too?"

Monk set the garbage bag down on the coffee table and browsed the bowl of apples that was beside it.

"Whom do you think he killed?" Geshir replied.

"He's Mr. Monk's shrink," I said.

"Then he should definitely be here," Stoffmacher said, and nodded his approval to the counter clerk. "Please call him as well."

Monk took an apple in his dirty hand and went over to look at the photographs in the collage. Mildred held on to the poster board protectively, as if it was some fragile artifact that Monk might break. I joined him and nodded towards the apple.

"You're not going to eat that, are you?"

Monk bit into it with a loud crunch.

"Does that answer your question?" he said with his mouth full.

"Do you realize that apple hasn't been washed and you're eating it with dirty hands?"

He took another bite just to be contrary and nodded at me.

I glanced at the collage. Dr. Rahner was in nearly every picture. He was very photogenic. There were a couple of shots of me, too, and in all of them I was being forcibly restrained.

"Those are nice pictures of you," Monk said to me, his mouth still full. "You should ask her for copies as souvenirs."

His suggestion gave me a wonderful idea. I smiled at Mildred.

"You take marvelous pictures," I said to her.

"Thank you," she replied cautiously. "It's my passion and my art."

"It shows," I said. "Do you happen to have your camera with you now?"

"I don't go anywhere without it," she said.

"Would you mind taking a picture of me and Mr.

Monk? This is an unforgettable moment and I want to be able to share it with all of our family and friends."

"It is?" she said incredulously. "Are you sure?"

"Absolutely," I said. In fact, I couldn't wait. "Will you pose with me, Mr. Monk?"

"Of course," he said and put his arm around me.

Mildred took out her camera and, once she did, she seemed to get into it. I think she realized that now she'd be able to show all of her friends the crazy swamp monsters she met in Lohr.

"Let's have some big smiles," she said, demonstrating with a smile of her own.

We smiled. Monk gave my shoulder a squeeze.

She took two pictures and, standing a safe distance away, showed one of them to me on the tiny screen of her digital camera.

Mildred got us in all our filthy glory. She even got the half-eaten apple in Monk's other hand.

"It's perfect," I said and gave her my e-mail address and cell phone number so she could send the digital photo to me. "I will cherish this and so will Mr. Monk."

"I'll send them to you tonight," she said. And, I figured, to everyone in her address book.

"Make sure I get one," Monk said.

"Oh, I will," I told him.

Dr. Kroger was the first to show up in the lobby. He let out a gasp when he saw Monk.

"Hello, Doc." Monk held out his arms. "Give me a hug."

"I think I'll pass," Dr. Kroger said.

"Come on, you know you want to," Monk said, gesturing him forward.

Dr. Kroger held his ground and looked past Monk to me. "He's on Dioxynl."

"Gee," I said. "How could you tell?"

Stoffmacher approached Dr. Kroger. "I am Hauptkriminalkommissar Stoffmacher and this is Kommissar Geshir. You are the doctor who prescribed this drug to Mr. Monk?"

Dr. Kroger nodded. "It relieves his anxieties and phobias and alters his personality to some degree."

"Some?" I said as Monk dropped the apple core into an ashtray and wiped his hands on his wet, mud-caked pants.

"But neither his judgment nor his competence is the least bit impaired by the medication, if that's what you are wondering," Dr. Kroger said. "He can be held responsible for his actions, though he's not a danger to himself or to others."

"How can you look at us and say that?" I said. "We were nearly killed tonight."

"That's not my fault," Monk said. "It's his."

He gestured to the stairwell, where Dr. Rahner was emerging. His hair was wet and his clothes were crisp and clean.

"Sorry you had to wait," Dr. Rahner said. "I was taking a shower."

God, how I envied him. I was cold, my hair was matted, and my entire body itched from the drying mud.

"Trying to wash off the odor of gasoline?" Monk asked him.

"My sweat," Dr. Rahner said. "I just got back from my nightly jog."

"And an attempted murder," Monk proclaimed.

Dr. Rahner glanced angrily at Stoffmacher and said something unfriendly to him in German.

"We're here because Mr. Monk believes you killed two people," Stoffmacher replied in English.

"Maybe three," Geshir added.

"I'm aware of that," Dr. Rahner said. "What sur-

prises me is that you're taking him seriously. I thought we discussed this."

"We did, and I've brokered a solution to the problem. I've offered him this opportunity to present his case in exchange for his promise not to harass you any further after tonight. He has agreed. Now it is up to you."

Dr. Rahner turned to Dr. Kroger. "He's your patient, Charles. What do you think is best?"

I spoke up. "I think it's a mistake. Mr. Monk is not himself. We should put this off until tomorrow when his medication has worn off."

"Adrian is the same man," Dr. Kroger said. "Only freed of his most obsessive-compulsive tendencies."

"And his detective skills," I said. "He might fumble something tonight that he wouldn't if he was at the top of his game."

"It doesn't take any skill to solve these murders," Monk said. "They are already solved. All the evidence is right here. I'm just presenting the obvious."

It was true that we already knew how and why Dr. Rahner committed the murders; all that was missing was the evidence. If Monk was right, and the evidence was in the room, there wasn't anything he had to deduce.

But that was a big, risky "if," and Monk would have to live with the consequences.

"I'd let Adrian proceed," Dr. Kroger said to Dr. Rahner. "He'll never let go if you don't."

"Very well." Dr. Rahner sighed and sat down on the arm of a chair. "This should be fascinating."

"First, a little recap in case you missed our last episode," Monk said. "Bruno Leupolz was a reporter who found out that you fudged your academic credentials and that you were swindling investors in your real estate venture—"

"Do you have any proof to substantiate that?" Dr. Rahner interrupted.

"None whatsoever," Monk said. "You saw to that when you burned Leupolz's notes and stole the hard drive from his laptop."

"So this is merely libelous speculation on your part," Dr. Rahner said.

Monk shrugged. "Well, Leupolz found the evidence, so I suppose that now that we know what to look for, we can find it, too."

"In other words, this is all fiction," Dr. Rahner said. "Please, go on. I love a good story."

"Three nights ago, under the guise of taking your evening jog, you went to Leupolz's duplex to find out what he knew, destroy the evidence, and scare him off the story. You used one of his pillows as a silencer and fired a gun into the wall to make your point. The pillow muffled the sound, but blew feathers all over you and the apartment. Even so, the gunshot scared Leupolz to death—literally—and killed the man in the next apartment."

Monk went on to explain how Dr. Rahner staged things to make Vigg's death look like a suicide, then returned to Leupolz's apartment to erase any signs of foul play. He also recounted how Dr. Rahner hid the body in the shack and ditched the feathers, pillowcase, and laptop in the pond.

"And here they are," Monk said, motioning to the bag like Bob Barker revealing a *Price Is Right* showcase. "Everything we need to convict you, tied up in a neat bow. The irony is, we might never have found it if you hadn't tried to kill us tonight."

"I'm curious," Dr. Rahner said. "Do you have any evidence to support your claim that I attempted to kill you?"

"You've showered and undoubtedly put your clothes

in the wash," Monk said. "So, no, I don't have any evidence of that. But I don't need it."

"You don't?" Stoffmacher said.

"I have this trash bag," Monk said and turned to Mildred. "Would you mind photographing the bag and its contents for the record?"

Mildred glanced at Stoffmacher, who nodded his consent. She took a few pictures of the trash bag.

"You'll notice the drawstrings are tied in a Norwegian Reef Knot," Monk said, making sure that Mildred got some pictures of it. "Just like the shoes that Dr. Rahner is wearing now."

Mildred took a picture of the shoes, too, eliciting a scowl from Dr. Rahner.

"I'm sure there are millions of people who tie shoes the same way I do," Dr. Rahner said.

"Maybe, maybe not." Monk giggled. "Knot, not—get it?"

Nobody saw the joke. Even on drugs, Monk had a lousy sense of humor. He swallowed his giggles and cleared his throat.

"Okay, moving on." Monk glanced at Stoffmacher. "Could I have a pair of rubber gloves, please?"

Stoffmacher reached into his coat pocket and gave Monk a pair.

Monk put on the gloves, untied the drawstring, and carefully opened the bag.

"Dr. Rahner didn't expect anyone to dredge the pond looking for this stuff and he figured that if it was found later, nobody would connect it to Leupolz or understand the significance of what was inside, assuming it hadn't rotted away."

Monk reached into the bag and pulled out a laptop, which was covered in feathers and had an empty slot where the hard drive should be.

"How do you know Leupolz didn't throw his own stuff in the pond?" Geshir asked.

"If Leupolz ditched his own laptop," Monk said, "why did he take the hard drive out first?"

"To save sensitive information," Geshir said. "Like passwords, financial information."

"Then why throw out his laptop at all?" I countered. "It seems kind of pointless if you are keeping the component that actually has all the content on it."

Stoffmacher and Geshir obviously didn't have an answer for that.

Next Monk pulled out the remains of the pillowcase and then the vacuum cleaner bag, everything covered with feathers and down.

"I'm sure your forensics experts will find gunshot residue all over this pillowcase. Assuming I am right, and you still don't believe me, I have a couple of questions for you," Monk said. "Why would Leupolz shoot his pillow and then try to hide the fact that he did it? Is shooting a pillow a crime in Lohr?"

Stoffmacher stroked his mustache. Geshir doodled in his notebook. But they couldn't hide that they didn't have an answer for those questions either.

"All of that might be suspicious, Adrian, and it might even indicate the poor man was murdered," Dr. Kroger said, "but it doesn't prove that Dr. Rahner was the killer."

"Exactly what I was thinking, Charles," Dr. Rahner said.

"His extra finger does," Monk said.

"There you go again," Dr. Rahner exclaimed, then rose from his seat and pointed accusingly at Monk. "Now we're getting to what this is really all about. This entire delusional episode arises from his irrational fear of people with physical anomalies. He pegged

me as a killer from the moment he saw me in the town square!"

"That's true," Monk said. "And I was right."

"You haven't proven it yet," Stoffmacher said.

"I'm not done. One of the problems with having eleven fingers is that you can't find a decent pair of gloves." Monk reached into the trash bag, pulled out a pair of used rubber gloves, and held one of them up for everyone to see.

There was a hole cut in it, right where Dr. Rahner's extra finger would go.

Monk dangled the glove in front of Dr. Rahner's face. "So you poked a hole in the glove for your extra finger, but you couldn't leave it uncovered, could you?"

He dropped the glove on a table, reached into the bag again, and brought out a severed finger portion from a rubber glove.

"So you cut off a finger from another glove to cover it with," Monk said.

Everyone turned to look at Dr. Rahner, whose face was reddening with anger.

"A hole in a glove and a piece of rubber don't prove anything," Dr. Rahner said. "You still can't put me in Leupolz's duplex the night when you claim the murder occurred."

"I don't have to," Monk said. "She did that for me."

He pointed to Mildred.

"I did?" she said, looking very confused.

"With your beautiful collage." Monk pointed to the picture she took of Dr. Kroger and Dr. Rahner together. "I was so freaked out by your fingers, and the sight of you with Dr. Kroger, that I didn't even notice the pillow feathers stuck to your clothes. But thanks to the wonders of modern pharmaceuticals, I did today."

Everyone but Dr. Rahner stepped up to examine the

picture. Sure enough, there were some down feathers clinging to his sweats.

We all turned back to look at Dr. Rahner, who just sat there, shaking his head in sad disbelief.

"Shoelaces and feathers," Dr. Rahner said. "That's all it takes to destroy a man."

Dr. Kroger looked at Dr. Rahner. "How could you murder two people?"

"I didn't intend to," Dr. Rahner said. "It was all a terrible accident. I'm not a murderer."

"So I suppose you accidentally locked us in a shack, accidentally doused it with gasoline, and accidentally set it on fire," I said.

"Things just kept getting worse," Dr. Rahner said, fixing his gaze on Monk. "If you hadn't followed your psychiatrist to Germany, nobody would have ever known how badly things went wrong."

"I doubt it," Geshir said. "You're underestimating the investigatory skill of our homicide unit."

"No, he isn't," Stoffmacher said.

"We're sharp," Geshir said.

"We're adequate to the task, most of the time. But if it wasn't for Mr. Monk's eye for detail and his relentless determination, we never would have seen these events as anything but a suicide, a natural death, and a tragic coincidence. Now we know the truth. It was murder." Stoffmacher tipped his head towards Dr. Rahner. "Arrest this man, Kommissar, and call the forensic unit up to go over his room. I'm sure we'll find more feathers and other trace evidence."

Geshir took out a pair of handcuffs, pulled Dr. Rahner's arms behind his back, and cuffed his wrists.

Monk stepped up and looked Dr. Rahner in the eye. "Did you kill my wife?"

"I told you, I'm not a killer," Dr. Rahner said. "At least I wasn't until three days ago."

Geshir led Dr. Rahner away. I put my arm around Monk.

"I'm sorry, Mr. Monk," I said.

"Don't be," he said. "I'll get him."

Dr. Kroger came up to us. "That was impressive work, Adrian. You might want to consider sticking with this medication."

Monk shook his head. "The case was solved before tonight. This was the easy part."

"It didn't seem easy to me," Dr. Kroger said.

"That's because you aren't the world's best detective," Monk said.

"I see the drug doesn't diminish the ego," I said.

"I'll have to make a note of that," Dr. Kroger said.

30

Mr. Monk Gets the Picture

There was no point in trying to salvage our clothes, but I actually had to argue with Monk about it when we got back to the hotel. I couldn't believe it.

"There's nothing wrong with these clothes that a little soap won't cure," he said.

"They're burned," I said.

"They look lived-in," he said. "It gives them character."

"I'm throwing them away," I said. "You'll thank me later."

He shrugged. "Whatever makes you happy."

I should have saved his clothes as a penalty for making that remark, but I took pity on him.

I went back to my room and had the longest, hottest shower of my life. I am pleased to report that I didn't find a single leech on my body.

Afterwards, I tried to do something with my hair because it looked like someone had given me a trim with a blowtorch. I made a few snips here and there with my scissors, but I stopped after a couple of min-

utes because I was only making things worse. There isn't much you can do to repair damage like that. You either have to shave it all off or let it grow out.

So I gave up and went downstairs to meet Monk for dinner. He was dressed in his lederhosen again and was eager to eat.

"Let's go to a different restaurant for a change," he said.

"But you hate change," I said.

"Everything in Germany is a change for us," he said. "So what difference does it make where we eat?"

He wanted a restaurant that was, as he put it, "as German as possible." We finally settled on a place in a lopsided half-timbered house with ceilings so low we had to practically crawl inside.

Monk insisted on ordering for both of us. He opened the huge menu. All the items were written in German and in heavy script. The light was so dim, and the cursive was so elaborate, that even if the menu had been written in English, I would have had a hard time reading it.

When the waiter arrived, Monk simply pointed at the items he wanted.

"We'll take this, this, this, and this, with some of this, this, and that," Monk said. "And this. And that."

"Do you have any idea what you just ordered?" I asked him after the waiter left.

"None at all," he said happily. "It's our last night in Germany, so I want to experience all the culinary delights the country has to offer."

"Does it have to be all in one night?"

"Do you have anything better to do?"

He had me there.

The entrées kept coming and coming. They finally had to pile the dishes on the table next to us. I sam-

pled only a few things and was stuffed, but Monk was insatiable.

He was still eating, and perusing the dessert menu, when I finally gave up and went back to our hotel and to bed.

I enjoyed my first good, full night of sleep since we'd arrived. I woke up at nine in the morning. I don't know if it was because I'd finally become adjusted to German time, or because I'd eaten a big meal, or because I'd escaped from a burning building into a pond full of mud.

It didn't matter. It was our last night anyway. Tomorrow I'd be fighting jet lag in San Francisco.

I showered again, just to be sure I was clean, and started packing, sad that I had to go home without really getting a chance to experience the country.

My phone vibrated on the nightstand. I picked it up and saw that Mildred had sent me the pictures of us in our muddy clothes.

And that's when I came up with my brilliant, if slightly nefarious, plan.

I zipped up my bag, went to Monk's room, and knocked on the door.

"Mr. Monk? Are you awake?"

"Unfortunately," I heard him mumble.

I opened the door. His bed was made, his bags were packed, and he sat stiffly on the edge of the bed, dressed in his usual attire, his hands on his knees.

"Is it time to go yet?" he said hopefully.

"We still have a few hours," I answered, sitting down beside him. "How was your night?"

"Now I know how Dr. Jekyll felt in the morning," Monk said. "It's a wonder he didn't kill himself."

He did, but I didn't see the point in telling Monk that.

"Look at the bright side. Yesterday you visited Ber-

lin, solved two murders, and proved that Dr. Kroger didn't betray you."

"So I really am psychologically unfit to return to the police force," Monk said. "Lucky me."

"You don't have to look at the negative side of everything."

"There is no other side," Monk said. "You should know that by now."

"Look at the big picture, Mr. Monk. You're in the center of Europe. Did you ever think you'd be here?"

"Trudy and I would talk about it sometimes," Monk said. "And then we'd come to our senses. We knew it would never happen."

"But it has, Mr. Monk. You're here. I'm here. We should take advantage of it," I said. "We might never have an opportunity like this again."

"That would be great," he said.

"No, it wouldn't," I said. "The hardest part of the trip is behind you. You've made the journey. Now France, Belgium, Switzerland, Poland, and Austria are right next door. There's a whole new world out there for you to see."

"That's very exciting," Monk said. "When is our flight?"

"We don't have to leave today," I said.

"Yes, we do," Monk said. "We have tickets."

"We can change our tickets," I said.

"No, we can't," Monk said. "It's strictly forbidden."

"The airline doesn't care," I said.

"I do," he said.

"We can be in Paris in an hour, Mr. Monk. Imagine that."

He shuddered. "I want to go home."

I sighed. "I didn't want to do this, but you have left me no choice. After last night, and my near-

death experience, I deserve a vacation. So we're going to Paris for a few days."

"I think not," Monk said. "In fact, I'm sure we're not."

I held up my phone so he could see the picture on the screen.

He screamed and scrambled away from me. "Sweet mother of God."

"All I have to do is press this key, and that photo goes to Stottlemeyer, Disher, and Ambrose."

"You wouldn't," he said.

"I might even send it to Julie," I said. "She could blow it up, have it framed, and hang it in our living room. She could make one for you, too."

"This is blackmail," Monk said. "That's a crime."

"Arrest me," I said.

"You're under arrest," he said.

"You're not a cop," I said.

"You're under citizen's arrest until we get back to San Francisco," Monk said. "Then you're going down."

"I suppose you could do that," I said. "But you will have to show the police the photo as evidence of the blackmail."

I had him, and he knew it.

"You are evil," he said. "What did I ever do to you to deserve such cruelty?"

I took a step towards him.

"Is that a leech on your neck?" I said and mimicked his laugh.

He winced.

"I was on drugs," he said plaintively.

"Too bad," I said.

He closed his eyes. "Okay, you win. We're going to France."

I smiled and put my phone in my bag.

"You won't regret this, Mr. Monk."

"You will," he said. "You can kiss your raise good-bye."

"You were going to give me a raise?"

"Eventually," he said. "But now all hope for you is gone."

"C'est la vie," I said.

Booking the flight was easy, but finding a place to stay in Paris that fit Monk's unique requirements was considerably more difficult.

Monk was a man of modest means and a notorious cheapskate, so I knew that a four-star hotel was out of the question.

I also knew he'd never stay in a three-star hotel, not because he was snob, but because it was one star short of an even number.

So I had to choose from the two-star hotels, which were probably more in his price range but less likely to meet his exacting standards of cleanliness and attention to detail.

On top of that, it seemed like every well-reviewed two-star hotel that I could find on the Web was fully booked. But I finally managed to locate a hotel on Avenue Carnot, less than a block from the Arc de Triomphe, that was relatively inexpensive, looked very symmetrical from the street, and that had rooms that appeared to be very clean. I booked two single rooms, and we were good to go.

We picked up our bags and drove to the airport in Frankfurt. Although the speed limit was one hundred twenty kilometers per hour, Monk insisted that I keep the speedometer at eight-six, which made no sense to me.

"That's thirty-four miles below the posted speed limit," I said.

"It's the equivalent of fifty-four miles per hour," Monk said. "That's the speed limit at home."

"No, the speed limit at home is fifty-five."

"Fifty-four is an even number."

"So is one hundred twenty."

"Not if you do the math," he said.

"What math?" I asked.

"One hundred and twenty kilometers is seventy-five miles."

"Okay, I'll go one hundred nineteen kilometers per hour."

"That's not an even number," he said.

"But it is in miles per hour," I said.

"I will still see the uneven number on the speedometer."

"So don't look at the speedometer."

"It's also twenty miles over the speed limit," he said.

"In America," I said. "We're in Germany."

"We're Americans," Monk said. "The law still applies wherever we go."

"No, it doesn't. We have to follow German law and right now we are violating it by driving dangerously slow."

"That's an oxymoron," he said.

"What is?"

"Dangerously slow," he said. "Slow is never dangerous. It's always safer."

"Driving this slow makes us an obstacle. A car could slam right into us."

"Only if it's going too fast," Monk said.

I didn't have any Advil or Rolaids handy, so I decided to give up on arguing with him.

I kept the car in the right lane and we puttered along at a steady eight-six kilometers per hour.

Furious drivers leaned on their horns as they sped past us in a blur, their cars sounding like shrieking animals.

Luckily, I'd overestimated how long it would take us to get to the airport, so we arrived there with plenty of time to spare. We even beat the flight crew to the gate.

The crew came in a group, walking in step with one another to an almost musical beat. It was as if they were modeling their uniforms for us rather than boarding the plane.

The pilots wore crisp, sharply tailored navy blue uniforms with stiff, shiny-brimmed hats and embroidered gold bands around their sleeves that made them look like military officers. There was no reason that I knew of why they had to dress that way, but I guess it was done to convey authority and imply that they'd been through rigorous training, were highly disciplined, and were men of honor.

By contrast, the stewardesses' tight-fitting knee-length dress uniforms had a kinky retro style that evoked the 1960s, martinis, Dean Martin, and the Playboy Club. It wasn't so much the dresses that gave it that feeling as it was the bright red berets, red leather gloves, and high-heeled shoes with sharp pointed toes. I was surprised the stewardesses didn't have bunny tails and whips, too.

The whole crew had matching rolling suitcases that were just the right size to fit in an overhead bin or under a seat. I admired how they could travel so light. It must be one of the benefits of wearing a uniform every day.

I knew Monk would be very happy if I wore a uni-

form, not because he was kinky, but because he liked uniformity.

Monk always wore the same thing.

His shirts were 100 percent cotton and off-white with exactly eight buttons and a size sixteen neck buttoned at the collar. His pants were pleated, cuffed, and they had eight belt loops. His sport coats were brown and so were his Hush Puppy shoes.

His unofficial uniform was every bit as crisp and sharp as the crew's and he wore his with the same sense of pride and authority.

He stepped in front of one of the pilots—the one with the most gold bars around his sleeves. The pilot was double chinned and slightly gray at the temples, and he had bags under his eyes that were big enough to check as luggage.

"Excuse me," Monk asked, "are you the captain of this aircraft?"

"Yes, I am," replied the captain.

The other crew members stopped to listen.

"Did you have a good night's sleep?"

"Yes, I did," the captain said with a polite smile. "Thank you for asking."

"Was it a full eight hours?"

"More or less."

"It either was or it wasn't. Are you always this confused?"

"I'm not confused."

"But you've lost track of time," Monk narrowed his eyes and sniffed. "Is that alcohol I smell on your breath?"

"It's mouthwash," the captain said.

"Would you be willing to take a Breathalyzer test to confirm that?"

"Who are you?"

"A concerned passenger," Monk said. "Very, very, very concerned."

I had to do something before things got ugly. I stepped up and flashed a big, cheerful American smile.

"Please forgive my friend, Captain. It's nothing personal. He's a little scared of flying."

"I understand," the captain said to me, then turned to Monk. "You can relax, sir. I assure you that I'm not impaired in any way. I have flown hundreds of flights in my career, and we haven't had an incident yet."

Monk held up a piece of paper with some writing on it and took several steps back from the captain. "Can you read what this says?"

"No," the captain said.

"And you still think you're fit to fly?"

"Have a pleasant trip." The captain tipped his hat and strode down the gateway to the plane.

"That's not what it says," Monk said, starting to go after him, but I blocked his path.

"Stop pestering the flight crew," I said. "You are going to get us in trouble."

"The pilot is a blind drunk," he said. "How much more trouble could we be in?"

"Lower your voice," I said, pulling him aside. "The flight will be over before you know it."

"That's what I'm afraid of," Monk said.

We heard the sound of a bell over the speaker system and then the gate agent, a man in a polo shirt with the airline's insignia on it, spoke for a minute in German, then announced in English that the plane would begin boarding from the rear of the aircraft, starting with rows twelve to twenty-four. While he was still making the announcement, people were already forming a line beside the ticket counter.

Monk approached the front of the line, where a man the size and shape of a refrigerator stood, his ticket in his huge hand.

"They are boarding from the rear of the plane," Monk said to him.

"I know," the big man said.

Monk motioned to the man's ticket. "You are in row seventeen. You're cutting."

"I was here first."

"That's irrelevant. You should be at least seven people back in line, forty-two if all the seats in the rows behind you are fully occupied. So please step aside while we get everyone in numerical order." Monk turned to face the line. "Let's see your tickets. Who is sitting in row twenty-four?"

Six people in various places in the line raised their hands and waved their tickets.

Monk ushered them forward. "You should all be up here in front. What were you thinking standing way back there?"

The big man growled. "Nobody is getting in front of me."

"If being first in line was so important to you, you should have bought a ticket in row twenty-four. But you didn't. You are in row seventeen. Live with it."

The gate agent stepped up to them. "What's the problem here?"

"This man is in row seventeen but insists on being first in line," Monk said.

"We're boarding from the rear of the plane, rows twelve to twenty-four," the gate agent said.

"Exactly," Monk said, turning the big man. "Now kindly move aside and let us get everyone organized."

The big man said something to the gate agent in German and then the gate agent addressed Monk.

"Sir, this gentleman was here first. As long as he's in the last twelve rows, he can be in this line."

"I know that," Monk said. "He just can't be first."

"Yes, he can," the gate agent said.

"You said you were boarding from the rear of the plane," Monk said. "He's in row seventeen. Don't you know how to count? Or is it the counting backward that's throwing you?"

I grabbed Monk by the arm and pulled him aside like a misbehaving child. I was beginning to regret that we weren't driving to Paris.

"What is the matter with you?" I said.

"Me? It's them. They can't count."

"They aren't boarding in order from the rear of the plane. What they are doing is allowing anybody in rows twelve through twenty-four to board."

"That's not what they said."

"It's what they meant," I said.

"Then that's what they should have said."

"Maybe they did in German but it got lost in translation."

"But the insanity didn't," Monk said.

While the passengers in the rear of the plane were boarding, Monk began to organize the remaining passengers into reverse numerical order based on their ticket numbers.

I let him do it because it kept him occupied and out of the ticket agent's way. Perhaps the passengers let him do it because they, like me, had lost the will to fight with him.

When the rest of the passengers were called to board, Monk led them in a single-file line to the gateway.

Monk glowered at the ticket agent as we passed him. "See how much smoother this went? I hope you've learned from this experience."

The ticket agent was wise enough just to smile and say nothing. He was getting off easy. It was over for him. But not for me and the rest of the passengers.

This was already the flight from hell and we hadn't even left the airport yet.

Obsessive.
Compulsive.
Detective.

MONK

The mystery series starring the
brilliant, beloved, and slightly off-
balance sleuth from the USA
Network's hit show!

Also Available in the series:

Mr. Monk Goes to the Firehouse

"The first in a new series is always an occasion to celebrate, but Lee Goldberg's TV adaptations double your pleasure. . . . *Mr. Monk Goes to the Firehouse* brings everyone's favorite OCD detective to print. Hooray!"
—*Mystery Scene*

"It is laugh-out-loud funny from the get-go. For *Monk* fans, this is a must. Totally enjoyable. Lee Goldberg has expertly captured the nuances of what makes Monk, well, Monk."
—Robin Burcell

"Lee has found the perfect voice for Natalie's first-person narration—sweet, exhausted, frustrated, exasperated, and sweet again. None of these feelings has to do with the mystery. They're all reactions to Monk's standard behavior as he wars with all the ways nature is trying to kill him. Lee Goldberg has managed to concoct a novel that's as good as any of the *Monk* episodes I've seen on the tube."
—Ed Gorman

"Can books be better than television? You bet
they can—when Lee Goldberg's writing them."
—Lee Child

Praise for the *Monk* Mysteries

Mr. Monk in Outer Space

"You say you don't read tie-in novels? You should give
the *Monk* books a try and find out what you've been
missing. They're funny, they're well written, they're
carefully plotted, and they're poignant." —Bill Crider

Mr. Monk and the Two Assistants

"Even if you aren't familiar with the TV series *Monk*,
this book is too funny to not be read."
—The Weekly Journal

Mr. Monk and the Blue Flu

"A must-read if you enjoy Monk's mysteries on the
tube." —Bookgasm

Mr. Monk Goes to Hawaii

"An entertaining and ruefully funny diversion that
stars one of television's best-loved characters."
—*Honolulu Star-Bulletin*

continued . . .